SON OF A DOPE FIEND 2

Renta

2

**Lock Down Publications and
Ca$h Presents**
Son of a Dope Fiend 2
A Novel by Renta

Renta

Lock Down Publications
P.O. Box 944
Stockbridge, Ga 30281

Visit our website
www.lockdownpublications.com

Lock Down Publications
Like our page on Facebook: Lock Down Publications @
www.facebook.com/lockdownpublications.ldp
Cover design and layout by: **Dynasty Cover Me**
Book interior design by: **Shawn Walker**
Edited by: **Jill Alicea**

4

Stay Connected with Us!

Text **LOCKDOWN** to 22828 to stay up-to-date with new releases, sneak peeks, contests and more...

Submission Guideline.

Submit the first three chapters of your completed manuscript to ldpsubmissions@gmail.com, subject line: Your book's title. The manuscript must be in a .doc file and sent as an attachment. The document should be in Times New Roman, double-spaced and in size 12 font. Also, provide your synopsis and full contact information. If sending multiple submissions, they must each be in a separate email.

Have a story but no way to send it electronically? You can still submit to LDP/Ca$h Presents. Send in the first three chapters, written or typed, of your completed manuscript to:

LDP: Submissions Dept
P.O. Box 944
Stockbridge, Ga 30281

DO NOT send original manuscript. Must be a duplicate.

Provide your synopsis and a cover letter containing your full contact information.

Thanks for considering LDP and Ca$h Presents.

ACKNOWLEDGEMENTS

I've been locked within this cage for the past sixteen years and as I reflect on all that I've had to face off with within the belly of this tarantula, I've come to understand that in order for *any* man, woman, or child to become great, they must first determine what greatness is to them, per se! Never judge your greatness or your success by the perspectives, success, or standards of the next mu'fucka. You'll lose every time! I truly appreciate my critics, *the good as well as the bad ones!* It's because of you that I keep this pen gliding across this paper. Yet, most importantly, I wanna give it up for my fans, those of y'all that fucks with me and my life's experiences that I place into these stories. I love y'all, fam! If it wasn't for you, I'd still be thinkin' dope is the only way to eat! A lot of people become so caught up in the fiction that they may not consider that the stories they're reading may derive from actual events, and no matter how much one adds to a story, the real will be able to separate the falsehood from the official. I give y'all thirty percent imagination, but seventy percent of the shit I've been through in my thirty-four years of thuggin'. *Black Diamond* was an actual mother - *my* deceased mother that was found dead in an alleyway in Florida. It's life! My name is Renta, pronounced Ren - Tay, an African American man from the slums, and I'm the brother, potna, and friend of a lot of gangstas, drug dealers, pimps, and hoes. I'm the King of my Queen, and son of a *few* women though! LOL! I gotta give it up for the women that I love with all of me. As always, Alexandria, I love you with all of me and will forever rep you. You're my ace, best friend, and rida. Stay ten toes, AR, and by the time you look back, you'll have everything you've ever desired.

Mama Helen, what you doin', woman? I love you like no other, and as I strive to get to you, just know I haven't forgotten your words of wisdom! I owe you the world and I promise to deliver - at least a piece of it! Mama Leah, what can I say? You're the epitome of strength and love! Stay strong, Queen. Kim, LOL, I ain't forgotten 'bout you, fam! Heard there's a man that I have to meet? Don't take him fast! LOL! Nisha, Kanika Cleo, Rachel, Terica, and

Granma Sharan, y'all know the business! As for my brothers? My niggas! Earl Gold Smith, Dunte "Solo" Daniels, I'ma rep you till they free ya! Lil Walter "Nukkey" Osborne, hold ya head, my "G", and keep ya Gators on tight! You're next up to hold the torch! Too Black, Papa, South Park Papa, Earlyboy head, Free Huncho, M-Lo, Papa, LeLe, Lil D, Lil A, Thug, Lil C, Wydell, Lil Yank, Yap, Big Vino, Sunny Bo Bo, E-man, 180, Juvenile, Beta, Lil Gatti, DJ Lil Red, and all you boys I ain't shout out…y'all know I gotta give it up for big bro Cash! Fam, it's anotha one for the books, OG! You opened the door for me and I'ma hold it down! Salutes, my G. LDP, WUD UP! I'm proud of y'all. They ain't fuckin' wit' US!

This one for B.I.T.S INC. *The Beauty in The Struggle* is what makes us family! That's Peace! Last but surely not least, my editor. You're official, ma, your work speaks for itself!

DEDICATIONS

This book is dedicated to Mama Leah. There's nothin' too big for God and He is in you! It's a fight, but you make it look easy, Queen!

Renta

Part I

The Starvin' Monkey and Roaring Lion

I was born way down in the ghetto deep,
Where my mama fucked my daddy, but when my daddy fucked
my mama the fuckin' was neva cheap!
Roaches were our company, and eviction notices came fre-
quent, my sister got pregnant at fourteen and since her baby's
daddy was ten years older, he didn't want her to keep it.
Yeeahh! I was taught the game waaayyy down in the Jungle
deep,
Where I encountered a starvin' monkey swingin' from vine to
tree, until one day his silly ass missed a vine and fell to the earth,
landin' next to a roarin' lion's feet.
That roarin' lion said to that starvin' monkey,
"You ugly monkey, if you dare step on my paw, I'll have you as
a treat! I'll have yo' monkey ass for breakfast, yo' monkey hoe for
lunch, and make dinner out yo' baby chimpanzee!"
That starvin' monkey smiled a humble smile.
"Ole lion, I don't mean to be disrespectful, but I'm a starvin'
monkey and there's a banana tree right behind you. I'd be mighty
grateful if you'd move yo' hairy ass and allow me to pass."
The lion bared its teeth before roaring,
"You untamed pest, you'd better be on your way, and I'm
talkin' fast, if not, I'm gonna
tell my lionesses to hunt and they'll no doubt tear into yo' mon-
key ass!"
Even with those big ole monkey nuts, that starvin' monkey knew
not to test the demand of the King of the Jungle, so he ran and he
ran, until he ran face first into the ass of a beautiful zebra that was
dehydrated. She was bending her head to have a drink
from a stream in the safari.
Yet there, lying in wait, was a giant crocodile that had the
tongue of a charmer
and was as swift as an imported Ferrari.

The croc rose to the surface and eased up just enough to that thirsty zebra and
whispered,
"Zebra lady, oh, how sweet are your stripes that you create magic in the loins of this here beast,
and if given the opportunity, I'll eat your sweet pussy from here till the last day of
next week!"
That dehydrated zebra stepped back in fright.
"Oh, you devilish fool, I'd never allow you to get even a whiff of this striped pussy, and you can bet that it tastes oh so sweet,
But you're a rough and treacherous beast that lacks manners when you eat!
You'd make a beautiful pair of shoes for a pimp, but surely you can't taste this pussy 'cause
You don't know how to refrain from usin' ya teeth when you feast!"
With that, the zebra was gone in the wind until she stumbled over that starving monkey.
"Ole monkey, I'm not tryin' to be funny but you sho'll is funky!"
she cried.
The monkey rubbed its sore head before replying,
"Well, lady zebra, I just may be, but you seem dehydrated, and if you will trust this ole funky monkey, I can lead you to a clear stream at which you can drink until you're rehydrated."
The zebra stared at him skeptically, but oh, was she dying of thirst, so she followed behind that starvin' monkey, thinking,
"What could it hurt?"
"Right this way, zebra lady, and by the way, has anybody told you how beautiful you are?
Your stripes are mighty pretty and ya ass is phat."
"Now wait a minute, you funky mu'fucka, I'm a lady with class, you ain't s'posed to
Talk to me like that!" the zebra snapped.
That starvin' monkey nodded his head feverishly.

"My apologies, zebra lady, the stream is right over here, just beyond this brush of high grass,"

He acknowledged as they stepped into a small clearing that caused the zebra to frown, but though her instincts set off an alarm, when she tried to confront that starvin' monkey, he disappeared too fast.

Out from the brush, a pride of lionesses surrounded her; she knew that she was doomed!

Not too far away, that roaring lion observed the hunt, and couldn't wait to be fed, and as he watched his Queens tear that zebra to shreds, a swinging silhouette cast a moving shadow over his head.

He gazed up just in time to see that ole starvin' monkey make it to a hanging vine of that banana tree.

He smiled before roaring,

"You ole funky monkey, you're a dirty, low down, sumbitch, but I sho' do like how you keep yo' game tight!"

That starvin' monkey laughed as he dropped a banana peel down onto the lion's head.

"Sho' ya right, you ole bushy tail, King of the Jungle, I gotta keep my game tight! Plus, I may be just a funky-ass monkey, but you and those dusty hoes of yours are the ones that fell for the banana in the tail pipe!"

He laughed as he stuffed his face with the bananas.

Renta

Chapter 1
2010

"Sista, I know you're pressed for time, but the good Lawd gonna smile down on ya if only you'll smile down on a poor man like myself," Leroy solicited as he stood outside the Walmart Supercenter. There was a tin bucket beside his foot for people to drop their blessings in. "Can you spare a few dollars so a man that's down on his luck can put somethin'' warm in his belly?" he begged, holding his stomach as if it ached from hunger pains.

The wind blew softly as an elderly woman took in his ragged appearance. The dirty overcoat he wore over a pair of dark slacks was stained with old dirt and his hair was matted against his head. She could see his big toe through the hole in the top of the busted shoes he wore and when he noticed the pity in her eyes, Leroy sheepishly attempted to hide his foot behind the bucket of coins and loose bills. The elderly woman's name was Ms. Essie and as her eyes rose to find the embarrassment that was written all over his face, she gave him an *aww, you poor baby* smile. The smudges on his face told the tale of hard times and being a product of the ghetto herself caused the old woman to sympathize with his struggle.

Ms. Essie's eyes trailed to the sign he'd made out of a piece of cardboard. It read, *"A man's pride is all he has after all that he's loved has been stripped from him, but when his stomach is empty, even that has a price! Luke 6:38."* Ms. Essie's eye's returned to Leroy's with a sad shake of her head. "Well, baby, I ain't got much, but I'm always ready to do the Lord's work," she began while opening her purse. "Just this mornin' I was tellin' the deacon we needs to do more for the poor folk. This *gotta* be ordained! Amen!" she spoke more to herself than to him. She searched through her purse until she found a ten dollar bill and with narrowed eyes, Ms. Essie held it out to him. "Now, Ms. Essie ain't got no problem with doin' for my peoples and thangs, but I ain't no fool. Make sho' you does right wit' the Lord's blessin' - hear me, chile?" she spoke while staring at him suspiciously.

Leroy reached out and gripped the other end of the bill, but Ms. Essie held tight to her end. They engaged in a slight game of tug of war as he gave her a tight smile in an attempt to assure her that he wasn't like the many others.

"No, ma'am, I would never do——"

Boc! Boc! Boc! Boc!

Four gunshots rang out in rapid succession, interrupting his spiel. Leroy's reaction was instinctive. As self-preservation kicked in, he snatched the money from her grip and in a full sprint, plowed over Ms. Essie. The old woman crashed to the pavement with a thud, the impact causing her gray, curly wig to pop off.

"Ohhh Lawd, have mercy, this nigga done knocked my hip outta place! I needs a doctor - a lawyer!" she cried as she reached out for her wig. The old lady glared in the direction Leroy had run. "Funky muthafucka, I'ma cut ya!" she spat before smashing the artificial hair back onto her head.

Leroy paid her no mind as he ran with all he had. He sprinted until he rounded the corner of the building and as soon as he saw the freshly-waxed G wagon he'd parked there, he snatched the stained overcoat off. Underneath it was a tailored pair of dark slacks and an off-white dress shirt.

"Nigga can't even put his hustle down nowadays without some crazy mu'fucka shootin' shit up!" he spat. Leroy hit the alarm on the foreign truck when the thought hit him. *Ain't this a bitch! Mu'fuckas done made me leave my earnings back there with that old heifer!* He was disgusted with himself as he stared down at the ripped half of the ten dollar bill he'd made off with.

Meanwhile, not too far away from the conman, the DEA was in tune with an entirely different crime.

"Shots fired! Shots fired! The suspect is armed and fleeing on foot! I repeat——" someone shouted into the headset Agent Mullowsky had around his head.

He snatched it off and slammed it down onto the makeshift table. "Goddammit, Hernandez, you see this psycho?" he spat in disbelief before springing from his seat. Agent Mullowsky flung the doors open on the rear of the florist's van and caused three bouquets of roses in glass vases to tip over and shatter against the stained pavement. Without so much as a glance back, he gave chase.

His sudden departure caught his partner unaware. Hernandez was mid-bite into the jelly donut when things went astray. He sat stunned for mere seconds after Mullowsky's quick departure, but it wasn't long before he flung the sweet cake to the side and followed suit.

Murda stared bewilderedly at the florist van as the scene unfurled like a bad movie.

"Freeze! DEA!" Slim's declaration stole his attention.

"If you move so much as a muscle, I'll blow your brains out!" The agent's voice was deadly as he trained his service pistol at Murda's thinking cap.

The crook's mind was a tornado of questions as he contemplated making a run for it, but the look in Slim's eyes revealed his hunger. He wanted Murda to try his luck so he could prove to him that true street niggas didn't have any.

"Do it. I *dare* you!" he challenged.

Murda was resigned to his fate as he threw his hands in the air. "A'ight, brah, don't shoot, my hands up, mane! My hands are in the air!" he shouted loud enough for the audio he knew was being recorded. Murda had a defeated expression on his face when Mullowsky and Hernandez flew by in hot pursuit of Sunjay. The killa had a good lead on his pursuers as he ran for his life. The parking lot came to life in a vicious game of cops versus the bad guy.

If these hoes catch me, it's ova for the kid! Sunjay thought as his heart hammered against his chest.

Scuuurrrr! An unmarked Ford Taurus skidded sideways in front of him and just before it turned the young goon into roadkill, he leapt into the air. Life took on a slow motion effect as he stared down at the hood of the car sliding underneath his airborne feet. Sunjay could hear his heartbeat in his ears and just when he thought he'd made it clear, gravity decided to make its appearance. He couldn't control the outcome as the motion of the car, coupled with his momentum, flipped him across the slick surface of the hood.

Sunjay landed awkwardly on the other side of the car, crying out in agony as the air shot from his lungs.

"Freeze, you son of a bitch, don't you——"

Boc! Boc! Boc! Boc!

Sunjay had snatched the FN off his waist and silenced the agent's threats. The stocky Caucasian man ducked behind the unmarked car and returned fire,

Boom! Boom!

The big .45 exploded with each pull of the trigger. Sunjay scrambled to his feet and moved off pure will.

"Freeze!" someone shouted from behind him.

Sunjay risked a glance back and spotted Mullowsky and his partner on his heels.

"Hey, watch——"

Ms. Essie's alarmed cry seemed to come out of thin air. Sunjay's mind told him to switch directions, but he was beyond slowing down, swerving, or doing anything to prevent the collision. He collided with the old woman with no mercy. All he could see as he rolled with the impact of the crash was a tuft of curly gray hair flying up into the air at the same time that Ms. Essie's floral-printed dress blew up and over her ashy ass cheeks. The clash caused the gun to fly out of Sunjay's hand and as he watched it slide across the pavement, it took all the willpower he could muster to disregard it. He scrambled to his feet and fled as a flaming bullet flew past his right ear.

Agent Mullowsky was desperate as he slowed his stride and in a moment of wild desperation, he took aim at the fleeing gangster's back. He tried to focus, but his old lungs weren't as healthy as they used to be. They burned as his finger tightened around the trigger and with one eye closed, the agent fired a wild shot that missed Sunjay by half an inch. Out of breath himself, Hernandez trudged up beside him. Mullowsky leaned over and placed his hands on his knees, tryin' to catch his breath. Both men watched in fascination as Sunjay proved that God sometimes had a soft spot for a gangsta.

Mullowsky shrugged indifferently as they were forced to watch Sunjay put on.

18

"I hope he runs himself into a wall at a hundred miles an hour." Mullowsky's bitterness was a deep fountain.

"Oh, Lord, these sons of bitches tryin' to rob me for my bingo money, protect me, Jesus, I paid a hundred dollars plus tax for that wig! Where's my glasses!" Ms. Essie cried as she crawled on her hands and knees, patting the ground in search of her belongings.

Agent Mullowsky bit his tongue to keep from laughing.

"Are you okay, ma'am? Do you need medical attention?" he asked just as she found her wig and smashed it back onto her head. Seeing that she'd placed the false hair on backwards, Mullowsky lost the war with self-control. He laughed in spite of his disappointment of Sunjay getting one up on them.

"I need a lawyer. Where's white folks when you need 'em? Police!" Ms. Essie screamed above his laughter.

***

Messiah's blood began to boil as his eyes captured the diamond necklace that adorned Justice's neck. It was identical to the one he wore outside of the diamond-encrusted leash connected to hers that held her captive, enslaved to her captor. A murder scene played within Messiah's mind as he envisioned what he'd do to the ones responsible. He took a step toward them, but a soft touch gave him pause.

"Don't." The word slipped from her lips in a hiss.

Frustration raced through his veins as Messiah glanced down at Persia's manicured hand that held him by the arm.

"Patience. Napoleon once said that the reason he beat the Austrians was because they didn't know the value of five minutes," she leaned toward him and whispered.

Messiah removed her hand but tamed his craving to get to his wife. His eyes rose to find Pimpin Maxwell unclasping the leash from the strange necklace, and as soon as she was liberated, Justice kicked off the heels she wore. She attempted to run toward Messiah, but at that moment, the band began to play a live piece by Stevie Wonder. Men and women paired off and rushed the dance floor.

"Ribbon in the Sky" was a sweet melody that caused Justice to get swallowed by the crowd. The brief interference caused Messiah's spirit to turn dark as his hand instinctively went for the tool he usually kept on his waist, but the absence of his burna reminded him how naked he was to his enemy. Impatience suffocated him before he began to force himself through the crowd in search of his heart, and just as his thought became a storm...

"Messiah!" Justice exclaimed as she broke through the crowd and into his arms.

He held her with all his might as she buried her face in his chest and cried. Seconds felt like eternity, but the embrace ended as quickly as it began.

Fuck all this lovey dovey shit! Messiah thought, ready to get to the gangsta shit. He held her at arm's length, studying her. The Catwoman mask was made of a soft material that accentuated her juicy lips. Her curly hair cascaded down past her shoulders and brought life to the sleeveless, black Louis Vuitton dress that complimented her every curve. As his vision digested her beauty, Messiah's mind ran wild with insecurity. *Why the fuck she wearin' this tight-ass dress! Has she fucked one of——?* He couldn't complete the thought. He fought against the darkness of his mind as he glanced around suspiciously, He knew the enemy surrounded them, hidden behind the illusion of masquerade masks and calculated dance steps. Couples danced around them as Stevie Wonder's melody was mastered by an aged black man that seemed to make sweet love to his saxophone.

"Have they hurt you, ma? Who is this nigga?" Messiah attempted to shout over the music.

Justice's eyes revealed her confusion. She couldn't hear him.

Messiah stepped closer and placed his lips close to her ear. "Baby, who the fuck is this boy? Tell me and I'm gonna put his brains all over this floor! On Black's life, I'm gonna——"

"No!" Justice interrupted him. She vigorously shook her head back and forth as if she was trying to eradicate the past few weeks from her memory. Justice reached up and pulled his head close to her mouth. "No, papi, I jus whan it to be over! Pay dem dey money and let's move far, far away from dis place...*please!* Dey have Karma, Messiah. Ah beg yuh to leave de game alone. Ah beg yuh!" Her accent was thick as her eyes pooled beneath the mask.

The devil spoke to Messiah's heart as her hurt fed his revenge. "Naw, Queen, I sent our seed to stay wit' your parents til this shit ova wit'. They ain't got our daughter, ma," he soothed her spirit as he plotted on their escape. Justice's face contorted into a confused mask at the revelation, but before she could question him, Messiah tensed. "Justice!" he called before pulling away from her. "What does Pimpin Maxwell have to do with this shit?" he inquired after remembering how his mentor held her with the leash.

Justice stared at him, perplexed. "Pimpin? Who yuh sayin', pa, why would Pimpin Maxwell be involved in dis?" she asked. "Wah going..." Her words trailed off as her eyes focused on somethin' behind him.

Messiah spun defensively and came face to face with an impec-cably-dressed man with eyes so identical to his that it shook him. The man's resemblance to Pimpin Maxwell was uncanny, but even more so, his common features to Messiah were frightening.

What the fuck! This boy looks like me - naw, like Pimpin! Maybe that's why Justice was so confused? Messiah's mind was a battle-field of confusion. The man's aura told Messiah that he was the puppet master and though Messiah wanted to crush him, the bulge under dude's dinner jacket warned off any rash decisions.

The stranger stepped forward with his hand extended. "Playa, playa!" he shouted over the music as if he and Messiah were long lost friends.

Messiah slapped his hand away and took a step forward to close the distance between them. Fire ignited in the man's eyes, but Mes-siah didn't give a fuck, he wanted that gangsta shit to pop off.

He was so lost within anticipation that he didn't notice when a couple to his right inched closer with a calculated twirl in their mock lover's dance. A sharp blade slipped from underneath the man's tuxedo sleeve and into the soft hand of his companion. She was a slender caramel-colored diva that was as poisonous as snake venom and beautiful as a poisonous flower. The man she danced with smiled down at her before bending her over his arm so far that she stared at Messiah from an upside-down view. Her partner lifted her upright before taking her hand and twirling her closer to her prey, a foot away from Messiah. The man spun her like a ballerina, but just when she spun with deadly intent, Justice saw the light that reflected off the sharp blade.

The deadly woman's evil plot was sabotaged when Justice pushed Messiah to the side. The edge of the blade missed his neck by inches but sliced through Justice's arm with ease. Confusion was evident in his stare when Messiah spun to confront the threat, but all he saw was the couple spinning away from them as they stared into each other's eyes. He turned to Justice and zoned into her eyes before glancing down at the blood that oozed from the slash. He was as lost as ever as he scanned the room frantically. He knew it was in their best interest to get out of the crowd, but when he moved to take Justice by the arm, another masked figure took her hand.

"Dance with me, beautiful," he demanded more than asked.

Justice attempted to pull her hand away, but the strange necklace came to life in various shades of burgundy, red, and green. The threat stole the fight from her as her eyes lifted to find Messiah's eyes trained on the glowing jewels on her neck, so much so that he didn't seem to notice his own neck glow with the Reaper's touch. His gaze lifted to find hers and within his eyes, Justice witnessed a bloodbath with her bathed in its substance. Yet she allowed herself to be pulled into the stranger's arms as he navigated their moves.

"Mr. Messiah, we have bidness to discuss, playboy."

The voice stole his attention. Messiah reluctantly turned to face off with the puppet master. He gritted his teeth as his eyes turned to slits. "I'm gonna whack you, fuck boy. I'm gonna knock your melon over the——"

"Sure, playa," the stranger cut him off before turning and walking away.

Messiah was puzzled, but stiffened when a pair of soft lips brushed against his ear.

"I think you should follow him," Persia whispered as her manicured nails scraped down the sleeve of his jacket. "And Messiah?"

Messiah turned to face her, Persia was an exotic feline that exuded sexual energy without seeming to notice. She smiled at him seductively. "When the charmer plays his flute, the cobra forgets that it's a poisonous snake and gets lost within its dance to the melody." She paused and stepped into Messiah's space. She wrapped her arms around his neck before leaning forward, her glossy lips grazing his neck as she spoke. "But when the music stops, the serpent remembers its nature and before the charmer is bitten by its deadly strike, it's in his best interest to remember as well," she spoke cryptically.

***

"Freeze!" someone shouted from behind him.

But Sunjay was all in as he ran for his life. He heard the growl of the engine before the crotch rocket zoomed into the lot. *If these hoes catch me, they're gonna strap me to Ole Sparky! Fuck all that! It's homicide or suicide now!* His thoughts were his motivation as he wrapped his mind around what he had to do. As soon as the rider was too close to slow down, Sunjay thrust his arm outward and clotheslined him. Dude tried to hold tight to the handles, but the bike slid from underneath him, causing him to go airborne. The bike took on a mind of its own as it swerved before falling and skidding sideways across the pavement.

The rider hit the ground hard. "Argh! Fucking-A, dude!" he cried his expletives, but Sunjay's heart was as cold as an Alaskan winter.

"My fault, my dude, but I need to borrow this mu'fucka. It's against the law to ride without a helmet anyway," he shouted over his shoulder as he ran over and snatched the bike up. The metallic paint had peeled off the right side of the motorcycle, but with a quick glance behind him, Sunjay saw that the appearance of the machine was the least of his worries. A slim DEA agent had dropped to one knee and was attempting to get a bead on him as he aimed his pistol. Sunjay's heartbeat accelerated. *Please, God, don't let these crackas kill me, fam. Today ain't a good day to die or go to jail, OG. Please fuck with me just this one time!* he begged the heavens as the adrenaline coursed through his veins. He straddled the bike.

"Hey, that's my bike, man!" the owner shouted as he struggled to his feet and attempted to shake the disorientation from his mind.

Sunjay ignored him as he gripped the throttle and pressed down on the starter. He gripped the handles tight as God answered his prayer.

Vroom! The motorcycle came to life with a menacing growl. Sunjay eased off the clutch and gave the machine some juice. The rear tire left a burn mark on the street as the bike jerked forward. He hadn't ridden a bike in years, but self-preservation was a good reminder as he sped out of the parking lot. Screeching tires could be heard like an angry demon, Sunjay leaned down on the bike while pulling back on the throttle just a little bit more. The crotch rocket responded to his touch and jumped up to sixty miles an hour as he weaved in and out of traffic on the George Bush Bridge. Sunjay glanced at the rearview mirror and damn near wrecked the motorcycle at what he saw. A speeding motorcade of law enforcement was on his tail and he knew it wouldn't be long before they had the ghetto bird flying above him. *Fuck it!* His resolve was singed in stone. The young gangster watched the needle on the speedometer ease up to eighty, ninety-five, a hundred, and finally a flying hundred and twenty miles an hour as the bike vibrated beneath him. "I need to get off this bridge!" he whispered to himself.

Sunjay wasn't naïve. He knew he couldn't outrun the Feds, but he also knew that at that point in his thuggin', shit was critical! He knew the military exit was up ahead and as he gunned for it, his greatest fear became his worst reality. The sound of the helicopter caused him to look up at the heavens. It was far off in the distance, but the aircraft would be upon him in seconds. He saw his exit and kicked the bike down to a rational speed, but just as he leaned the monster to make the exit, Sunjay came to realize that Lady Luck was just as treacherous as every other cutthroat bitch that attempted to love two different men at the same time.

The Feds were the second man in their lover's triangle and they proved to be a formidable force. They'd anticipated him going for the exit and had blocked it off with two black SUV's. As cars sped by, Sunjay eased the bike to the side of the exit. A red Honda Civic slowed down to be nosy and Sunjay smiled at the two bad-ass kids that had their faces plastered to the window, pointing at him excitedly. He nodded at them before gazing down at the blockade of cars. He could hear the DEA surrounding him from behind and turning the Bush Bridge into a congested movie scene. Civilians stared from their car windows, fascinated at the showdown.

Sunjay's mind was dark. *"Sunjay Carter...we, the state of Texas, condemn you to death by lethal injection!"* His mind foretold the conclusion of his story. "Shid -- they may as well get the coroner ready!" he grumbled as he glanced back at the deadly assemblage of officers. They took aim at him from behind their vehicles. *A firing squad!* his mind concluded. Sunjay watched as a lanky black man in a cheap suit placed a megaphone to his lips.

"This is the Drug Enforcement Agency! You will get *one* opportunity to comply before we——"

Sunjay laughed to himself and made the motorcycle roar. Without warning, he kicked the crotch rocket into gear. He'd made his decision. The rear tire created a cloud of smoke when he pushed it forward. The looks on the agents' faces were priceless as they stared with their mouths agape at the madman's intent. Sunjay was on a kamikaze mission as he leaned down low on the bike. His hands gripped the throttle tightly as he gave a little twist to his wrist. The front wheel eased off the ground as Sunjay pushed the bike up to eighty miles an hour. He vaguely heard the shots that were fired as he rode the wheelie with survival on his mind. There was a four foot gap between the two SUV's that they hadn't expected him to recognize.

An agent stood in his path to freedom and after seeing his intent, he began firing at the wild young cat. What he didn't anticipate was Sunjay's concept of life or death being beyond the fear of meeting the Reaper, but he caught on quickly. The agent dove out of the way

25

at the last minute as the motorcycle zipped through the small opening.

Sunjay had one thing on his mind. *If I make it to the hood, I can lose these hoes. They'll never catch me if I get to the cliff!*

Chapter 2

"Cedric, nooooo!" Ruth's frantic screams filled the room.

The hot lead tore into Cedric's stomach, causing him to double over. The loud explosion of the burner was profound to Blow's ears as he squeezed the trigger a second time. He watched as Cedric's shoulder exploded into a bloody mess before he crumbled to the floor. Blow rushed into his clothes before turning to finish the job.

"Noooo!" Ruth screamed for the second time as Blow took aim at her husband.

The gun jumped in Blow's hand as he fired for the third time, but at the last moment, he tried to divert his aim. Ruth's desperate attempt at protecting her man earned her a grazed side as she dove on top of him. She cried out in agony before trying to plead with the devil.

"Please. Please! We'll get you your money. We have kids, Blow. We——"

Boom! Blow pulled the trigger.

The explosion of the gun snatched him out of the reoccurring nightmare he'd been having for the past four years. Blow had to swallow his own screams in order not to wake his cellmate. He sat up in his bunk. Sweat saturated his skin as he stared at the chipped paint on the aged walls. He took deep breaths as he reached underneath his pillow and pulled out the only sense of sanity he had to hold onto. He studied the words inscribed on its cover as if they were life sustaining: *Holy Bible.*

Blow glanced at the digital clock on the desk. "Four in the A.M.," he whispered to himself.

"I see you still havin' those nightmares, brotha." Jihad's words were deep, but low. "Allah is most gracious and most merciful," he acknowledged.

Blow wasn't surprised that the old man was up and one with the darkness. He slid from the bottom bunk and turned to face the humble Muslim.

"The same one. And each time, I——" He paused before casting his demons into the atmosphere. "Each time, I can see myself pullin' that trigger, Jihad. I spilt that man's blood on behalf of my very own sins, and now it's become my greatest regret," Blow admitted before using his back to slide down the wall until he sat on the cold floor. He gazed up at Jihad, who was already sitting upright in his bed with his legs crossed Indian style as if he were meditating. He had a black Kufi on his head and his Quran open in his lap. The fifty-four years of his life had been good to him and it showed in his youthful appearance.

Jihad nodded his understanding. "Sura two, aya two hundred eighty-four says that to Allah belongs all that is in the heavens and on the Earth. Whether you show what is in your mind or conceal it, Allah calls you to account for it. He forgives whom he pleases, and punishes who he pleases, for Allah has power over all things." He recited his favorite verse from the Quran. Jihad studied Blow. They'd been cellies on the Estelle unit in Huntsville, Texas for the past few years and Jihad had grown fond of the slick-talking hustler. Jihad envied the blessing Blow viewed as a burden. While the younger brotha stressed about going back to the streets and atoning for his past ways, the older man would give his nuts just to have the opportunity. Yet it was Blow that had the opportunity. He'd be free from that cage when the sun rose on their side of the world, free to obtain the redemption his soul thirsted for.

Jihad glanced up at the small, narrow window. It was a mocking contraption, as if whoever designed the prison *wanted* each man there to see how beautiful the sunshine was, but also remind him of the simplest pleasures he took for granted. His gaze returned to Blow. "The night only lasts for twelve hours, ock, so when things seem at their worst, just remind yourself that it only remains dark for seven hundred and twenty minutes. If you can stand tall until then, the sun *must* shine your way in the thirteenth hour," he spoke before closing his Quran and climbing down from the top bunk.

Jihad made his way to the sink and washed his hands before splashing cold water over his face. Blow watched as the old man cleansed his nose, washed behind his ears, and rinsed his mouth. He'd performed that same ritual every day for the past twenty years

28

in preparation for his conversations with God. After drying his face, Jihad's eyes found Blow.

"You'll be free in a few hours, and the moment you step foot on the other side of those gates, ock, the real war begins," he spoke before walking over and extending his hand to him.

Blow studied it for mere seconds before accepting the gesture and allowing the OG to help him to his feet. The men faced off as they waited for the sun to make its way to their side of the world.

Jihad placed a hand on Blow's shoulder. "Never allow your regrets to blindfold you to your survival, black man. The eyes see, the ears listen, and the mouth is drawn to the flame, but what if the eyes could hear? What if the ears could see, and the mouth understood that the flame could incinerate it? Maybe then we'd understand why the mute person uses more sense than people that possess all their senses," he jeweled him. The old man turned and took his prayer rug off the shelf before glancing up at the window. "You came into this prison a savage the streets knew as Blow, but you're leavin' out as a changed black man," he whispered while resting his rug on the floor. Turning to look at his younger friend and fixing him with a penetrating gaze, Jihad asked a question that many men never *truly* had an answer to. "Who are you?"

Blow glanced up at the small window. The heavens had turned a pale gray. The thirteenth hour. His eyes returned to the humble man. "I'm Deacon Robert Matthews," he professed.

Jihad smiled a half smile. He wished he could have brought Blow over to the community, but knew that Allah was an omnipresent deity that chose his warriors no matter the culture. Jihad nodded. He was aware that he himself would never see the sun rise on the other side of that gate again, but had come to find peace in that reality. *When you roll the dice, sometimes you lose more than just the rent money*, he thought as he prepared to humble himself before God and ask him for just one more roll.

***

The man had introduced himself as King, but Messiah knew that was merely another deception within his castle of lies.

"Let me ask you somethin', playa, real talk." King was the first to break the silence.

Messiah didn't respond. His attention was more in tune with the scene before them. They were in the vast backyard of the mansion, and the picture that Messiah's eyes were capturing was beyond anything he'd ever seen before. The yard was illuminated by octane-fueled torches that cast dancing reflections on the surface of a massive swimming pool. The clear waters shimmered as its inhabitants engaged in their choice of pleasure. Messiah stared in shock as in and around the chlorinated water, eroticism intermingled with the taboo.

This some real Sodom and Gomorrah shit, man! he thought as he witnessed two men doing the abnormal.

King chuckled at the expression on Messiah's face. The party outside was just as outlandish as the masquerade theme on the inside of the house. Outside of their masks, the crowd out back were as naked as a baby fresh out of its mother's womb. Same-sex freak shit was in full swing as well as pornographic displays of men versus the women. They fucked, sucked, and explored their wildest fantasies, all from behind the cover of the strange masks they wore. No one would recognize who they were giving themselves to. All they had to distinguish man from woman was the genitalia, so it was an untamed fantasy to fulfill without the fear of being judged in the morning.

"Do you know that *everyone* wears a mask in one form or another? Think about it, playa: most of the men you know, the majority of young brothas you know out here in these wicked streets, hide behind big guns, their money, and the lyrics of rap songs. Behind all that bullshit, they're merely men in search of an identity," King spoke as he pointed at the freak show and singling out a thick, creamy-skinned woman. She sat at the edge of the pool, mouth agape in ecstasy, and though her face was covered by a cocaine white feather mask, one could see the hunger in her eyes as her legs spread eagle and a muscular dark-skinned cat sucked her clit. "A lot of these women spend thousands of dollars on artificial hair, nails, and body enhancements because they don't understand true beauty, Messiah, but just beyond all that Barbie doll persona resides a beautiful woman that merely seeks the attention of a solid brotha," he stressed.

King paused to take two glasses of champagne from a tray of cocktails a waiter offered. He attempted to pass Messiah one, but he merely glared at the host from behind the evil mask. King shrugged before chuckling and downing one of the drinks. He pointed the empty glass at Messiah. "It's the mask, playa. It gives people refuge from who they truly are. Even you, baby boy. *You* wear a mask. You carry yourself like a true businessman. You hide behind a soft smile and that lucrative business you started. Yet, just beyond the surface, you're a murdering pimp that uses your women to move narcotics for you and those Jamaicans that——"

Messiah's hand was a blur when he reached out and slapped the champagne glass out of King's hand. "Look, fuck boy, I ain't here to hear 'bout your intel on my life. Fuck you think you are, Sherlock Holmes or some shit?" he growled. Messiah had lost his patience and he took a step forward. "Fuck that shit you talm'bout. I'm here for my wife, and after that?" He left the threat hanging in the air as he shrugged and gave dude a wicked grin.

King's deadly stare rose from the shattered glass at his feet and focused on him. He raised an open palm in the air as if to wave someone off, causing Messiah to glance behind him. A masked waiter had drawn down on him and if that wasn't enough, the strange necklace began to light up.

"This little rendezvous was just a show of what you're up against, lil daddy. Tomorrow we'll make the trade. I want the rest of my chedda, playa, and don't forget the diamond." King's words left no room for negotiation.

When Messiah turned to him, he was surprised to see the man stripping down to his boxers. Messiah was beside himself with that other level shit. *This hoe nigga playin' me like a sucka! On God, I'm gonna whack this boy!* Though his thoughts were homicidal, he held his composure. "So, this was all some kind of game?" Messiah wondered aloud before rubbing his hand over his bald head. "Why the fuck you keep talm'bout a diamond I ain't got? All I got for you is some hot lead for ya head, homeboy!" He tossed caution to the wind.

King laughed before making his way over to the edge of the glowing pool. A slim woman with a curvaceous, athletic build swam over to him and King smiled at Messiah as her hand slid underneath his boxers.

"Ya boy Sunjay can tell you where the ice is, playboy. Let's just hope he hasn't done anything foolish, or..." King returned the suggestive threat. He smiled wickedly as the slim woman liberated his nature and wrapped her lips around him. "Your wife..."

He paused before looking down at the wild blow job. "Now she has some nice lips," he murmured.

Chapter 3
2010
THE NEXT DAY

Marcella stepped off the Greyhound bus with a suitcase that contained the only possessions she had left. After Assata's death and Jazzy going to prison for the murder of Freedom, the city of Denton, Texas wasn't safe for her. Marcella hated the shit she'd caused and regretted allowing her envy and lust for Assata to bring the snake out of her, but she knew that regrets don't have the power to change shit. She was just glad to have escaped with her life. She'd heard about the hundred thousand dollar ticket on her head and knew that her own reflection would whack her for that kind of bread.

Marcella's sharp eyes took in the glass towers of downtown Dallas as she inhaled a lung full of its promising air. "Long time, no see, triple-D. It's good to be home," she whispered to the city that had birthed her. Marcella placed an oversized pair of glasses on her face before heading out of the bus station.

She hadn't seen her mother or brothers since CPS stole her from her crying mother's arms, and she couldn't wait to see the look on their faces when they saw her after twenty years. *I wonder what my brother Messiah looks like now?* she wondered as she hailed a cab. Marcella Dashia Ridge was broke and on her last leg, and when a serpent was cornered, it only had one basic instinct.

***

Messiah entered the room with a heavy heart. Coffee had already prepared him for what to expect and it fucked with his mental. Black was on her deathbed, and no amount of his money could create a donor for her. He stood with his back to the door and studied her. His mother had aged over the course of weeks. Her hair was graying and her still form appeared fragile. *All this money I got and I can't pay for what she needs to live. Mane, God don't give a fuck about nothin' but the collection plate!* he thought harshly.

Slowly, Messiah made his way over to where she lay. Black's eyes were closed and if Messiah wouldn't have glanced at the EKG machine, he would've thought she'd already checked out on him. He felt the pressure building up behind his eyes as his soul cursed God. Messiah leaned down and placed a soft kiss on her forehead and before he could catch it, a lone drop of water fell from his left eye and splashed against her face.

Black's eyes cracked open. Confusion was evident in her stare. "Who...are you?" Her voice was scratchy, distant.

Messiah's heart crumbled to pieces, but he smiled a sad smile in spite of himself. "A friend, Queen. I'm just a real good friend," he replied before pushing a strand of hair out of her face.

"Did God send you?" she asked. "If...if he did, you need to tell that muthafucka that I ain't ready yet." She frowned, but seemed too weak to move.

Messiah's vision blurred at her words. *Baby, God stopped giving a fuck 'bout us way back in '87,"* he wanted to say, but he kept it in his head. "Yeah, Queen, God sent me, and he wanted me to tell you not to give up just yet, 'cause he has big plans for you," he spoke with a heavy heart.

Black's eyes filled with wonder as Messiah walked over to the chair and pushed it next to her bed. Messiah sat and when he looked up at her, he noticed her eyes were fixated on the black book he'd laid in his lap.

"Did he tell you?" She broke the silence before lifting her sleepy eyes to his. "Did he tell you what plans he has for me?" she asked.

The question almost folded him, but Messiah disguised the turmoil by opening the book to where they'd left off. "God never tells us any of his plans, ma. He's a secretive dude that allows us to go through certain shit before we figure out His intent." He pointed as he spoke from the diary. "Maybe his plans will be revealed in this book, 'cause if not..." He paused and looked down at the cursive script. "If not, shid, they gonna put us in the same coffin!" he declared before he began reading.

***

Entry 7:

It's December sixteenth and the breath of winter can be felt on the wind. Today was a long day, but even with my trials, I observe you, Messiah. I'm proud of you, baby boy! Let me tell you a secret that's not so much a secret as it is the truth. Messiah, you have been molded for the life of a crook. You are what many men aren't. You have too much heart to be a successful pimp, but not enough heart to not play the game. See, baby, the thing with Pimpin Maxwell, Suave, and every other man that claims to be an avid connoisseur of women is they've become a victim of their own lies. A lot of men have convinced themselves that they truly understand the nature of one of God's most complex creatures: a woman! Yet if you ask a man why a woman cheats, he'll simply give you the reason "men" cheat! If you ask a man why a woman is more emotional than men, he'll give you some psychobabble bullshit of estrogen versus testosterone, rather than merely forfeiting his pride and admitting that he hasn't the slightest clue!

A man will act as if he knows what a woman wants, needs, and deserves, but how would he know that when no one woman is like the last or the next? You can't fuck, kiss, make love to, or love the next woman as you did the woman before her, Messiah. You must see beyond what a woman has between her legs and that's where you'll find her self-worth. I've always wanted you to change the game and not let the game change you. That's why I named you Messiah. A savior! Never forget this, son: a woman is twenty percent initiative, thirty percent emotional, and ten percent crazy. She's twenty percent physical and twenty percent of things you'll never figure out. Altogether, that equates a hundred percent of a perfect woman. Before I end this, know this, baby: God didn't create a woman to be independent. He created the woman only because he saw that man wasn't shit without her, even with ordainment over everything in the Garden of Eden. He created the woman from a man's side - his rib! If she was meant to be behind him, God would have molded her from his backbone. If she was meant to lead, don't you think the creator would've shaped her from the man's brain? God meant for her to be his helper, and 99.9 percent of the time, Messiah, The only reason a woman tries her hand at independence is because outside of his dick and materialistic tokens, most men don't give their women much to be dependent on.

Mama

***

1991

"Messiah...Messiah, wake up, baby."

Black's voice was distant to him. She called him a few more times before her voice seeped into the waters of his sleep. Messiah's eyes fluttered open, confused. "Huh? What's up, Mama?" he grumbled in frustration. He turned his back to her and attempted to drift back to sleep.

"Boy, I ain't gonna tell yo' black ass no mo', wake up!" she demanded more firmly.

Messiah's mind registered the threat and he laughed. He was beyond the fear of a whoopin' from his mama, but he cracked his eyes open and rolled over to face her nonetheless. "'Sup, Ma, what time is it?" he questioned while rubbing sleep from his eyes. He'd just fallen asleep and wasn't feeling his Queen disturbing his rest.

"Boy, it's time for you to open the gift I brought for you. With your heart broken, I didn't want to give it to you last night. You wouldn't have known how to appreciate it," she spoke as she studied him. *I wish you were here to see your son, Ced. You'd be proud,* she thought.

Messiah looked up at her with a puzzled expression on his face. "That's a bet, Ma, where is it?" he asked as his eyes fell to her empty hands.

Black giggled before turning and making her way to the door, but paused and looked back at him before opening it.

36

Candy stood in the doorway with a seductive smile on her face. There was a big red bow tied around her perky titties, and as she strutted into the room, Messiah couldn't take his eyes away from the imprint of her lower lips. They seemed to pout behind the red material of the thong. The young Puerto Rican was just as gorgeous at twenty-seven as she was when he'd first laid eyes on her when she was twenty-three. She sashayed over to where Messiah lay and with her eyes at half mast, she gazed down at him with a freak show playing in her pupils.

"What's good, papi chulo? I hear you're the new nigga to see in these streets," she spoke before placing her manicured hand on her slim waist.

Messiah looked to his mother with a curious expression before his eyes made their way back to Candy. "Hoe, I ain't got no conversation unless you got my compensation!" he spat a line Pimpin Maxwell had taught him.

"Your convo is not only your gift, pimp friend of mine, but it's also your hustle. Hoes out here are deprived of a mutual beneficial conversation, so when you bless 'em with the gift of your tongue, you're developing the hoe's mind. Never – never - cheap talk. Your words are diamonds, and why would you give diamonds away for the sake of frivolous chit chat? Mack hard, mack buddy!" Messiah momentarily reflected on the jewels the old man had dropped on him.

Candy was taken aback. She'd known the young'n since he was an eleven-year-old pup, hustling packs for Blow. Now he was a budding boss and she'd been gifted to him. She nodded before turning to Black.

"I got it from here, Black Diamond," she whispered huskily with a predatory expression on her face. Her vision returned to Messiah. "Daddy wants my choosin' fee," she whispered before runnin' her tongue over her top teeth.

***

Sunjay's eyes opened with a struggle. The meds they'd given him had Sunjay feeling lovely as he tried to shake the cobwebs from his memory. He was confused and just beyond the fog of the anesthesia, he could feel the pain of his wounds. He attempted to get up, but the pain became more pronounced. He fell back flat against the hospital bed. He tried to recall how he'd gotten in that position. *Fuck am I doin' laid up in the hospital? Damn, my head knockin' like the police!* he thought.

A deep growl escaped his lips as he gritted his teeth against the pain. Sunjay couldn't understand why he was in the hospital feeling like a human piñata. His eyes traveled the room, capturing his surroundings, and that's when he saw her. There was a caramel-hued girl asleep in a chair beside his bed. Sunjay studied her. Her hair was pulled back into a tight bun that left her long bangs free to curve over her eyes. The curve of her pink lips was just enough to send his mannish mind on a journey through a pornographic fantasy. As if she'd felt his stare, shorty's eyes slowly opened. Sunjay didn't blink as he tried to place her, but he drew a blank. *Damn, lil mama's eyes match her skin*, he thought as his eyes fell to the small diamond piercing in her nose.

She gave him a soft smile. "Damn, lil daddy, I thought you was gonna die or somethin'."

Sunjay merely glared. "Who are you?" His voice was foreign to even him.

She rolled her eyes before crossing her legs. The act caused her already short mini dress to ride up her thigh. The material had a small slit on the left side and Sunjay could see a darker shade of her skin that led up to paradise. It was a test of his willpower. *Shawty can get it, on gang!* His thoughts were explicit.

Crossing her arms over her chest, the mystery girl began to bounce her foot. "I'm the bitch that saved your life, nigga. At least you can say thank you, fuck you, *somethin'* other than givin me all that 'tude!" she sassed with a snake of her neck.

Sunjay found it cute and the crooked grin on his face was the evidence. "'*Tude?* Fuck that mean?" He chuckled. "Naw, I ain't on that otha shit, ma, I just don't know you. Where I'm from, talkin' to strangers will get you down bad." He offered a cease fire, but the lady merely giggled.

She made a point with emphasizing her words as she swept her hand around the room. "Well, I can see that you didn't take heed to that shit 'cause this sho' look down bad to me." She gave him a "now what" expression.

Sunjay laughed at the pun intended. "Shit!" he moaned as pain exploded at the back of his head.

The girl rushed over to him at the pained expression on his face. "You okay?" she asked as she stood above him.

Seconds passed before the pain eased into a distant throb. That's when his mind reverted to his greatest curiosity. "Why am I here? I don't remember shit," he asked as confusion eased into his facial features.

She studied him peculiarly. "First off, let's focus on one thing at a time, lil daddy." She placed her elbows on the guard rail of the bed and rested her face in the palms of her hands. "My name is Dream. And you are…?" she inquired with a sexy smile.

Sunjay rubbed his hands down his face. "My name Sunjay. But fuck that, answer my question," he demanded.

"Cute," Dream whispered before runnin' a finger over his busted lip. "Your name," she clarified with a smirk. "To be real with you, all I can tell you is I found you in that apartment over there in Best for Less. You were tryin' to make it to the hallway and you were drenched in blood. You was——" she was sayin' when Sunjay was plummeted into days past.

Everything came flooding back to him like a horror movie. *"Nooo, Stebo! You said we was just gonna take his shit! Don't kill the boy, baby!" Tamika's voice filled his head as if he was back there in that living room.*

I gotta get to my burna! he remembered thinking.

Sunjay's eyes blinked against the onslaught of thoughts as the scene unfolded in his mind. Dream stared in confusion as his hand gripped the guardrail on the side of the bed as if it was his only anchor to sanity.

Sunjay remembered crawling to the open door and the face of the girl that had come to his aid. "Hey...can you hear me?" she'd asked the night she found him bathed in his own blood. "Hey, can you hear me?"

Her voice brought him out the waters of the past. Sunjay blinked before his eyes focused on her.

"You remember, don't you?" she asked.

Sunjay responded in a way that she wasn't expecting. He tore the IV out of his arm and pushed the safety rail down on the bed.

Dream stepped back in surprise. "Wh-what the hell you doin', Sunjay?" she stuttered.

He ignored the sharp pain that raced through his body, but paused when he got his feet on the floor. The meds had him sluggish, but murderous intent and street smarts enflamed his motives. Sunjay's eyes were sharp as they bore into Dream's.

"Look, mama, I need to get outta this hospital before they have the law in here questionin' me 'bout shit I can't explain. Plus..." His words faltered as he struggled to stand.

She studied him before making her way to him and wrapping her arm around his waist to help him keep his balance. Sunjay placed an arm around her neck, using her as a brace. He looked down at her with appreciation in his stare. "Plus?" she asked curiously.

He studied her for moments of eternity before somethin' evil bled into his gaze. "Plus..." He paused before runnin' his hand over the split in the back of his head. He winced at the instant throbbing of the gash. "Plus, I'm gonna whack them niggas *and* that bitch that did this to me," he vowed.

***

1991

"Ain't you gonna unwrap your gift?" Candy asked after Black had excused herself.

Messiah sat up and tossed the blanket away from him before slipping from the bed. His face was void of emotion as his eyes rolled over her beauty. The plumpness of her lips, the roundness of her breasts, and finally, the imprint of her pussy lips. "Ya ass don't determine your class, hoe. I don't like to repeat myself. Where my trap before you start runnin' your mouth?" he spat. Though his words were firm, anyone with a set of eyes would've recognized the nervousness in his posture. Pimpin had schooled him to perfection, but play time was over. He was standing before his first whore.

Candy was digging his ism as she ran a manicured nail down his chest. "Okay, daddy, I got my choosin' fee, but let me give it to you *after* I give you your gift," she cooed seductively.

Messiah studied her for only a moment before doing something he used to fantasize about when he was younger. He reached out and pulled the bow on the ribbon. The silk material unraveled and fell to the floor.

First mistake! Candy thought as the ribbon pooled by her feet. Candy knew that Black and Pimpin Maxwell were watching and listening to their boy's first introduction into the life, and she was turned on by the thought of an audience. Messiah stood lookin' awestruck as his young mind spoke to his dick head. Candy smiled as his eyes bore into her protruding nipples. She slowly slid out of the red thong and allowed it to dangle from her finger. The primal hunger in Messiah's adolescent eyes was a dancing flame as the red panties slipped from her grip and joined the ribbon at her feet. She smiled a freak's smile when his gaze traveled to her bare treasure and became lost within her garden. His boxers tented when Candy slipped her fingers behind the waistband of them and eased them down his thighs.

Messiah tensed. *Awww, he's embarrassed!* she thought. She knew he'd never had any pussy before and as Candy glanced down at his hardened six inches, she licked her lips. She crawled onto the bed and laid on her back before eyeing him from between her creamy thighs. *Umph! Lil nigga just like every other man: tough when his pants up, but putty when his dick is in the hands of a real bitch!* she mentally concluded. The promiscuous Latina smiled at the uncertainty in his eyes before taking his hand and pulling him on top of her.

"Relax, daddy. It's not the pussy you should fear. It's the bitch that it's attached to that's dangerous," she whispered as she pulled him down for a sloppy tongue kiss.

Their tongues tangoed for a few seconds before Candy eased her hand on top of his head and softly pushed down. Messiah was confused, but she was a gifted navigational system. "Put your face down by my pussy, papi, kiss her!" she moaned deeply. At that time in the early nineties, it was against a playa's law to suck pussy, yet just as with every other cat before him, Messiah figured the bitch could keep a secret. He was about to learn a valuable lesson of being conned for his tongue as he did as she instructed. He slid down Candy's body until he was face to face with her paradise and as soon as his eyes captured his first glance of the weapon that women used to take down some of the world's strongest of men, he couldn't take his vision away. Candy's essence resembled a pink budding rose, slightly moist from the morning's mist. Her pussy lips puckered as if they *wanted* to kiss him.

"Kiss her, daddy!" she encouraged while gazing down at him.

"Nigga, you can't hit the blunt, dawg, you got yuck mouth! Coochie breath-ass nigga!"

Messiah could already hear Sunjay clowning him, yet he bowed his head to taste her nonetheless. Messiah's lips were inches from her lower lips when a confused expression eased onto his face. He studied her femininity. *Fuck! Somethin'' ain't right!* he thought as he studied the short string that hung from between her clam. His eyes shot up to Candy's grinning face. *"Never* lick on a pussy that you ain't cutting *exclusively,* Messiah," she gave him some boss game. Candy toyed with her stiff nipples as she watched him. "A bitch will be fucking two or three different men and you'll never know 'cause we have our ways to shrink and take the stink from our kitty," she whispered. "Open her, daddy." The freak in her cried as she placed the tip of her manicured nail between her teeth.

Just beyond his confusion, Messiah knew that the jewels she was bestowing upon him would be paramount to his success. He used his thumbs to spread her lips open, and there, staring back at him, was Candy's choosing fee. He pulled the string and the knot of money eased from her heaven. "This is a diamond for you, Messiah. A sneaky bitch will try your ism, and this is one of the many stash spots to look in if she's lookin'' to cuff on you," she revealed before propping herself up on her elbows. "Now, come give me that dick."

***

"Fuck me, nigga. Fuck…meee!" Porsha screamed as Rock ran dick in her from the back.

They were so lost within erotica that neither heard the front door open and Tasha, Porsha's mother, enter the living room. She'd come home early from work and all she wanted to do was shower and hop in the bed with her man. Tasha and Rock had been rocking for four years and she loved his thuggish ass. She believed that she'd finally met the man of her dreams.

"There! Right…there!"

Tasha could hear the passionate cries of her young daughter. Tasha tossed her purse on the couch before slipping off her flats. *I know this little ungrateful bitch ain't fuckin' none of her nothin'-ass niggas in my house!* she thought as the sounds of lovemaking navigated her steps. *Where the hell is Rock at anyway?* she wondered as rage blossomed in her heart at the realization of the cries coming from *her* room. *This stank bitch has the audacity to have her lil ass in my bed? Oh, hell naw!* Her thoughts enflamed her pace as she made it to her bedroom door.

"I'm cuminnnng!" Porsha's climax was an odyssey to the heavens, but it was the second voice that was a suicidal fall from devastating heights for her mother.

"Yeah, come on wit' it, cum on that dick for daddy! Wet this mu'fucka up!"

Rock's pleasure pushed Tasha into a pool of reflections.

"Mama, you need to check ya man. When you be goin' to work, he be lookin' at me funny," Porsha confided one day as she and Tasha sat with her eyes glued to the TV, watching General Hospital.

She reluctantly glanced over at her daughter with disgust in her stare before taking a drag from her Newport 100. "Porsha, quit lyin' so damn much! Rock ain't worried 'bout yo' fast ass! You've been walkin round this muthafucka wit' those short-ass clothes on tryin' to get his attention!" she admonished while dumping the ashes in an empty beer bottle. Tasha sucked her teeth at the surprised expression on her daughter's face. "What you need to do is start lookin' for somewhere else to stay 'cause you gettin' way too grown 'round here. Your fast ass ain't payin no bills and up in my face lyin' on my man! Girl, bye!" Tasha spat before exhaling a fluffy cloud of nicotine smoke. She gave Porsha a roll of the eyes and a "girl, be gone" hand.

"But, Mama, he's doing nasty stuff to——"

"Bye, Porsha!" She'd cut her off with a piercing glare.

"Damn, lil mama, you's a beast!"

Rock's voice brought Tasha back to the present. As she stood at the door that would castrate her happily-ever-after, her heart became a turbulent ocean that drowned her. She pushed it slowly open and the smell of their betrayal slapped her in the face harder than a physical blow as her eyes captured the treason that was taking place in her own bedroom. Rock's face was contorted in euphoria as Porsha gave him sloppy head, and at that moment, Tasha's sanity died.

"You scandalous *bitch*!" she stressed the word.

"Shit!" Rock spat in surprise when he heard the hurt that resonated from Tasha's heart. He damn near choked Porsha with his length when he jumped.

"Mama!" Porsha shouted as she tried to get off her knees.

Tasha's reaction was the same as every other woman that's ever been in her position. She blamed her daughter for the sins of a no good-ass nigga. She rushed Porsha and grabbed a fist full of her hair before delivering a powerful uppercut to her face. Porsha tried to fight back, but her attempts were no match for her mother's rage. All the while, Rock had slipped into his clothes and was escaping from the civil war his trife ways had created.

***

"No, baby, slow down!" Candy moaned in his ear. "Why are you rushing? The pussy won't disappear," she schooled.

As soon as Messiah had slid inside her, he took off like a jack rabbit. Candy placed her hands on his ass to control his pace. She spread her legs wide. "Now *stroke* this pussy, daddy. It's all about the stroke." She guided him. She could feel him losing control as her walls constricted around him, her ocean baptizing him until a demon shot from his nut sack in a squirt. Messiah's eyes rolled to the back of his head as Candy's lower lips milked him.

"See, young blood, that feeling you're experiencing right now is the reason some of the world's greatest hustlas are merely broke niggas with rich histories today." Pimpin Maxwell's voice caused Messiah to roll off Candy and attempt to cover himself.

"Damn, Pimpin, get out of here!" he demanded as Black's laughter followed her into the room.

She leaned against the wall and watched the exchange. "We watched your performance, and——"

"What? Why the fuck would y'all do some freak shit like that?" Messiah interrupted him.

Pimpin Maxwell raised his palm, demanding silence. "It was imperative to your game, mack buddy. How else would we know your flaws?" he asked before reaching into the breast pocket of his suit coat. Pimpin came out with two cigars and handed one to him. "Congratulations. You now know why wars have been fought over what's between a whore's legs, daddy." He chuckled before placing the Cuban between his teeth. "Let me school you to your three mistakes so you'll be able to play at higher stakes," he jazzed before pointing at Candy. "When this whore disrespected your spit by flashin' you her tits, you made a sucka's decision, lil daddy."

His words carried Messiah back to the moment the OG was speaking of. *"Okay, daddy, I got my choosin' fee, but let me give it to you after I give you your gift.* He remembered Candy's words.

Pimpin saw that he understood and nodded his head in acknowledgement. "Never choose pussy over your money, Messiah. I've never met a hoe that was born with a million dollar pussy between her legs, but I've met plenty of chumps that will pay a mill for some good snatch that they could have gotten for free," Pimpin spoke before reaching down and retrieving Messiah's boxers. "Your second mistake was kissin' this hoe, pimp buddy. *That's* a violation!" he said as he nodded toward Candy. Pimpin tossed the underwear to him. "A hoe's mouth has tasted more cum than Trojan condoms. Never taste a whore's lips for the sake of exotic trips, lil daddy. *Never* allow a bitch's sex appeal to blindfold you to what's critical. That's how a lot of these niggas get caught with their pants down and left with nothing to call their own but a wet tally whacker." Pimpin Maxwell's words were the gospel as he turned and headed for the door. He paused in the doorway and glanced back at Messiah. "You was born with one dick to fuck a woman's twat with, but today..." His words trailed as he pointed the unlit cigar at his protégé. "Today I'm giving you a second dick, one you'll be able to fuck her mind with, and there's no deeper orgasm than a mental one, young blood," he schooled before making his exit.

***

Porsha laid on her stomach with her face in her pillow. She couldn't seem to find her way out of the maze her mind had become. *This bitch put her hands on me because her nigga can't keep his dick in his pants!* she thought. Her young mind couldn't wrap around the wrong in her own sins.

"Get out!" Tasha spat. She stood in the doorway of Porsha's room with a half-empty bottle of Thunderbird in her hands. Her eyes were bloodshot from crying, but as she attempted to drown her pain with the cheap liquor, she wondered more of Rock's return than she did of her daughter's heartbroken melody.

Porsha turned and sat up in the bed. "Wh-what?" she stuttered.

"Bitch!" Tasha took a threatening step closer. "I won't repeat myself. You couldn't wait to fuck him, I saw how you used to look at him." Her drunken words were low.

"No, Mama, he——"

"Shut up and get the fuck out of my house!" Tasha cut her off. She turned the bottle up to her lips and guzzled from the spirits.

Porsha slid from the bed and slipped her foot into her shoes. "Where would I go, Mama, huh? It's two in the morning!" she pleaded with tears streaking down her face.

Tasha glared at her without responding. Porsha understood. Her mother didn't give a fuck.

"Okay, Mama, but don't come to my funeral when they find me dead somewhere," she sniffled as she slid into her coat.

Tasha stepped to the side to let her pass. "I hate you!" she shouted.

Porsha dropped her head before running out of that room and into a cold world that didn't give a fuck about her tears, age, or innocence.

Chapter 4

Sunjay glanced around to ensure no one was watching before he pushed some canned goods and a big bag of cooking flour aside. He pulled a brown paper bag from underneath his shirt and stuffed it as far back in the cabinet as he could before rearranging things how he'd found them. He closed the cabinet door before making his way to the refrigerator and opening it. *I'll come back for that shit later*, he thought of the nine-and-a-half ounces of crack cocaine he'd just stashed. Sunjay grabbed the cold pitcher of watermelon Kool-Aid and took a sneaky look around before turning the jug up to his lips. He got two good gulps in.

"Sunjay Carter, what the hell I tell you 'bout puttin' ya nasty lips on my pitchers!" Ms. Betty fumed in her southern drawl.

Kool-Aid shot from Sunjay's mouth and nose at the sound of his sixty-six-year-old grandmother's soulful voice. Even at that age, she moved as if age was merely a blessing from God rather than a robber of youth.

She stormed over and smacked the back of his head. "You betta clean that mess up too!" she admonished as she pried the pitcher from his hand.

Sunjay laughed before wrapping her in a tight embrace. "My fault, Granny, but you know *nobody* makes Kool-Aid like you do!" he tried buttering her up. He released her and let her put the pitcher back in the refrigerator.

Ms. Betty took the dish towel off the counter and handed it to him. "There's no special way to make no damn Kool-Aid, you heathen!" She rolled her eyes at her baby. "Besides, what does that have to do with you puttin' ya filthy lips on that pitcher, Sunny?" She addressed him by the nickname she'd given him when he was just a young pup.

Sunjay squatted down and began wiping the Kool-Aid off the floor.

"You've been doing that mess since you were a lil boy, and all those ass whoopin's ain't did you not a lick of good." She shook her head in mock disbelief. "What you doin' here, boy? You don't show up until you're hungry or somethin' crazy has happened to you. I'm tellin you, Sunjay, ain't nothin' out there in them streets, and the devil ain't nobody's friend," she told him before stepping over to the dish rack for a plate. Mrs. Betty made her way over to the stove. Sunjay watched as she began scooping red beans onto it before adding a nice helping of chitlins to the side. She then scooped two helpings of cabbage onto the plate before topping it off with a sweet slice of hot water cornbread. "The hot sauce is already on the table," she spoke as she handed him the plate and turned to leave.

Sunjay watched her departure. *Yeah, she's 'bout to give me a sermon,* he thought before glancing down at the plate. He laughed and set it down on the counter. Hardheaded as ever, he took the Kool-Aid back out of the refrigerator and turned it up to his lips. *I gotta leave Granny a few chips before I leave,* he reminded himself.

"And you bet' not be in there messin' with that Kool-Aid again, Sunny!" Ms. Betty's voice was stern.

***

Rock snorted another line of the tan powder off the scarred table. Its potency caused him to fall back against the couch and lay his head back. He stared up at the ceiling as the room began to spin. He was so high that he was oblivious to the loud knocking at the door. It sounded distant to him.

"Rock, open the door...*please.*"

The soft voice swam into the halo of his high. The heroin he'd just snorted was an attentive lover that rode him better than any woman he'd ever met.

"Rock, I know you're in there," the voice pleaded.

With effort, Rock stumbled to his feet and made his way to the door. Flinging it open, he glared at her. "What!" he spat, as if she'd interrupted him.

Porsha studied him curiously before a sad smile eased onto her face. *This nigga high as Pookie was on* New Jack City! she thought as her eyes registered the barely visible film around his right nostril.

"What you want, Porsha? I'm busy!"

Porsha's eyes scanned the breezeway of the neglected housing projects. The smell of piss was ever powerful, but it was the filth that littered the ground that was the evidence of how fucked up things were for the Section 8 tenants of Fishtrap. Ironically, there was an empty Old English forty ounce bottle and tainted syringe discarded a few feet away from Rock's front door. The glassy look in his eyes told the tale of how blitzed he was. Rock was so lit that he damn near went into a nod while standing at the door. Yet he wasn't so far away from reality that he missed the look of disgust on Porsha's face as she stared down at the dirty needle.

"Why you actin' like this, Rock? We ain't gotta sneak around no more. You said you was gonna leave her and we was gonna be together anyway, right?" Her words were skeptical as her eyes found him.

Rock began scratching his arms as if he had a terrible itch, but it was merely the opium-induced high that made love to his senses. "Riiight...right, but you gotta let me get some shit together first, lil mama, then it's just me and you," he promised while scratching his neck. "I'm busy right now. I'll get up wit' you later."

His words sounded like some bullshit that even she knew was a fantasy that would never be fulfilled. Porsha shook her head sadly. "Well, you're 'bout to be a lil busier." She paused to stuff her hands down into the pockets of her hoodie sweat shirt. "I'm pregnant, Rock, and guess who's the daddy?" She laughed bitterly.

***

Sunjay was as full as an anorexic white girl at an all you can eat buffet. The Beans was active as usual when he stepped out of Ms. Betty's apartment. Bad-ass kids terrorized the hood and as he stood and took in the life of the ghetto, Sunjay knew he had to find a way to get his G-lady away from the place she'd called home for the past twenty years.

"Break yo'self, punk!" a squeaky voice declared.

Sunjay hastily went for the burna on his waist, but as he realized who was sticking him up, he fell into a fit of laughter. The young boy aimed a plastic cap gun at him, holding it sideways. Lil Zetti stared at him defiantly. "Give me five dollars or I'ma shoot you like bang bang!" he shouted.

Sunjay had a soft spot for the young'n that ran deep. They shared the same story that ninety percent of people from the slums had as a reality: a drug-addicted mother and a father that just didn't give a fuck. He strolled over to the nine-year-old and stepped behind him. "Here, let me show you how to put ya G down, lil nigga." He took the toy gun from the child's hands. Sunjay placed the toy gun in Lil Zetti's right palm and closed his left over it. "Hold it like this and aim straight, lil daddy. All that holdin' a gun sideways shit only works in the movie, you can't get ya mans like that," he schooled him as his eyes fell to the boy's feet. He shook his head in frustration. "Lil Zetti, where them shoes I just bought you, bro?" He fumed at the sight of the boy's bare feet. *I'ma kill Felicia's hoe ass! Always takin' from her seed to feed her habits!* he thought as he dug in his pocket and pulled out a knot of money. "Did yo' mama take ya shoes?" he asked.

Lil Zetti's eyes grew wide as he viciously shook his head no.

"Don't lie to me, Lil Zetti. *Never* lie to me. We're family, and family don't lie to family, feel me?" He gave it to him raw while peeling forty dollars from the bankroll.

Sunjay watched as Lil Zetti dropped his head and looked down at the ground. He nodded his little head as if he'd been scolded, but Sunjay placed a knuckle underneath the little one's chin and lifted his head until they were eye to eye. "A man doesn't blink or look down when the pressure thick, lil bro, and *you* are the man of your house. You gotta be strong out here, Lil Zetti, 'cause these streets don't give a fuck 'bout our struggle." He spoke his heart before rubbing his hand over the boy's nappy head.

Lil Zetti glanced up at him with eyes that held a story that a child his age shouldn't share as a reflection. "Nobody does, Sunjay," he whispered before dropping the toy gun by his leg.

Sunjay's heart cracked from the admission - not because it came from a nine year old, but because it was a truth that not even he could dispute.

"Mama said she gonna buy me them LA Gear's that light up!" Lil Zetti's words were complemented by a smile, but Sunjay witnessed the uncertainty just beyond his facade. He nodded at the boy before stuffing the money in his pocket.

"Don't tell ya mama you got this. Give it to your sister and tell her I said get y'all somethin' to eat. I'm gonna get you some more J's tomorrow, fam., make sure you meet me right here." he spoke before the door opened behind him.

He and Lil Zetti turned to find Ms. Betty standing in the doorway. "Sunjay Carter, what I tell you about leavin' me all this money, boy? I'on need none of yo' devil's money. When you gonna get an honest job, huh?" his grandma scolded. Sunjay saw her eyes fall to Lil Zetti's bare feet. "Zetti, baby, where ya shoes at, chile? I know Felicia's crazy butt ain't lettin' you run round here barefoot! Where's ya sista Tweety?" She shot off question after question as she fanned herself with the six hundred dollars Sunjay had snuck into her purse.

Lil Zetti's eyes trailed to the parking lot, where music blasted from someone's car stereo. A group of people, mostly men, surrounded the thirteen-year-old girl as she twerked to the beat. "Lord have mercy, won't you look at this chile?" Ms. Betty's shocked voice came out in a whisper.

Danger bled into Sunjay's stare. He rose and contemplated storming over and snatching Tweety by the little bit of hair she had tied into a ponytail, but as he weighed his options, another young female stepped into the circle. A year older and twenty pounds thicker than Tweety's slim frame, Tanisha placed her hand on her knees, bending at the waist, and began bouncing her ass. She seemed to be extra with her movements and when her skirt lifted up, frustration ate at Sunjay's mind. Tanisha wasn't wearing any panties and as she danced, the men were tryin' to get a glimpse of her fourteen-year-old thickness.

"Go Tanisha, go Tanisha, go girl! That's my baby. I taught her that move!" a dark-skinned older lady raved as if her proclamation was some cool shit.

Sunjay shook his head, ashamed for her. *This bitch has her daughter out here naked and poppin' her ass for niggas that's old enough to be her daddy!*

The woman's encouragement was the spark the fuse needed to ignite. Tweety brought her dance to a halt as she turned to face Tanisha.

"Bitch, why you always tryin' to jock my style. You need to stay off my clit!" she spat.

The music died when Tanisha's face balled up and she stepped closer to Tweety. "Bitch? Yo' mammy's a bitch - bitch!" she retorted with a snake of her neck and a snap of her fingers.

Tweety wasted no time going in her mouth with a crisp three piece. The two girls went into a fall-out brawl, blow for blow, before Tweety reached out and grabbed a handful of Tanisha's dookie braids. She yanked the girl's head down and began delivering wild hooks to her face. "Bitch...you... asked...for...this...ass whooping!" she emphasized with each blow.

"Uh-uh, Tanisha, you betta get that lil hussy off you!" the girl's mother shouted before kicking off her dirty house shoes.

"Tweety!" Lil Zetti screamed while attempting to go to his sister's aid, but Sunjay held him tight as Tweety worked clean.

Just another day in the slums, he thought as he dragged Zetti over to Ms. Betty.

"No! Noooo, Sunjay! Tweety, Tweety, Sunjay!" he cried as he fought against him.

Ms. Betty took his hand. "Zetti, you betta calm ya butt down. *Now!*" Her voice was authoritative.

Zetti instantly calmed, though in tears. "But Tweety, Ms. Betty, she fight!" he whined as she pulled him into the apartment.

The old woman turned to Sunjay. "Boy, these streets don't love nobody," she told her grandson. When he didn't respond, Ms. Betty turned and headed into the apartment, but wanted to leave him with something to ponder. "Them white folks got a place for you and if they don't get ya first, God sho'll will," she spoke over her shoulder before the door closed.

Sunjay shook his head. *I love you too, ole lady*, he thought as he made his way to his car.

"Sunjay! Hold up, nigga, let me bark at you, dawg!" a short, dark-skinned kid called to him.

Sunjay instinctively reached for the banger on his waist, but calmed the animal in him when he recognized Murda. "Saayyy, blood, don't be runnin' up on me like that. I almost put ya shit on flat line!" He laughed. Sunjay kept it pushing toward his Crown Vic as Murda followed him.

"Yeah, whateva, nigga, I saw yo' slow ass reachin' for that burner, but if I was comin' for yo' head, I would've had my mans!" Murda bragged as he passed him the blunt of corn he was taking to the face.

Sunjay laughed without replying to the jab at his slow reaction. He'd been hearing Murda's name ringing in the streets and knew the young boy was wit' it. He'd known the young goon since he and Bam, his twin brother, had moved to the hood with their grand-mother, and he G'ed for their get down. "What's the business, bro bro, you said you tryin' to fuck wit' me?" he asked as he slid into the driver's seat. Sunjay leaned over and unlocked the door when Murda ran around the car to get in.

As soon as he plopped down in the seat, the boy reclined the seat. *Just like a nigga, always makin' themselves at home in another person's shit!* Sunjay thought as his eyes returned to the chaos out-side the car. He took another pull from the blunt before shaking his head in dismay. Somehow Tanisha had wound up on top of Tweety and was going to town on her face.

"Another day in the slums, huh, brah?" Murda's voice stole his attention.

Sunjay nodded as he exhaled and passed the blunt back to him. "No doubt, but I know that's not what you wanted to fuck with me 'bout?" he responded before putting the key in the ignition.

Murda nodded his confirmation. "Yeah. Yeah," he spoke over a lung filled with cannabis smoke. "Say, fam, you remember that hoe Tamika that set you up a few weeks ago?" His question was rhetorical.

Sunjay exhaled a hot whoosh of breath before lookin' at him with a suspicious gaze. His hand went to the back of his head and grazed the healing reminder they'd left him. *"Rule number one: never show an outside bitch where you rest yo' head!"* He seethed at the thought. "Brah, fuck I'm gonna forget 'bout the bitch that left me to meet the reaper!" he growled.

Murda laughed before easing the blunt clip out the window and glancing back at Sunjay. "I know where that hoe rest her head, blood. We can go rock her to sleep tonight!" he vowed.

***

"Hey, lil girl, you okay?" a dopefiend named Peabody asked as he stood over Porsha's bloodied body.

She laid on her side, curled up in the fetal position, on the side of the ragged building that she'd fallen beside. As he studied her, he knew she was on her last leg by the way her blood stained the material of her pants. He was confused. For a moment, he wondered if she'd been shot or even stabbed, but his concern was fleeting as the call of his addiction overpowered his morals. Peabody's eyes rolled over her until they landed on the Jordans on her feet. Sinister thoughts played in his mind as he looked up at her face. It was swollen beyond recognition and the blood that oozed from between her legs had begun to pool around her.

"Need...help!" she cried as she clutched her stomach.

"Now, you just be still, baby girl, ole Peabody got this." His words were loaded. Peabody saw something dark in her eyes as she stared distantly at him. Little did he know, Porsha's mind had reverted back to that moment - back to that moment when her vision of love became a shattered picture of a thousand pieces.

"Pregnant? What that gotta do with me?" Rock's voice seemed strained.

Porsha detected the danger in his tone, but misplaced love blindfolded her to the reality that lived just outside of the fairytale she craved to be true. She smiled up at him with an uncertain look on her face. "Can I come in?" she asked while ignoring his indirect rejection of the seed that was forming in her womb.

Rock stuck his head outside the door and glanced around before stepping to the side. After she'd stepped in, he closed the door before turning to face her. "How you know you're pregnant, Porsha?" he asked.

Porsha allowed her eyes to digest the reality that Rock faced every day. The interior was just as bad as the exterior. "I missed my period, so I took one of those prego tests from the corner store and it came back positive. I ain't fuckin' nobody else, so..." She left the conclusion hanging in the air as she turned her eyes to him.

Rock nodded his understanding. "Who else knows 'bout this?"

His question seemed out of place, but Porsha merely walked over to him and wrapped her arms around his neck. "Nobody, baby, I ain't told nobody. Im just glad we ain't gotta hide no more. Ain't you happy we're pregnant?" she asked before resting her face against his chest. "I love you, Rock," she purred before looking up to gauge his reaction.

Rock reached up and pulled her arms from around him before putting some distance between them. "Yeah, that's cool, but you're not planning to actually have no baby, are you?" he asked skeptically.

Porsha's face instantly balled up into a frown. She couldn't wrap her young mind around why the first man she'd ever loved was speaking on the fate of their creations as if it should have been questioned. "Wh-what!" she stammered before placing her hand on her hip. "Nigga, what the hell you mean? Really? You damn right I'm keepin' my baby! You wasn't worried 'bout that shit when you was runnin' up in me raw, but now that——"

Rock knocked the words back down her throat with a punch to the mouth and followed it up with a jab to the eye. Her right socket instantly swelled up.

"Uhhhh!" she cried out as Rock went crazy. His next punch dropped her to the floor and he began stomping her in the stomach.

"Bitch! You... won't... be... havin'... no... muthafuckin'... baby ... by... me!" He growled each word with a more forceful kick.

Porsha cried as she curled up into a protective ball, but life was an unforgiving observer that allowed fate to take its course. "You said... You, you said you love me!" she cried as Rock robbed her of what she tried to hold tight to.

"You said you love me! You said..." Porsha kept repeating as she came back to the present.

Peabody was confused at the repeated chant as he scratched his arms. As her unborn's life oozed from her essence, so did hers. If she didn't get medical attention soon, she'd be just as dead as the life in her stomach.

"Can you hear me? Hey!" Peabody called to her as he glanced around for prying eyes. Once he was sure no one was watching, the old fiend revealed how uncaring life could be. He went into Porsha's pockets and took the last she had, and as if that wasn't enough... "You won't be needing these where you're going, lil mama. Heaven got golden streets you can walk on barefooted. When you get there, tell my no good-ass mama that ole Peabody smokin' fifties till the reaper comes to get me!" He chuckled at his own twisted humor as he slipped the pink and white J's off her feet.

Porsha was oblivious to the heartless act as she stared blindly into the night. "You said you love me. You promised," she mumbled.

***

The sun had turned in for the day, but the heat and humidity was typical of a Texas night. Sunjay and Murda were parked a few houses down from the one they were stalking on the corner of Lagos street. They watched and waited on their prey as they passed a blunt back and forth.

"Dawg, you wanna know what's crazy?" Murda broke the silence.

Sunjay glanced over at him through the thick fog of smoke, but didn't respond. Murda smashed the stick in the ashtray before his eyes fell to the wires of the exposed steering collar. He was an expert car thief and loved to exploit his craft. He reached down and gripped the handle of the nickel-plated .380 before his eyes lifted to stare out the windshield.

"Sometimes when a nigga out here in these trenches, we be moving so fast that we miss the signs of treachery that be right - *there!*" He pointed at his eyes to emphasize his point. "Bet if you think about it, this hoe Mika had the scent of a reptile out the gate, but your dick head only allowed you to see how wet that pussy was, huh?" he asked before easing the window down to allow some of the smoke to escape.

For a moment the car was bathed in silence, but Sunjay's admission disturbed it. "You know I ain't leavin' nothin' breathin' when we leave up out this bitch, right?" Sunjay's words were lax as he reclined in the passenger's seat of the stolen Honda.

Murda glanced down at the blue steel of his burna. There was a thick layer of duct tape wrapped around the handle and the serial number had been scratched off, but the lives he'd stolen with the gun were a testament to its reliability. "What's your point, blood?" he asked challengingly through the cloud of smoke that hovered around them.

Sunjay flipped the lever on the side of the Uzi and released the extendo from the bottom of it and studied the golden talons that were stuffed down into the clip. "I don't know what type of work you've put in, my dude. I hear ya name out here, but I know niggas just be dick ridin'." He shrugged indifferently. "I fucks wit'——"

"You sayin' I'm a pussy or somethin', Damu?" Murda cut him off.

Sunjay chuckled. He knew that Damu meant Blood in Swahili, but figured that Murda was merely tryin' to flex with the knowledge. He was on the verge of responding when the loud music from an approaching vehicle caused him to focus on the approaching headlights. A dark expression eased onto his face as he got low in his seat, tapping Murda's shoulder so he'd do the same. They watched as the car pulled into the driveway of the targeted house. The bass emitting from the royal blue Caprice Classic was monstrous as it idled in the night. The driver killed the ignition as a short, curvaceous woman slid from the passenger's side. She was thick in all the right places and though the night shadowed her face, Sunjay would recognize her slutty walk anywhere. His blood began to boil at the sight of the heavily-jeweled cat that slid from the driver's seat. He strolled over to Tamika as if he was the flyest thing since the airplane.

This bitch nigga shinin' off my hustle. He gotta think shit sweet! The darkness of Sunjay's mind was murky waters, and without much thought, he reached for the door.

"Fuck you doin'!" Murda's words came out in force. That gangsta shit surged through Sunjay, but the hand gripping his arm was firm. "Hold up, dawg, you'll have ya mans in a minute," Murda spoke before glancing out at the couple. "Don't blow the spot up wit' dry shots when we can get up close and personal."

His words simmered the taste of blood that enflamed Sunjay's murderous intent. He shrugged Murda's hand off. "You right, blood, this shit just got me ready to get on that dumb shit!" he seethed before sitting back in the seat.

Together they watched as dude slapped Tamika on the ass, causing her to glance back at him with a promising smile, before they entered the house. Murda's chuckle brought Sunjay's heated gaze to him. The young boy aimed the .380 at the windshield and pretended to pull the trigger.

Sunjay's thoughts became treacherous. *Is this boy trustworthy? Fuck it. Before we leave up out this bitch, I'm gonna slump him too!* he thought as he shared a laugh with the same nigga he was plotting to leave face down.

***

The pungent smoke wafted through the air as the flickering flame on the candle cast dancing shadows on the walls. The candle was the only light source in the foul-smelling room and as Black sucked the smoke from the metal stem, her cheeks sank in from the force of her inhale.

"Damn, bitch, don't hog the candy, we only have that dub left!" Creamy complained before sucking her teeth.

Black's eyes told their own story as she held the smoke of her escape in her lungs. She craved just one more blast from the pipe, but knew that if she did, Creamy would be smoking air. She handed the white woman the pipe before exhaling the tainted smoke. The high was instantaneous as she closed her eyes and let the waves of crack cocaine's euphoria wash all her stresses, emotions, and thoughts away.

Slowly, her eyes cracked open and took in the reality of what life had become for her. Her gaze found a dirty man and woman in a far corner. The man had just tied a stained bandanna on the woman's arm. After it was secure and he found a healthy vein among the many track marks, he slowly sank a filthy-looking needle into her flesh.

"Ahhhh!" A soft wash of breath slipped from her lips as soon as dude eased his thumb down on the plunger of the syringe. The clearish brown liquid was freed into her veins and as Black watched, the woman's chin fell to her chest in a blissful nod and tears came to her eyes.

"Cedric, why'd you leave me, baby, here in this cold room of a crack house?" she silently cried to her late husband. She shook her head slightly before reaching down and picked up the black diary that she'd been spilling her life into. Opening it, Black found the pen and stared down at the cursive handwriting.

"What is that shit anyway, Black Diamond? Every time we get high, you go to writing in that book. Is it a diary?" Creamy inquired as she tapped the end of the metal pipe against her open palm in hopes of some crumbs falling out.

Black smiled a sad smile before picking up the pen and allowing all that she'd been hearing about her son's progress to spill upon a blank page. "No, Creamy, this is my sanity," she whispered as life spilt out of her thoughts.

***

"Yeah, beat it up, nigga, don't stop till you nut in this… this…pussyyyyy!"

Tamika's cries were passionate as Stebo ran dick deep inside her. He had a handful of her hair in his clutches as he pumped at a feverish pace.

"Take this dick, bitch, yeah, throw that shit back," he growled as Tamika threw her ass back on his nature.

Sunjay smiled as he eased into the room as silently as a lion watching his lioness hunt. His gloved fingers held tight to the handle of the black steel as he looked to Murda and placed his finger to his lips as if to tell him to keep quiet. Murda nodded his understanding before turning his eyes to the primal act of ecstasy.

"Oh shit! I'm 'bout to cum, Mika, I'm 'bout to bust!" Stebo shouted as he pounded into her.

But Tamika had other plans. She forced his hands away from her waist before slipping away from his masculinity. She turned and dropped her head to his lower self. "Let... me... suck... this... dick!" she moaned over a mouthful of his nature. Tamika sucked, stroked, and talked to it while creating a symphony of sounds with her wet mouth. She became manic on his dick, soaking it with so much spit that it dripped from Stebo's shaft. She bobbed her head on the head as her mind spoke to her confidence. *He's almost there! Look at this nigga's eyes rollin' to the back of his head. Yeah, nigga, I'm that bitch, huh!* she thought while increasing her pace.

Stebo's body tensed. Tamika was determined to push him over the edge, but a sudden movement out of her peripheral slowed her form of encouragement. Her lips popped when she pulled away from his hardness. She was still stroking his dick when she looked to her right and came face to face with the reaper.

Sunjay leaned around Stebo with a golden smile on his face. "Long time no see, mama. I got next or what?" His words were mocking as a murder scene danced in his pupils.

Stebo jumped at the sound of his voice. "What the fuck?" he shouted as he attempted to dive for the burner he kept under the pillow.

Whack!

The butt of Murda's tool sent him into a pool of darkness. Stebo spasmed as he fell face forward into the bed with his naked ass cheeks in the air.

"Oh my God! Wait, Sunjay, baby, I'm *soooo* glad you found me! I've been all over the D lookin' for you!" Tamika cried as she scampered out of the bed and over to him.

Confusion was evident on Murda's face as he glanced at his boy. *Is this hoe serious?* he wondered.

Sunjay merely smiled as he eyed her. "Oh yeah? Why you been looking for me, lil mama? You got my work and the fifty bandos you and this fuck nigga stung me for?" he spat as he nodded toward Stebo's sleeping form.

Tamika's naked body shone from the freak session her and her dude had just indulged in, and with her nigga's sweat still drying on her skin, she threw her arms sound Sunjay's neck. "Yes, baby, I've been tryin' to get at you to let you know how I tried to talk this nigga out of that foul shit he did to you, but he——"

"Ain't this boy yo' BD?" Sunjay cut her off. The look on her face was priceless as Sunjay chuckled. He smiled as Tamika fidgeted. *Lyin' bitch!* he thought.

"Y-Yeah, he's my son's father, b-but what he did to you was some hoe shit and he gotta pay for that. I-I don't——"

"Shhhh!" Sunjay quieted her deception before winking at Murda. He disentangled her arms from around his neck and looked down at her.

"Noooo, Stebo, you said we was just gonna take his shit! Don't kill the boy, baby!" He reflected on the words she'd spoken the night they'd left him drowning in his own blood. The scene was still playing in his mind when Sunjay eased the barrel of the Uzi down the side of her face. "That shit ova with. We're 'bout to see what the bidness is though," he whispered.

"Wh-what the fuck is -- aghhh!" Stebo stole everyone's attention as he fought his way back from his short nap. The blood that escaped from the gash in the back of his head told the tale of the devil's presence.

"'Sup, homie, remember me?" Sunjay asked with a sarcastic smile on his face.

Stebo flipped over onto his back. "Nigga, who the fuck are——" His words died in his throat as his eyes narrowed and familiarity set in. "Ain't this a bitch!" he spat in disbelief.

"Naw, nigga, *you* a bitch! I told you that you was wrong for that bullshit, and now look, you're 'bout to get your ass kicked!" Tamika's retort was animated as her neck rolled with each word. She looked from Stebo to Sunjay. "Beat his ass, daddy, hit him in his——"

"Tamika, shut yo' dumb ass up! These niggas ain't here to beat nobody's ass. They're here to kill me *and* you, you dumb-ass bitch!" Stebo cut her off as he drew the line.

The silence battled the energy that hovered in the air, and though Tamika attempted to mask it, everyone in that room recognized the uncertainty and the fear that radiated from Tamika's eyes. She laughed a nervous laugh when she looked to Sunjay.

"Naw, Sunjay wouldn't do *me* filthy like that." She paused to study him.

Sunjay smiled to give her reassurance before smacking her bare ass with the side of the gun. "Come on now, lil one, you know I wouldn't do you dirty like that, especially when you've been lookin' *all over the D* for me." He emphasized his words with a chuckle.

"Yeah, I was tryin' to find you. I even begged Stebo not to do you like——"

"Snake-ass bitch!" Stebo raged as he lunged for her.

Crack!

The sound of his nose snapping was resounding when Murda brought the pistol down on the bridge of it. Blood shot everywhere.

"Arrrrgh! Fuck! Bitch-ass nigga!" Stebo wheezed as his hands shot to his face. He glared at Murda, who merely shrugged with an evil smirk as he aimed the tool at dude's noggin.

"You spooked me, blood," he acknowledged, but Stebo's attention had diverted.

As blood gushed from his nose, his eyes became a captive to the sins of the woman that bore his seed. Confusion etched into Murda's features as his vision followed the man's betrayed stare.

"Dawg, fuck you on, blood?" he asked Sunjay in confusion.

Tamika had just freed Sunjay's dick from his sweat pants and Sunjay seemed to not give a damn about his audience. His eyes went to his mans at the sound of the surprise in his voice.

"Chill, bro bro, this hoe got some of the best head in the trip! You need to get some of this shit. I promise ya life won't ever be the same!" he said with mirth as he grabbed a handful of Tamika's hair as she swallowed his nature.

Stebo's eyes turned black at the sight of the treacherous act, and as his heart melted in his chest, no one noticed his hand slipping underneath the pillow until it was too late. He sprang up from the bed with the pillow in front of the .357.

"Fuck you, niggas!" he shouted as he squeezed the trigger *relentlessly!*

Boom! Boom! Boom! Boom!

The pillow exploded in a storm of feathers. Blood shot from Sunjay's shoulder as one of the slugs pierced him, but Murda answer with a few shots of his own.

Blocka! Blocka! Blocka!

The .380 jumped in his hand as a murder scene was created within a hail of bullets and feathers.

Chapter 5

1992

"Top of the day, baby doll. Don't you got somethin' that belongs to me?" Sweet Eddie, a veteran pimp, called to Candy.

The seductive Puerto Rican glanced over her shoulder at him with a mischievous glint in her eyes. The '92 Fleetwood crawled slowly beside her, causing Candy to take notice of the Jolly Rancher red paint that glossed under the radiance of the sun.

"Oh yeah? And what is it that I'm s'posed to have that belongs to *you*, daddy?" she purred as her eyes fell to the triple gold D's that reflected off the street as he followed her.

Sweet Eddie maneuvered the big machine closer to her. "Let's not waste time wit' the baseline, hoe, you've heard of Sweet Eddie as sho' as a bitch is messy, and I can sniff a vet bitch in the midst of a bad stench." He paused to run a jeweled hand through his long hair. "And bitch, you got the familiar aroma." He wasted no time getting slick. Sweet Eddie's long hair was freshly pressed and tumbled about his face in a mass of curly Shirley Temples and as he glanced down at the gold face of the Presidential on his wrist, she noticed the big diamond on his pinkie. Sweet Eddie glanced up at her. "You can't waste my time 'cause this Rollie will last foreva, but if you don't hurry up and choose ya part, our time is better off spent apart." He shrugged.

Candy smirked suggestively. She respected his *ism*, but knew that Messiah was destined to be the king of the stroll. "You know betta than to be shootin' at anotha playa's whore, Sweet Eddie. Or have you become so desperate for a boss bitch that you've forgotten the rules of the game, suga?" she shot before pausing and turning to fight him.

Sweet Eddie's response came at the speed of light. He was in such a hurry to get out of the car and put his stomp down that when he pushed the door open on the Caddie, he forgot that he hadn't stopped and put the slab in park. It continued to roll as he put his

Gator-covered foot on the asphalt and caused him to scuff the reptile-skinned shoe as he hurriedly corrected the error of his haste. After the car was in park, Sweet Eddie was even more furious that he'd scraped his Now and Later-colored shoe. He was out and in Candy's face so fast that he could have been the spokesperson for a Jimmy John's commercial. She only had a moment to appreciate his manicured nails and unisex hairstyle before he got on that other shit.

"Bitch, the name of the game is cop, lock, and blow, and I ain't *eva* heard 'bout no rules of this here life when it comes to knockin' anotha nigga for his hoe!" he seethed before flicking his nose with his pointer finger. "Funky whore, I'm tryin' to take you from a name of shame and induct you into the hoe Hall of Fame!" he pimped hard while wiping invisible lint from his shoulder. He glared at her with his next words. "But if you don't tame that rogue tongue of yours, I'll put these Gators so far up ya ass, you'll have a reptile pattern on ya funky asshole, hoe." Sweet Eddie arched his jeweled hand back to slap her.

Candy tensed for the assault, but...

"You may wanna tame this wild mitt of yours, cat daddy. Puttin' ya filthy mitts on one of my bitches will be detrimental to ya pimpin'," Messiah spoke low as he gripped Sweet Eddie's wrist.

The old pimp's eyes shot to the young cat with malice in his stare, but Messiah was unbothered. The old head snatched his arm free.

"Get yo' filthy hands off me, sure chump, I'm too pretty to let you hit me, but if you put yo' funky hands on Sweet Eddie again, I'll cut ya too short to see and too thin to pee!" he spat before putting some space between them. *It's official. These hoes under the management of a Junior in pimp's attire!* he thought as his eyes digested Messiah. He'd heard of the protégé of the great Pimpin Maxwell, but didn't believe the hype.

"Candy, front and center, hoe, and I'm talkin' put some haste in ya pace!" Messiah demanded as his eyes studied Sweet Eddie.

Candy rushed over to him. "Daddy, I——"

"Hoe, I ain't ask you for no explanation!" he cut her off. She gazed down at his Gators submissively. "Is the street talkin' to you, Ms. Lady?" he responded.

She looked up into a set of young eyes that had seen too much.

Messiah placed a finger under her chin, demanding unperturbed attention. "You know you're in violation, don't you?"

Candy nodded her confirmation, but Messiah wasn't satisfied.

"Bitch, are you a mute or just think my mackin' a fluke? Answer me!" He was hard on a hoe.

Sweet Eddie observed the exchange through envious eyes. *Who the hell this young punk think he is?* he wondered, but held his tongue when his eyes fell to the bulge underneath Messiah's shirt.

"Yes, daddy, and I'm sorry!" Candy whined in hopes of her puppy dog eyes softening his get down.

Messiah recognized the ploy and smiled at her as he stroked the side of her face. He understood that the psychology of his lifestyle surpassed the physical aspects of it.

"And how are you in violation, baby?" His tone was soft as he swept a stray strand of hair out her face.

"I should've never gave another pimp my attention unless he paid for it because to do so encourages his pursuit for a prostitute." She reiterated the jewels he'd instilled into each woman of his stable.

Messiah's eyes drifted to Sweet Eddie, but his verbal was for Candy. "Hoe, you betta get out there on this here stroll and work until you snap the straps on them pretty lil stilettos. Don't short change me, baby doll, or the next tongue lashin' won't be in this fashion." He pimped hard before slapping her on the ass, dismissing her. As she sashayed away, Messiah's sharp eyes narrowed. "Now, to address yo' guerrilla tactics, pimp, it's against the law to put ya hands on anotha playa's bitch."

He spoke with a smile, but Sweet Eddie didn't notice the friendly expression. He was more in tune with Messiah's hand, which had inched down toward the bulge underneath his shirt.

***

Maxwell's juke joint was alive with the gamble as its patrons placed everything on the line for the sake of leaving the establishment with a bankroll.

"Hot sex on the beach makes the night complete. I'll trick for the six! Hit dice!" a lanky bright man shouted with a roll of the dice. He was one of those biracial men that had inherited more of his European attributes than his father's Negroid features.

All eyes fell to the cubes as they rolled across the polished wooden floor. They tumbled before one landed on a full six and the other one spun on one of its edges. Brothaman held his breath. *Come on, come on, I can't lose this rent money, Shonda gone kill me!* His thoughts were a silent plea. The cube flipped before stopping on the devils eye. "Man, hell naw! Let me see that mu'fucka. One of y'all suckas done put some shit in the game!" he exploded when he crapped out.

Pimpin Maxwell chuckled at the theatrics. He'd grown accustomed to people's reactions after they'd gambled all they had, only to walk away with the reality of them having just squandered the money for the light bill. He watched Bear make his way over to the disappointed man and school him to the fact of the house not taking too kindly to accusations of foul play. Pimpin Maxwell sat at the bar of his establishment, observing the hustle. He spun around on the bar stool and smiled at the bartender everyone knew as Big D.

"Some cats just don't know how to take a loss," he acknowledged with a nod of his head.

Big D nodded his agreement before sliding Pimpin a glass tumbler with three fingers of E and J cognac swimming inside it.

"But they sho'll know how to take a win." He completed the statement with a chuckle.

Pimpin Maxwell lifted the glass to his nose and inhaled deeply before slightly tipping the edge of it at his longtime friend. "Sho' ya right, cat daddy. That's what separates the government from the investors up there on Wall Street," he gave his opinion before downing the amber liquid.

Big D was confused by the ideology and it showed in his facial expression. Pimpin Maxwell slid him the glass back before clarifying.

"When an investor places all he has on the line, he's not only gambling with *his* dough. He's also wagering the bread of those that trust his judgment. If what he invests in plummets or the stock market crashes, the loss becomes too big for his sanity." They shared a chuckle as Pimpin accepted his refilled glass and took a gentleman's sip. He swirled the liquor in the glass before nodding at Big D. "The government, on the other hand…those slick suckers take a loss and all they're gonna do is cut the budget on government aid and raise the taxes on our black asses!" He laughed at the reality.

Big D couldn't help but join in as he wiped the bar with a dry towel, but when he noticed that his boss had become silent, he glanced up at him. Pimpin Maxwell's eyes had strayed to the mounted TV behind the bar. He gave Big D a quick glance with a nod at the screen.

"Turn that up, pimp buddy, Looks like it's some heavy shit goin' down up there in the Golden State," he requested.

Big D complied and the news anchor's words created a tense atmosphere in the room filled with people of color.

"This is Cathy Bennett with Channel Four news. I'm devastated to report the insanity that's taking place up in South Central Los Angeles. As I speak, the streets of that beautiful city are ablaze with pandemonium. It's April 29th and a grand jury has just acquitted four Caucasian police officers on all but one count of police brutality in the 1991 beating that was caught on film. These four white officers are shown brutally beating the defenseless black man that we've come to know as Rodney King. Riots have erupted all over the city and the death toll has now reached fifty-three. The violence doesn't seem to be letting up and businesses are aflame as others are being plundered. The city screams for justice, this is a sad day for people of color and——"

Pimpin Maxwell eased a cigar from his breast pocket and placed it between his teeth before his eyes drifted behind him to the inhabitants of his spot. All gambling had stopped and the silence spoke louder than the tension of the Cold War. All eyes went to the seemingly-white man that had disturbed the groove moments before.

He glanced around suspiciously. "What? My mama was a white whore and my old man was the unlucky black pimp that couldn't keep his dick out of her! I'm a nigga with light skin -I swear it!" he swore.

At that moment, Pimpin wondered why it always took a person of color to be beaten or murdered to remind the people that though slavery had been abolished, the great-great-grandchildren of the ones that advocated for it to continue now held the majority of the seats in Congress!

Chapter 6

Next day - 7:50 a.m.

"I don't know what it is that you've done to me / but it's got me actin' in such a crazy wayyyy / whatever it is that you do, when you do what you're doing / it's a feeling that I don't understand / 'cause my heart starts beating triple time, with thoughts of lovin' you on my mind..."

Dream sang along with S.W.V.'s newest single. She patted the finger wave hairdo she'd gotten the day before as she sashayed around the room, cleaning up the mess she and Sunjay had made. Clad in nothing but a G-string and baby tee, her plump ass cheeks jumped with each step she took. The shine of some good loving radiated from her vibe. The wee hours of the night had been filled with her pleasured testifying as Sunjay punished her essence so good that she couldn't distinguish the floor from the ceiling. The power of that good dick had her up early on that Saturday morning, cooking and cleaning as Sunjay slept peacefully.

The aroma of sizzling bacon and hash browns wafted through the small apartment as she danced her way to a pool of clothes Sunjay had discarded during their session, and when her eyes fell to the tool that rested beside them, Dream sucked her teeth in irritation. *This nigga so reckless! I've told his ass ova and ova to stop leavin' all these damn guns layin' everywhere!* she thought as she reached down and picked it up. Studying it, she rolled her eyes at the length of the clip.

"I get so weak / blood starts racin' through my veins / I get soooo weak / boy, that's somethin' I can't explaaain," she sang along while laying the burna on the coffee table. Dream picked up the pants and black tee Sunjay had worn and headed for the dirty clothes hamper. Checking the pockets to ensure they were empty, she found a thick wad of money.

Dream tossed the clothes in the hamper and was about to stuff the money in her bra when something out of place caught her eye. It was a folded piece of paper tucked in between the many bills.

"*Knocks me right off of my feeeeeet / can't explain why your lovin' makes me weak / I try so hard to fight it / no way I can deny it,*" S.W.V. crooned as the young queen unfolded the paper. Her pretty features instantly contorted. *Oh hell naw! Fuck is Latavia?* Her thoughts were aflame as her eyes turned to slits. The name was scrawled in a cursive script and sealed with a blood red, lipstick-stained kiss. Yet it was the burgundy streaks that gave her pause. It looked as if someone had sprayed the dark substance from a distance. Dream hurriedly retrieved the pants from the hamper and studied them. Though they were black, the tiny speckles of blood had congealed so thick that they stood out like small bumps against the jean material. She brought the jeans closer to her face for a closer look and her nose scrunched up as she inhaled deeply. As soon as the distinctive rust smell invaded her nostrils, lil mama's mental couldn't have been further from the truth.

Uh-uh! No this dog-ass nigga ain't out here fuckin' these nasty-ass hoes while they're on their period, then coming up in this mu'fucka stickin' his nasty-ass dick up in me! Surely he ain't! Her assumptions were a false prophecy.

Dream turned on the balls of her feet and stormed back to the living room. She snatched the black steel off the table and with bloodstained money and the note in her other hand, she stormed into the room where Sunjay was getting his Beast rest. He slept peacefully on his stomach and as she stared down at him, the serene expression on his face almost made her change her mind. The fresh design he'd had cut into his tapered haircut turned her on, but it was the thoughts of his sins that pushed her over the edge and down into an ocean of misplaced insecurities.

Dream flung the roll of loot at the exposed side of his face. It burst into a storm of loose bills. Sunjay exploded up from his sleep. His sharp eyes were bloodshot as he searched for the threat, but all he found was a sexy lioness with evil playing in her stare as she aimed the Uzi at his dome.

"Who the fuck is Latavia, bitch? Yo' dog ass got me oh so fucked up, nigga," she hissed.

It took Sunjay a few seconds to register the situation. His alert eyes fell to the scattered money before lifting back to his rida.

"Bitch, is you crazy?" he gritted. "You gonna make me fuck you up. Fuck wrong wit' you, ma? You better keep yo' hands to yo'self!" he growled.

"Bitch, huh?" she hissed as she squinted one eye and aimed the compact machine gun.

Sunjay rubbed sleep from his eyes as Dream's manicured finger wrapped tight around the grip.

"Naw, boo, the *bitch* is the nasty *bitch* that got blood on yo' dick!" Her words were sassy as she snaked her neck. "Stop trying to avoid the question, bitch! Who is this hoe, Sunjay? I'm not gon' ask you no mo'!" she spat while mugging him.

Sunjay was unbothered. He fell back against the pillow and exhaled a hot whoosh of air. "I don't know no mu'fuckin' Latisha, man, stop buggin', fam." His response was nonchalant as his eyes drifted shut.

Dream slapped the shit out of him. "Nigga, I said, *La-tavia*! You heard what the fuck I said! Don't worry 'bout it? Uh-uh! It's all good, lil daddy. I'ma give Bam's sexy ass some of this good pussy. I bet he got some fiya dick!"

Her tune was tinged with vindictiveness and ran Sunjay as hot as the sands of Egypt. His reaction was instantaneous. He sprang up and slapped the gun away from his face. Naked, he scrambled out the bed, causing Dream to stumble backwards a few steps. Sunjay was hungry in his hunt, so much so that when he lunged for her, the sheets tangled up around his legs and tripped him up. He fell hard on his naked ass, causing Dream to giggle. Sunjay's relentless pursuit stole the humor from her when he rushed back to his feet, she attempted to turn and bolt from the room, but he was a flash of speed when he reached out and caught a handful of the back of her shirt.

"Come here, bitch! You was tough just a minute ago!" he spat through gritted teeth.

Sunjay yanked her backwards and in desperation, Dream swung the Uzi back at his head. He weaved just in time as she spun and tried again. He slipped the attempt and hit her in the mouth with a stiff jab.

"Ahhh!" she cried out before dropping the gun. Dream's hands flew to her lips as time stood still.

Sunjay pointed a stiff finger at her. "Look what yo' dumb ass made me do! Sit yo' ass down somewhere!" he demanded.

But Dream was a product of East Dallas projects and the beef was on. She rushed him. "Fuck you, bitch, you hit me?" she screamed as if the question was justified.

She began swinging wildly and in the heat of battle, her nails raked across Sunjay's face and created raw, wicked scratches. Sunjay grabbed her by the front of her shirt and slung her at the bed. The shirt ripped down the middle and caused her succulent titties to fly out. He was beside himself.

"I'm 'bout to beat that ass now!" he cried out in frustration.

Sunjay slapped her across the face. Dream's wild swings landed some of everywhere, but one caught him square in the mouth.

"Bitch!" he growled.

Dream kicked at him before turning and hurriedly crawling in the opposite direction of his assault.

"Naw, don't run now, you *wanted* this shit!" He chuckled with that gangsta shit just beyond his words. Sunjay caught her by the ankle as she fought to get away and in her urgency to escape, his eyes captured the violent jiggle of her ass cheeks. *I know just what yo' ass needs, Dream Catrina!* he thought as his swinging dick began to harden. Sunjay yanked her backwards and she fought against him, not knowing that his war had melted into his surrendering to an untamed ecstasy.

"Let me go, Sunjay!" Dream cried.

At that moment, Sunjay realized that no matter how tough a woman portrayed herself to be, it was the heart of that gangsta that revealed the heart of that woman. He paid her no mind as he pulled her to him.

"Sunjay, let me——" she was saying before she felt his nature knocking against her. Tears stained her face as she rolled her eyes at his audacity. Dream fought against his intent, but feebly. "Get off me nigga, uh-uh!" she cry-moaned. The thin string of her parties snapped when Sunjay yanked it with force. She reached back and weakly pushed against his chest. "You heard me, boy!" Her words were weak. "Unnn!" her moan escaped through the rage of her gritted teeth when Sunjay slid his dick deep inside her.

He folded himself over her, his chest against her back and his face in the crook of her neck. She reached back and dug her nails into his neck, but Sunjay grabbed her wrist.

"I ain't tryin' to hear that shit!" he growled while stroking that pussy. Sunjay played with her pleasure while giving her the peace she craved. "I told you…" He fought for words as he dug deep and created a whirlwind on her clit. "I…don't…know…no…Latisha…Latavia…none of that shit!" He was losing control. His words sounded strained as her waters bathed him.

Dream's fingers twisted the sheets. "I hate yoouuu, Sunjay, I hate…I hate yo' black ass!" Her moans were passionate. She attempted to escape his pound game, but Sunjay had an arm tight around her waist, pumping like a wild dawg. "Fu-fuck you, nigga!" Her anger tried to slay the pleasure he was giving her as her eyes rolled to the back of her head.

Sunjay bit down on her neck. "Shut up, bitch, and take this dick! Tell me…tell me you love this dick. Tell me!" he demanded as his pace quickened.

Dream lost the battle as her explosion surged through her. "Yasss, I love this diccckk!" she testified. "I love *you*, bae!" she cried as she bit down on her swollen bottom lip.

It was ghetto love at its finest.

***

The day was dusky with a slight chill when Ms. Betty stepped out of her apartment. It was the fifteenth and she was on her way to the mailbox to see if her SSI check had come in, but she paused when she saw Lil Zetti.

"Zetti, baby, what you doin' sittin' out here so early?" she asked. He'd been sitting there since before sunrise and was posted like a light pole.

"I'm waitin' on Sunjay, Ms. Betty. He said he gonna buy me some more J's. He say meet him right here." His excitement was evident as he smiled.

Ms. Betty studied him. *Lord, have mercy on this chile and his sister. They need you, Father,* she prayed silently. "Well, baby, Sunjay ain't come by yet, but you be careful out here, Zetti. Where's ya sista at?" she asked as her eyes fell to the worn, old shoes on his fee.

Lil Zetti pointed.

"She ova there wit' Pee Bo, Ms. Betty. They kiss too!" he told her.

Ms. Betty's eyes followed his slim finger until she found the answer to her question. Tweety was hugged up with a man that was old enough to be her daddy. Ms. Betty shook her head sadly. It wasn't the simple fact that the girl was out fucking a man fifteen years her senior, but more because the ghetto was a robber of people that never looked back at the lives it ruined.

"Okay, chile. You make sho' you stay where I can see you, ya hear?" she spoke over her shoulder as she headed to see if her check was in.

***

"Sunjay, can I ask you something, bae, without you gettin' mad?" Dream whispered while resting her head on his chest.

The day had passed them by in flashes of fuck sessions, weed smoke, and more fucking. It was crazy how war between a hood nigga and his bitch could create a loyalty beyond conception.

"What's good, ma?" He opened the door to her inquisition.

Dream stroked his chest before dropping her leg over his. "There was, umm…" She struggled to place her thoughts into words.

Sunjay glanced down at her. "Stop biting your tongue, fam, that shit only makes me think you 'bout to lie." His words were firm.

"First off, I'm not ya *fam*, Sunjay. Leave that for them niggas in the streets. Secondly, I ain't gotta lie to no nigga. It's just, when I was cleanin' up earlier, I picked up yo' pants, and…" Her words trailed off as she circled his right nipple with her finger.

"And?" Sunjay's patience was running thin. He lifted her head so they could be eye to eye. "Listen, lil mama, wheneva it gets to the point that you can't speak your mind to yo' nigga, that means either you don't trust him or you don't trust yourself. A woman that gives herself to a nigga she don't trust is a bitch that shouldn't be trusted at all," he jeweled her as he ran a finger over one of the gelled finger waves on her head. "If you can't trust you, then you're a hazard to every man, woman, or child that trusts you." His words were absolute.

Dream nodded her understanding. "No, boo, all I'm sayin' is when I picked up your pants to put 'em in the hamper, I noticed blood on them. That's why I wigged out earlier," she confessed before sitting up in the bed. "Look, Sunjay, I'm four years older than you, but your lil ass got something 'bout you that I "G" for. You're a young nigga gettin' to a bag and I *know* you're gonna fuck other bitches. Naw, I'm not fuckin' wit' that, but I'm grown enough to know how niggas are." She shrugged. "You have to slow down though, dude. Respect is all a bitch asks for and if you can't give me that, we may as well tap out now." She paused to allow her words to sink in. Sunjay touched her swollen nipple and she slapped his hand away. "You can't be out here in these streets runnin' dick in these hoes while they're on their period!" she spat in contempt.

Sunjay was lost until her words dawned on him, and then he burst into laughter. Dream's eyes narrowed, but Sunjay playfully tackled her to the mattress.

"So that's what all the smoke 'bout!" He laughed before kissing her. *Damn, I'm slippin'! I gotta toss that burna and burn them clothes!* he thought.

"Boy, stooop!" she moaned as he kissed her neck before confessing his sins.

"Since I was a lil nigga, all I eva wanted to be was a gangsta. That's the life I know." It was his turn to shrug. His words caused Dream to stare at him, her heart beating against her chest. "You remember the shit I told you 'bout that hoe settin' me up?"

His question was rhetorical, but Dream nodded nonetheless. "Yeah, I remember," she confessed.

Sunjay studied her before admitting to the type of shit that he shoulda took to the grave. "I murked 'em. That was their blood on my jeans. I fed 'em every slug in that clip, ma. That's why the gun was empty.

***

"Zetti, baby, why are you still out here?" Ms. Betty stuck her head out the door.

Lil Zetti sat in the same spot he'd sat in all day, waiting for Sunjay to keep his word. He glanced back at her with disappointment in his big eyes. *"I'm gonna get you some more J's tomorrow, fam. Make sure you meet me right here."* Sunjay's voice played in his head.

"Zetti? Zetti Tyrone Jackson, don't you hear me, boy?"

Ms. Betty's voice shook him from the reflections of broken promises. His eyes watered. Sunjay was his hero and while Lil Zetty's mind was too young to understand that even superheroes let you down sometimes, his heart understood the betrayal of being lied to.

Ms. Betty made her way over to him, her sharp mind replaying why he sat out there on that curb. His excitement! "Come here, baby," she beckoned.

Lil Zetti climbed to his feet and turned to face her, staring up at her with wet eyes. He seemed to be fighting not to blink. "Sunjay said family don't lie to family, Ms. Betty. Ain't I family too?" He lost the war with his emotions as a slow stream ran down his face.

Ms. Betty took him by the hand and led him toward the apartment. "Cryin' is good fa the soul, chile. Don't *ever* let nobody tell you different," she spoke as they entered the home she'd nurtured from the seeds of the ghetto for the past twenty years. Ms. Betty closed the door before turning to face him. "You gotsta understand that peoples is gonna let you down, Lil Zetti, but that's a good thang, baby. How else you gonna learn how to stand up on ya own if nobody ever lets you down to try? You understand, chile?" she asked, though she knew he didn't.

As if he could prove her wrong, Lil Zetti nodded his head yes and got a good laugh out of the old woman.

She used her thumbs to wipe the tears from his face -- "Boy, go on in there and wash ya hands while I makes you somethin' to eat. Ya hungry, ain't ya?"

Lil Zetti nodded again. "Yes," he whispered.

Ms. Betty gave him a stern look that made him correct himself. "Yes, ma'am!" he shouted before running off.

Ms. Betty watched him until he disappeared around the corner before turning for the kitchen. She shook her head. Her thoughts were a harsh reality. *So much like Sunjay was at that age - forced to turn to the streets for what he'll never find at home!*

***

The crime scene tech snapped numerous shots from different angles, the flash of the camera giving the stiff bodies a grotesque appearance in the dim room. Detective Spinx silently observed as he envisioned how the gruesome murders had taken place.

"It's craziness like this that reminds me that this beautiful city of ours has gone to shit!" a gruff voice spoke from behind him.

Spinx gave a brief nod, but didn't have to look to know who the speaker was. He'd known DPD's Sergeant McBeth for the past three decades and while he respected the man's ambition, he didn't much care for the man himself.

McBeth eased beside him with a solemn expression on his face. "Whoever did this is a sick son of a bitch, that's for sure." he spoke as they watched the coroner and her team deal with the dead.

A strange look eased onto his face as he studied Tamika's still face. Her vacant eyes had paled over and her skin appeared hazy, but neither abnormality held his attention as powerfully as the rotting piece of flesh that was stuffed deep into her mouth.

The sergeant took a few steps closer to get a better look. "Is that what I think it is?" he asked no one in particular.

"A penis?" Kim, a dark-skinned woman, inserted. "Yes, some sick fuck shot our John Doe's wee-wee off and stuffed it down the poor gal's throat." She pointed a gloved finger toward the deceased girl.

Stebo lay cold beside her with an expression of agony forever immortalized on his face. Both their souls had divorced their bodies and moved on to wherever spirits went after death. Rigor mortis had set in, causing Sergeant McBeth to shake his head in pity. He placed a finger against Tamika's stiff body to get a feel for the dead before covering his nose with his other hand. The stink of their decomposition violated the air. Kim gave him a humorous glance. She'd been Dallas's coroner for the past four years and though she respected McBeth, she had a thing for Spinx.

"Whoever did this believes in overkill," she acknowledged before pointing a gloved finger at the bloody hole in Tamika's forehead. "See here? This dark ring around the entry wound?" She made a small circle around the dark hole. "This indicates that the shooter placed the barrel of what I believe to be a .380 caliber directly against the poor girl's head and pulled the trigger," she gave her thesis before gazing at Spinx.

His eyes never left the dead couple. Though his face was void of any emotion, his mental was a volcano. *What the hell's gotten into you, Sunjay? You've graduated from petty gang shit to premeditated murder!* he thought as he pulled a pack of gum out his back pocket and pulled a piece free. His dark eyes strayed to her as he popped the gum in his mouth.

"I assume there's more you're trying to tell us than merely this girl's head being blown away." He gave her a brief smile before his usually serious expression fell back into place.

Kim gave him a sarcastic smile in return. "You must have graduated from Johns Hopkins?" She gave him the finger to punctuate her words. She stepped over to Tamika and carefully took hold of the severed organ. It was work, but after a few stiff tugs, it eased from the girl's cold throat. Kim held Stebo's dick out to them in mirth. "The Jane Doe was dead long *before* her brains were blown out."

The revelation caused sergeant McBeth's face to ball up in confusion. He didn't understand the claim. "So if she didn't die from a friggin' bullet to the head, how'd the Jane go?" He shook his head in amusement before placing a finger to his temple as if he were in deep contemplation. "Wait, let me guess…" McBeth dramatically hit his forehead with the palm of his hand. "That's it! She died from asphyxia while giving a suicidal blow job!" He laughed at his own morbid humor.

All eyes shot to the dead woman. Kim's left eyebrow shot up before she gave McBeth a sarcastic smile. "Now aren't you a modern day Einstein!" She laughed at the puzzlement etched into his features. "In fact, based off the semen samples we took from her, this young woman had just engaged in not only a sexual act by penetration, but also oral. As I said, these two were already tied up before death, which means the Jane was already bound when her jaw was broken and this thing was stuffed down her throat." Kim shrugged   indifferently. "She choked to death." She waved the swollen organ at McBeth.

He cringed and stepped back. "Get that thing away from me, Kim!" His words were heated.

She laughed before her eyes strayed to Spinx. The man's eyes were fixated on Stebo's rigid form. The boy's body was riddled with bullet holes. The detective's vision then fell to a bright, discolored spot on the carpet, and curiosity held him captive.

"Oh. That?" The coroner shook her head as she made her way to the bleached carpet. She dropped the piece of flesh into an evidence bag as she made eye contact with both officers. "The perps used bleach to clean up after themselves. Whoever this psycho is, he didn't leave unharmed, but he was smart," she revealed as she looked to Detective Spinks.

The detective merely nodded before turning and heading for the door. *I'll catch up with you, Sunjay Carter, and when I do, we're gonna have a nice little sit down. Me, you, and ole Messiah,* he thought as he made his exit.

***

The constant ringing of the phone pulled her from her sleep. "Hello?" Tasha answered thickly. She had to shake away the sex-induced cobwebs in order to focus.

"Hello, may I speak to a Ms. Tasha McDade?" the caller requested.

Tasha removed the man's arm from around her waist before sitting up. She glanced at the clock on her nightstand. 1:30 a.m. Her eyes traveled to the man that slept beside her, and her heart melted as she listened to his wild snores. "Who is this playin' on my damn phone askin' all these damn questions!" she demanded.

"This is Cathy Jones. I'm a nurse up here at Parkland Hospital, and we have a patient up here that has you listed as her emergency contact."

"Me? Maybe you have the wrong person. All my family either dead or in Atlanta," Tasha lied.

"Well, maybe so, but our records shows that Porsha McDade is your daughter, am I correct?" Nurse Jones asked.

A cold expression fell over Tasha's face. "No, I don't have any kids. As I've said, you have the wrong number," She reiterated.

"But, she's been admitted here since late last——"

Tasha disconnected the call before lying back down. She pulled dude's arm back around her as she snuggled up against him. She gently eased her backside against his nature and to her surprise, he was as hard as Chinese arithmetic.

"Who was that, baby?" Rock asked groggily.

Tasha reached back and stroked his masculinity. "Nobody, boo, they had the wrong number," she whispered.

Unbeknownst to her, her deception brought a smile to Rock's face. He knew she didn't give a damn about her daughter any more than he did. There was a thin line between loving someone and loving them to the point of stupidity, and Tasha had surpassed the latter. She'd long ago transgressed the obligation to her only child, and as Rock slid deep inside her, she cried the words that should have been more reserved for a proclamation to her daughter than a declaration to a man that was more in love with her pussy than he was with her as a woman.

"I...I love you!" she cried with abandon.

Chapter 7

2010

After they'd left the hospital, Messiah had demanded to be taken to see Pimpin Maxwell, but the old pimp wasn't at his apartment and no one seemed to have seen him in days. The Bentley coasted like a ship upon tranquil waters as Paradise navigated it through the slippery, dark city streets. Messiah stared absently out the window, gazing out at what sex, money, and murder had done to the once beautiful landscape. The drizzle fell from the clouds and gave the scenery an even drearier appearance, and as the heavens cried, so did his soul.

Picket lines / Picket signs / Don't punish me, with brutality / Talk to me / and you will see / ohhhh what's goin' on / what's goin' on... Marvin Gaye's voice serenaded them as Paradise glanced up at him through the rearview mirror. Messiah appeared in control, but she knew the appearance of a man was merely a mirage that blindfolded the observer to the storm that raged just beyond the illusion. Between the dark shades of the night and momentary flashes of the street lights that illuminated his features, she wondered why men were so prideful.

Father, father, there's way too many of you dyin' / mother, mother, there's way too many of you cryin' / Youuu knowww, we gotta find a way, to bring some lovin' here todaaayy / what's goin' on... Marvin's words mirrored his reflection.

Paradise turned down Saner Street and eased the SUV underneath the overpass, slowly pulling it beside an old man that appeared to be down on his luck. Fast Freddy was a fallen star of the slums who wore tattered clothes complete with a dirty skull cap on his head, and as he stood on that curb, he fidgeted from whatever addiction he'd fallen victim to.

Messiah eased the window down and gave the OG a jeweled smile. "What ya know good, Fast Freddy? You seen that ole fool round here?" he asked.

Fast Freddy's snaggle-toothed grin should have prepared Messiah for the bullshit. "Ole Fast Freddy done seen all the good, the bad done been my hand to play for the last twenty years, and I done shed my last tears, young buck, but you—" He paused to allow his eyes to take in the kilo-white Bentley before looking back to Messiah. "But I see you, young Messiah, you profile in style, and an ole man like myself sho' would appreciate some spare change to knock the cold from my veins," he spoke while doing a two-stepped tap dance.

Messiah chuckled at the finesseful extortion, but respected the game nonetheless. He dug in his pocket and peeled a twenty from the bankroll before holding it out to the old man.

Fast Freddy's hand was lightning fast in relieving him of the bill and nodding toward a spot deeper underneath the bridge where a group of dirty men stood warming themselves by a crackling barrel of fire. Even from afar, Messiah recognized his mentor. Pimpin Maxwell's voice carried on the wind as he spoke jewels in the form of a ghetto hymn.

"See, a lot of mu'fuckas can't tell you the difference between the trees, the birds, or the bees, but I'm here to bring sight to the blind man that thinks he sees. I'ma tell you brothas, it all dates back to the baddest bitch that eva pissed between two knees. Yeah, my daddy was a rollin' stone that owned a cocaine-white Cadillac that brightened my day. Brah, man, I'm tellin' you, this that down home blues shit that Otis Redding was talkin 'bout as he sat on that dock by the bay!" He paused with a mischievous expression on his face. Pimpin made eye contact with each man before smiling and speaking with some pizzazz. "See, the book of Genesis tells a nigga that God created man from the dirt and his bitch from his rib. It speaks of life before our people were brought into bondage. What it don't speak of is after God created the two, why the hell he forbid them of partakin' of the tree of good game, the fruit of knowledge! He even gave Adam ordinance over *everythang* in the garden! Even tells the lame he could partake of any food of the land, but then turns around and denies him the tree that produced the substance the Book of Proverbs feeds to the soul of man!"

88

He chuckled before spreading his arms out wide and staring into the flames of the barrel. "William Tyndale was the mu'fucka that translated the New Testament of the Bible into English. His translation is the basis of the King James. White folk musta had somethin' to hide, for that reason the poor son of a bitch was locked in chains. See, Adam didn't sin by partakin' of the fruit, but more because he didn't jewel his hoe to the slick ways of snake niggas. That's the main reason that ole serpent was the best man for the job, 'cause he gave it to the hoe fresh from the hip, didn't waste time wit' spittin' lame riddles."

Pimpin Maxwell allowed his audience to digest his authenticity before tapping the shoulder of the man closest to him. He began to snap his fingers to a created beat until they all caught on and followed suit.

"Dig me like a grave, mack buddies, let me pour you gents a sip from a pimp. See, the snake was the first mu'fucka to bless a hoe with some bonafide game, so every hoe after her is born wit' that same trait. It's just that some dames know how to keep it in bed, 'cause that's how a few was bred. Yet, if the snake was the first nigga to bless Eve wit' the power of her pussy, and she was the first lady, every bitch after her has a serpentine gift. It just takes her usin' her head."

"Talk that shit, Pimpin! That's that food fa the mind, brotha man!" one of the bums encouraged to the nods of the other four disheveled men. He paused to pass Pimpin a bottle of Thunderbird that was concealed by a worn, brown paper bag.

Pimpin Maxwell took a deep swallow before passing it to the next man. He popped the collar on the wrinkled suit jacket he'd worn for the past few days and allowed the burn of the liquor to warm his belly before speaking.

"That ole devil told the Jane, bitch, you have a treasure of pleasure between ya legs that's gonna make niggas kill, steal, and do anythang to cop a feel. Whether slim, trim, or as fat as a bat with more hair than a jungle cat, it's gonna bring some of the most powerful men to their knees!" Pimpin stomped his right foot as he gave it to 'em. "That serpent schooled that lady to thangs that at the time must've been hard for her to believe, but the mind of a good hoe is a true playa's playground, for his words opened Eve's eyes to the truth of the birds and the bees."

The bum to his left clapped his hands feverishly. "Church! Preach, Pimp, preach that shit!" he shouted as if he had the Holy Ghost.

"Hallelujah!" Someone else sang their praise.

Pimpin Maxwell nodded. "In the third chapter of Genesis, it speaks of how Eve's eyes were open after eating of the fruit that left between her legs smokin', but I think that was just a clever way of sayin' she gave that ole serpent some pussy while he showed her the value of her essence while her legs were opened. That's why it's looked upon as the forbidden fruit, because after the deed, Eve had to share the feelin' of a good nut wit' Adam's tender dick ass so she wouldn't be the only one that folded, and after they fell in love with the feelin' of pussy and dick, they sewed fig leaves together to cover themselves 'cause they heard God approachin'."

Pimpin Maxwell's eyes drifted to the curb. It was a moment of deja vu. He chuckled in shame at the sight of the idling SUV. His eyes returned to the crowd. " 'Where are you?' God demanded. 'I heard you in the garden while me and my bitch were naked, so we hid ourselves!' Adam's response was weak. 'Who gave y'all the knowledge of dick and pussy? Have you two sons of bitches eaten from the tree that I commanded ya dumb asses not to eat?' God spat." Pimpin laughed while rubbing a hand down the side of his face. He knew he had some explaining to do, so he brought his spiel to an end. "See, pimp friends of mine, Adam was a sucka. Not only did he allow his bitch to mislead him, but he was the first nigga to ever snitch and this what he told God: 'The woman whom you gave to me, she gave me fruit and I ate!' 'What have you done?' God called to Eve after Adam sealed the bitch's fate. Eve frowned. 'I was deceived and fell victim to the game of the snake's message. He told me that you lied when you said we'd die if we partook of the fruit. He even told me my pussy was precious!' God turned a wicked eye to Adam. 'Nigga, I created the bitch to follow your lead, but you allowed a lowdown, snake mu'fucka to use her to trick you!' He paused to eye the skirt Eve had made. 'Now ya funky ass gotta get up outta this here garden, and take this treacherous bitch wit' you!' " Pimpin Maxwell ended to an offbeat round of applause.

Messiah observed him and even from the darkness of the Bentley, he could tell the old man was as high as Neil Armstrong was when he claimed to step foot on the moon. Messiah reflected on the older man's promise to never put another pipe to his lips. Feeling her eyes on him, he glanced up to find Paradise staring at him through the rearview mirror. Their eyes spoke a language that needed no verbalization, but Messiah felt obliged. Messiah toyed with the VVS heart-shaped diamond ring on his pinkie finger that Pimpin gave him for his fifteenth birthday. Though he'd had it resized since then, it still stirred the same nostalgia that it had ever since he'd matured enough to understand its true meaning.

"Sometimes, a man's greatest enemy is the shit he loves the most," he whispered to the confirming nod of Paradise.

***

Sunjay had hidden the bike behind the trap house before sneaking through the back door. He'd beaten the odds and though he'd escaped the clutches of Johnny Law, he knew that Murda was the thread that could connect him to his sins.

"What's goin' on, Sunjay?" a soft voice whispered from the darkness of the living room.

Sunjay flinched in surprise. He'd forgotten he'd called Dream and told her to meet him there.

"Shhhh!" he blew through his teeth while placing a finger to his lips. He stalked over to the burglar-barred window and peered out the bedsheet they'd used as window curtains. "Chill, ma, I'll explain in a minute, just sit down and——"

"Nigga, why the fuck you whispering'? Uh-uh, Sunjay, yo' black ass betta get ta talkin'! You done had me leave work early and now you got me cooped up in this raggedy-ass house on some real suspicious shit! I'm the bitch that's gotta lie to them white folks if they come lookin'! I'm the bitch that gonna be harborin' a fugitive

when dem nothin'-ass niggas you run wit' start eatin' the cheese!"
Dream cut him off as she crossed her arms over her chest and impatiently bounced her right foot. Her face was shadowed by the dimness, but Sunjay could see the frustration in her pretty features.
He made his way to the couch and plopped down. "Shit ugly, fam. It's crazy right now and I may have to dip for a minute to let shit cool off," he fumed before burying his face in his hands.

Dream's face contorted as she became completely still, but that drama shit was there. "*You* may have to dip? Fuck we stop bein' a team, bae? Naw, naw, that's not how this shit go! If you gotta dip, *I'm* dippin' right——"

"Umph...uh...mm!"

A muffled cry interrupted her explanation and gave her pause. Dream's eyes shot in the direction the noise was coming from before her suspicious gaze ping-ponged back to Sunjay.

"What kind of shit you done pulled me into, Sunjay Carter? You betta skip all them theatrics and keep it funky with me. Like now!" she demanded while placing her hand on her shapely hip.

Sunjay climbed to his feet and tossed the couch cushion aside and with something sinister playing in his pupils, he snatched up the throwaway plastic Glock he'd stashed there for these just in case situations.

"Look, mane, I may be a wanted man. I don't know what Murda tellin' them folks, but what I do know is, I ain't *ever* goin' back to nobody's cage!" he vowed before turning and storming off.

Dream didn't understand, nor was she feeling Sunjay dancing around the complete truth. *Oh hell naw, he gonna give me some real answers today! Why is this boy always into some bullshit?* Her mental surged with thoughts as she followed Sunjay's departure. The old adage - *don't go looking for trouble or you just might find it* - proved to be undisputed truth when she made it to the door of the room Sunjay had slipped into. There, tied to a wooden chair in the middle of that empty space, an attractive, light-skinned woman cried a muffled cry. Dream watched as big tears slid down her pretty face and down over the thick strip of duct tape that held her lips shut.

Diamond! Recognition dawned on her as her surprised eyes flew to Sunjay. She'd grown fond of Messiah's girls and though she knew that her man and his brother from another mother were at odds, she didn't think it had become something so evil that they'd begun to shoot so close to home. Sunjay paid her no mind as his eyes took in Diamond's condition. The girl had lost a pound or two from lack of food and her left eye had swollen to the point that it seemed as if her tears had to squeeze out the slits it had become. Dream lost it.

"Sunjay, are you fuckin' crazy! Why the——"

"When I was a lil nigga, me and Messiah used to play this game where when either of us would fall asleep first, the other would use toothpaste, hot sauce, shaving cream, or anything messy to smear it all over the other's hands and face," he cut her off.

Dream bit her tongue even though she wanted to spazz.

"Um, pweeze et me ooo!" Diamond's words were almost indecipherable.

Sunjay's heart held no sympathy as he clutched the burna tight. *Quick and clean, or let the hoe live?* The question blew through the streets of his mental like a feather drifting on the wind. "When one day he got me, I wasn't feelin' that shit and we fought like rams. I hated that I'd become a victim of the same shit I'd once served, fam," Sunjay whispered. "In that squabble, I learned to never sleep on a nigga. Even family will do you. That game me and fam played was indirectly teachin' us trust."

Sunjay paused in deep thought. Dream watched as the burna lifted and…

Boom!

It exploded in his hand, but his eyes didn't blink as they trailed to her shocked expression. Her hands flew to her mouth to muffle the scream that clawed its way up her throat. The bullet had knocked Diamond's head back, causing her last thoughts to splash against the wall.

"Sometimes a mu'fucka can't trust *nobody*," Sunjay spoke more to himself than to her.

Boom!

Renta

The gun jumped in his hand for the second time. Vomit shot from Dream's mouth and nose from the pressure of the kill, and before Sunjay could make it to her, she fell into a pool of darkness.

***

The Bentayga slid over the wet streets as the street lights disturbed the darkness in momentary flashes. Paradise navigated through the drizzle as Messiah stared out the tinted window, watching as the streets of the ghetto rotted away. On the corner of Illinois, a second group of bums warmed themselves by a barrel of fire, and as Messiah digested reality, his heart cracked at the sight before him. The contained fire sent wild sparks up into the night as the shadows of its flames cast dancing silhouettes across the men's faces. Messiah's eyes were trained on a dark, haggard man that had just placed a glass pipe between his lips. He cupped his hands around the front of the stem before leaning forward and allowing the flames to heat its tip. Messiah watched as the man's cheeks sank in with his inhale, and as he allowed the tainted smoke into his lungs, it seemed as if the old man's eyes looked up and into the dimness of the luxury truck.

Messiah reached inside the pocket of his suit coat and came out with a golden cigar case. *"A playas choice"* was engraved across its surface. He opened it and freed a cigar from its golden captivity. Messiah placed the sweet leaf between his lips before lighting its tip and gently puffing a fluffy cloud of smoke.

Pimpin Maxwell's eyes were bucked, and the shame of his broken promise was written all over his face as he stared down at the golden cigar case. It once belonged to his mentor before it was passed down to him, and as he sat within the exact spot he had the day Messiah had pulled him from his lowest moments, Pimpin remembered the day he'd passed the token down to his young apprentice. The reflection seemed to steal the energy from the OG and he fell back into the soft leather seat.

"You wanna know why the year of 1963 was one of the most vital years of the Civil Rights movement?" His voice castrated the silence.

Messiah didn't respond. Though he was listening, his attention had diverted out the rain-pelted window where the truth of what the hood had become couldn't be denied. There was an Afro American woman along with a young child huddled together at the bus stop and as the Bentley eased by, Messiah's mind toyed with a question that he could never answer. *So many kids havin' kids these days. I wonder if lil mama knew what she was signing up for when she was giving herself to the type of cat that would allow her and their seed to sit at a bus stop in the rain?* he thought.

"Back in '63, May 2nd, I think, our people started the march for our Civil Rights up there in Birmingham, Alabama where that Klansman, George Wallace, was advocating to keep colored folk from eating, shitting, and drinking from the same places the pink folks were. That day in that hick town is what lead to the abolition of segregation."

Pimpin Maxwell's words caused Messiah to nod in acknowledgement. The old head reached over and freed one of the freshly-clipped cigars. He placed it underneath his nose and inhaled deeply, savoring the distantly familiar aroma before his thoughts took him back to days when being black made you a target not only to the police, but to the public as a whole.

"By June 11th, all hell had broken loose, young blood, and only when shit turnt violent did those white folks make that racist-ass governor George Wallace step aside. The sacrifice wasn't made without compensation though, naw..." His voice became distant. Pimpin paused to place the cigar between his teeth before speaking again.

"The very next day, the sneaky mu'fuckas hit us hard!" he spat while slamming a clenched fist into his palm for emphasis. "They took ole Medgar Evers from us, shot that ole boy dead like a rabid dog!" But Pimpin Maxwell's passion was deeply rooted as he attempted to smooth the wrinkles out of the suit he'd worn for the past few days. "Our people was resilient, and by August the 28th, two hundred thousand different shades of black beauty was marchin' our colored asses through D.C. right behind that good ole doctor with the big dreams. My black ass was right there, Messiah, thick-ass afro, bell bottoms, and all. I stood tall, proud, at Lincoln Memorial, where that black man spoke of a dream that was bigger than the man that envisioned it."

Pimpin's words drifted through the silence of the truck as he turned to stare out the window. The streets were slick with heavens tears as they rode through the ghetto. Messiah exhaled a thick mushroom of smoke before glancing at him.

"What does *any* of that shit have to do with you puttin' that crack pipe back to your lips, OG?" His words cut through the fog of smoke and caused Pimpin to chuckle.

"Everything, young'n. You..." He paused to lean over for a light.

Messiah obliged him as he awaited a rationality to why a man would sell his second chance at grace to the same thing that robbed him of it in the first place. Pimpin puffed the cigar before speaking.

"Addiction is one of the most powerful mind games one can play on themselves. See, them Caucasians had become so fixated on the power they held over us that it became an addiction. So much so that on the day of September 15th, eighteen days after that "I Have A Dream" speech, them crackas bombed the 16th Street Baptist church up there in Birmingham. They killed four young black girls just to show us how much they respected a nigga's dreams!" he spoke before looking to see if Messiah was feeling him.

He wasn't! The younger man knew that the history lesson was merely a deceptive way of setting the stage for an excuse. He gave Pimpin a knowing gaze that caused him to chuckle before bringing clarity to an otherwise murky explanation as to why he'd broken his promise.

"I lost my way, baby," he admitted while rubbing his hands down his face as if wiping invisible tears away. "Back then, I stood and fought for our people because I was tired of the control them white people had over us, and now that this hardened white bitch has strong-armed my *ism,* she's kickin' my ass for the same mu'fuckas that introduced her to the hood," he admitted as the SUV slowed and made a sharp turn down a graveled drive.

Pimpin Maxwell glanced out the window curiously. He wondered if he'd reached the end of his two step as he took in the scenery. The cemetery seemed to emit a colder temperature than the rest of the city and as the truck glided over uneven earth, Messiah eased a pistol from underneath the thick Prada sweater he wore. Cigar smoke snaked from his nostrils as he studied the night. The Bentley pulled to a stop and the heavens cried. "Today is my Pops's birthday." His words were mellow. The admission gave the older man the peace of knowing why they were visiting the dead. "Gambling was his addiction, Pimpin. It's the same addiction that led him here," Messiah whispered with a wave of his hand.

He pushed the door open to the night and allowed the icy kiss of the night's mist to invade the confines of the truck as he stepped out onto the grounds that had swallowed so many. Lightning streaked across the sky as he spoke over his shoulder.

"Addiction ain't nothin' but a prelude to the things that will eventually kill you, Pimp. It's the slowest form of suicide known to man and the fucked up part about it is, mu'fuckas so crazy that they convince themselves that their want for whatever they're into is more powerful than their self-control."

He gritted his teeth as cold drops of rain bathed his bald head. It didn't take long for the tears of heaven to soak through his clothes as Messiah stood clutching the burna by his thigh. He gazed out into the wet graveyard before slightly turning toward the truck. "Come on, ole man, let's go make peace with the devil," he spoke before walking out onto the darkened grounds.

***

"Der together, I told Jah, Star, him fuck boy bomba clot is serpentine! Who Jah av me do, whack him, fun boy?" JonJa asked eagerly. He'd been following Messiah all that day. He felt it in his gut that he had been in on the stolen diamonds and the meeting in the cover of night only confirmed his suspicions.

"Be easy, yea, no blood should be spilt jet, JonJa. If him boy is guilty of thievery, Jah will have him head. Patience is what will lead us to me precious diamonds, son. Those stones are very special to me. Jah hear?" Gator's voice came through on the other side of the phone.

JonJa gritted his teeth against the retort on his tongue. He felt that Gator was becoming weak in his old age and would be the cause of the organization's downfall. He burned to have Messiah's head on his blade, yet he knew, in due time, he'd have his wish.

***

The rain splashed against Sunjay's shirtless upper body as he knelt down by the headstone. When he'd gotten the text from Messiah to meet him there, he'd been leery, but he knew that if he and his bro were to shed each other's blood, it wouldn't be there - not on that night. He ran his fingertips over the engravement: *Cedric Ridge - a man gone before his time*, it read. The rain splashed over his skin, but even more, it camouflaged the silent tears that fell from his eyes as his mind ran wild.

"Messiah, don't come in here, baby, you and Sunjay go play!" *Black had screamed, but it was too late.*

Messiah ran into the room with Sunjay on his heels.

"I'm sorry, baby, I'm soooo sorry!" Black cried a melody that only a woman that had known the defeat of true love could cry.

Sunjay stood stuck in place, shocked as he watched her rocking back and forth with her husband's head cradled in her lap. Cedric's blood stained her clothes as she stared up at them with a river of pain flowing down her face.

Messiah rushed over to his slain hero. "Daddy, get up, man!" he cried as he fell to his knees and tried to will life back into the only man that had ever given a fuck about him.

"I'm sorry, baby, he's gone. He can't get up, Messiah!"

Sunjay could still hear her words in his head.

"Thought I told you to stay low until I could figure this shit out, brah. Why you always gotta tempt fate like this?" Messiah's voice brought him back to the present.

Sunjay's dark skin shone under the moonlight as the rain washed over him. With nothing but three diamond necklaces, a presidential Rollie, and a VVS diamond pinkie ring on to shelter him from the drizzle, Messiah had to respect his potna's need to be one with the night. They'd made it a ritual to meet at Cedric's grave every year on the fallen hustler's birthday and Sunjay didn't give a damn what threats awaited him after the fact. He wasn't gonna miss it.

He didn't respond immediately. Instead, he twisted the cap off the half gallon of Seagram's gin and took it to the head. He cringed at its powerful punch before standing and holding the bottle out to his childhood friend.

Messiah studied him though the slanted rainfall and after a brief assessment, he accepted the offer. Both men were drenched as they stood freely underneath the open sky. Turning the bottle up to his lips and allowing the liquid fire to burn its way down his throat, Messiah quietly acknowledged his boy's gangsta. *This nigga ain't gonna eva change!* he thought.

As if he could read his thoughts, Sunjay spoke his piece. "What, you my daddy now, Messiah?" He chuckled. "Don't disrespect me, my G. As long as there's air in my lungs, I'm gonna be here for this boy." He nodded down at the grave. "I don't give fuck 'bout no fate, nigga. I'm here to give it up for one of the livest niggas we knew," he professed as his gaze rolled over his day one in quiet observation. Sunjay smirked when his eyes paused on the burna in Messiah's hand. "Since when did we greet each other with our bangas on deck, fam?" he questioned with a nod at the Nina Ross.

Messiah's eyes were searching before he tilted the bottle to his lips and took a deep swallow. "Arrrrgh!" he growled as the liquor burned through his chest. He wiped his lips with the back of his hand. "When did we start snatchin' up each other's people, *fam*?" he replied in kind while putting emphasis on the title.

Sunjay couldn't control the look of surprise that blossomed on his face, but he shrugged nonetheless. He knew that Messiah would find out about Diamond sooner or later, but had to admit the boy's intel was fancy.

Messiah handed him the bottle back before stepping around him and over to the headstone. The rain had slowed to a soft cry as he knelt down beside it and rested that tool on top of it. He almost broke down from the pressure of the past few weeks, coupled with the sight of the cold marble that rested on top of his old man's physical.

"All you've ever wanted to be was a gangsta, Sunjay, a dope boy. Now that you've become who you've always wanted to be, you seem to not give a damn 'bout nothin' else but a bag," he spoke softly. Messiah wiped rain from his face. "But money don't make a nigga real, family. Your recklessness has not only placed your neck on the blade, but also mine! All over a punk-ass few dollars, brah," he whispered.

Sunjay's face instantly contorted into a mask of confrontation. He gritted his teeth. The gin swam through his veins as he watched Messiah turn his face up to the sky and allow the wetness to wash away his own tears.

"I see you still takin' those pussy-ass Jamaicans' words over mine and that ain't how it's s'posed to go, dawg," Sunjay seethed.

His words were a sharp blade that cut through Messiah's heart and without warning, he scrambled to his feet and shoved the shirtless man with brute force.

"You think this shit a game? Huh!" he spat in rage.

The surprised look on Sunjay's face melted into one filled with that drama shit, but his brother's next words rocked his world and simmered that gangsta's call inside him.

"Nigga, somebody done snatched my wife up and got a ticket on her head. Mama laid up in a hospital and can't remember me, you, or who the fuck *she* is, and all yo' punk ass talm'bout is them folks. But your greed has *always* been bigger than your brain, fam, even when we was kids!"

His words were a sword that drew the line. Sunjay chuckled, but it was merely a prelude to his response.

Bam!

He hit Messiah with a stiff jab, and there, in a dark cemetery illuminated by streaks of lightning, two men that were closer than a soldiers' formation fought their damndest.

Pimpin Maxwell stood a few feet away, biting down on a wet cigar. He watched the battle with an understanding that only few could accept. *Sometimes it takes war to give a man the peace he needs*, he thought as the two men fell to the wet earth in a hail of flailing blows.

Chapter 8

Beep! Beep! Beeeeep!

The heart monitor's alert was hysterical. Coffee, along with a few others in the nursing staff, rushed into the room expecting the worst, but what they found was merely the closest thing to the worst.

"Empty!" The word slipped from Coffee's lips in an astonished whisper. They stared bewilderedly at Black's empty hospital bed before Coffee timidly stepped deeper into the room. "How the hell did she——"

"Look!" a slim white guy interrupted her.

They all paused to see what he was so unnerved about and as their stares followed his outstretched finger, the answer to their mutual questions were answered. A thick, braided mass of hospital sheets were tied to the leg of the hospital bed. Coffee's heart fluttered as she made her way closer to Black's deception. She walked over to the open window and gazed down at the deserted street. The makeshift rope swung lazily back and forth as it descended toward the wet pavement. A soft smile played at the corners of her lips as she realized she'd been duped.

"What's going on here? Is Ms. Ridge——" Dr. Sung's voice was panicked when he burst into the room, but he paused when his slanted eyes landed on the empty bed. Alarmed, his stare shot to Coffee for answers she couldn't give.

***

The room was eerie as a single light bulb illuminated the dark basement. It occasionally dimmed before glowing bright again with an annoying humming buzz.

"Tony Little, a.k.a. big, bad-ass Murda out the Butta Beans!" a deep baritone voice sounded from a far corner of the room.

Murda tried to lift his head, but without his consent, it fell back down, chin close to his chest. He was bound naked to a wooden chair and was in bad shape. They'd beaten him unmercifully, but continued to bring him back to consciousness. They wanted him to feel every ache of the torture. Through swollen eyes, Murda searched for the speaker. His heartbeat was like the rapid strides of two runners vying for the finish line. With a strange familiarity, the sound of that voice struck a chord with him. *Hell naw...can't be! This nigga s'posed to be dead, buried underneath a ton of federal max concrete!* His mental was a typhoon of fear intermingled with a touch of disbelief.

Agent Mullowsky's face came into view as he stood over him. The dirty cop's features were bathed in sweat and speckles of Murda's blood. He'd taken a break from the beating he was administering when the demand for him to ease up was made. He smiled wickedly at his destruction.

"Who was that scum bag that got away? You're gonna tell us, or will you die for——"

"I said that's enough, Mullowsky!" The deep voice sliced through the threat.

Mullowsky glanced toward the darkest corner of the room as a muscular, dark, bald-headed man eased into the light and fixed him with a cold stare. The man's presence seemed to suck the air out of Murda's lungs when he beheld the devil in the flesh. The ex-agent Spinx had aged in numbers, but his muscled body seemed to cling to its youth. The fifteen years he'd spent behind the walls of super max federal prison had not only blessed him physically, but it also allowed his dark mind to blossom into a beautiful evil that he couldn't wait to reveal. He smiled down at the bound man.

"There's no need to ask questions we already know the answers to, partner. The one that got away is a very good friend of ours. Ain't that right, Murda?" He chuckled with the question.

Murda's eyes were blurred from the blood clots in them, but even with the stains in his vision, one could see the questions tumbling through his mind. He began to rock back and forth as if he was attempting to tip the chair over. "Mmmph!" he mumbled from behind the duct tape over his mouth.

Spinx reached down and snatched the silver strip away.

"Argh!" Murda's cry was deep and painful as the tape peeled free with a layer of his skin stuck to it. He cried incoherently as he mentally prayed that the devil blessed him with the chance of a bloody revenge.

Spinx laughed at the manic look in his eyes, but nodded his acknowledgment. He knew that the young killa was 'bout that action and would sign it in blood if given the chance.

"What's poppin', *dawg!*" His words were tinged with sarcasm. The rogue detective jacked his slacks in order to be comfortable and squatted down so they'd be at eye level.

"Didn't think you'd ever see me again, huh? You lil niggas done really grow into your own. Y'all could have at least sent ole Spinx some love while I rotted away in that concrete coffin!" His words held a hidden danger. As he studied the young goon he'd watched grow from a cub and evolve into a vicious lion, he gritted his teeth at the flood of memories that submerged his mental within treacherous waters. The shock, the embarrassment, but most dominantly, the betrayal came flooding back.

"Agent Spinx, you're a disgrace to our country and a betrayer of your fellow officers. I hope you rot in that cell you're going to! God knows you deserve it!" the DEA director declared as Spinx was being cuffed and placed into the back of an unmarked car.

The red and blue police lights flickered over his face as Spinx stared out the window. The larcenous stares from his fellow field officers that once trusted him with their lives did nothing to his enflamed pride, but it was the triumphant gazes from other sets of eyes that wounded his crooked heart. Messiah, Sunjay, and Murda stood amidst the gathering crowd of onlookers, watching as their plot unfolded before their eyes. It seemed as if the entire hood of South Oak Cliff had turned out for his going away party, and as he sat chained at the wrists, he could hear the round of applause from them. They clapped their hands and shouted victory cries. They hated him for the injustices he'd inflicted on them, and as Spinx's eyes moved, they found Sunjay. The young killer formed a gun with his fingers and mockingly pulled the trigger before turning and disappearing into the crowd. Likewise, Murda followed suit, but the boy Messiah observed him with intelligent eyes. At that moment, Agent Spinx knew that the young'n was the brains behind the scheme. The young pimp saluted him before following behind his partners in crime.

"Argh!" Murda's tortured cry was the music that pulled the vengeful rogue back from the poisonous memory. It surprised him to find himself grasping a handful of Murda's testicles, squeezing them as tight as an anaconda's squeezing hug.

Murda panted as his eyes bulged out of their swollen sockets. His lungs contracted as he fought to stay conscious. "Please! *Please!*" he moaned.

"Huh? I can't hear you, bitch, say it again! Beg for mercy, nigga!" Spinx growled in sickening elation.

Murda rocked viciously in the chair, but the pain was unforgiving. Spinx laughed maniacally as he roughly released him.

"I'ma kill yo' bitch ass, on God!" Murda exhaled the sentence as if it was one word. He whimpered softly.

Spinx delivered a powerful punch to his midsection.

"You gonna tell us where those punk mu'fuckas Messiah and Sunjay rest at!" he spat before wrapping his fingers around Murda's throat and applying pressure. "The trap spots! The hoes. Them pussy-ass Jamaicans! I want it all, mu'fucka, or you 'bout to die up in this bitch right now!" he promised with spittle flying from his mouth.

A soft touch on his arm caused Spinx to glance at Mullowsky.

"He's tryin' to say something." The agent nodded at Murda.

All eyes went to the goon as Spinx released him.

Murda coughed and sucked in precious air before glaring up at the heartless man. Something played within his stare that only he and the devil smiled upon.

"A'ight…a'ight. I'll give you what you want, but leave me and Sunjay out the equation! We gotta walk free from this shit. Messiah and them hoe-ass Jamaicans though?" He paused to give them a bloodied smirk. "Them boys dawg food!" he professed with a passion that caused even Spinx to raise an eyebrow, intrigued.

Chapter 9

"Damnnnnn, nigga, you…you ain't nut yet? Get that! Get that off, boo," Tutts moaned more out of irritation than pleasure.

"Shut…shut up, bitch, and take this shit! Take it!" the young hustla growled as he feverishly pumped in and out of her essences. He had her bent over the arm of a worn couch with her dingy miniskirt pulled up over her ashy ass cheeks. The young'n could feel his escape surging from his nuts as he watched her juicy ass jiggle with his every thrust.

"Well…well, hurry the hell up so I…I can get mine! Boy, you tryin' to make love to this pussy. You gonna have ta bless me for this!" Tutts snapped as she felt him pull out and squirt on her backside. With no regard, she bent down and scooped her panties off the floor and used them to clean herself.

"Damn, Tutts, you know you got that fiya!" the young hustla declared with a chuckle. He tucked his nature back inside his boxers before glancing over at their spectator. Black sat at the other end of the couch with a disgusted expression on her face. "You look familiar, ma, what you tryin' to do?" He eyed her lustfully.

"Montray, come on wit' my shit so you can get ya mannish ass out my house. And you bet not tell Junnie 'bout this shit neither!" Tutts spoke with a suck of her teeth.

The young'n pulled a sandwich bag from his jeans pocket and pulled a chunk of tannish rock from inside it. He used his thumb nails to chip a smaller piece from it and handed it to her.

"Tutts, I'm grown. I turned my first stone when I was ten. She ain't gave a damn 'bout me since she started fuckin wit' that nigga Walter. Why would I tell her my bidness?" he jazzed his truths while handing her the smaller piece of crack.

Tutts glanced down at the stone before glaring at him. "Uh-uh, nigga, all that humpin' you done did, and you got the balls to give me this small-ass shit!"

The young hustla's eyes bounced from Tutts to the quarter ounce of hard he held. "Man, Tutts, you always roachin'. I'ma need some head for this!" he fumed as he chipped another dime piece from the rock.

As soon as she had it in her hands, Tutts gave him a stained-tooth smile. "Later, baby. Right now, I gots thangs to do. Yo' young ass done wore an old woman out!" She laughed as she ushered him to the door. "Montray, don't forget that I watched ya lil bad ass grow from Pampers to blue jeans! You're my son's friend and you lil new niggas don't even know how to hold ya liquor, let alone yo' business!" she spat before slamming the door in his face and turning to face Black. "So what brings you to my humble abode, fat cat? Last I heard, yo' ass was laid up somewhere in one of them crazy houses." Tutts didn't mince words as she shuffled across the stained carpet.

Black watched her take something off the coffee table before stepping into the kitchen.

"You know you can't always believe the talks of the ghetto's hot line, Tutts. Dependin' on the gossip of the beauty shop won't get you nothin' but a pretty hairdo and a head full of illusions!" she spat in irritation. *Mu'fuckas ain't got nothin' betta to do other than busy themselves with other folk business!* she thought as Tutts returned, using a slim object to stuff something down into a clear pipe. She made her way over to the couch and sat at the other end, the same end which she was just bent over. Black's heart began to pound against her chest and her palms begun to sweat as she watched Tutts put the glass dick to her lips and glance down at it.

No...no, I ain't goin down that road again. That shit almost killed me! I'd be a damn fool to give my life back to that shit! Her thoughts were a rapid river beyond the point of control.

The flame danced off the lighter as Tutts took a deep pull from her dark heaven.

Just one hit won't hurt nobody, will it? I'm just gonna take a small hit to ease my mind and then I'll leave this demon alone forever! Black's thoughts were a powerful current as Tutts exhaled a thick cloud of tainted smoke. She held heaven out to Black knowingly.

"If that's so, suga, that there hospital gown you're wearin' is either evidence of the truth or you're tryin' to start a new trend that nobody's gonna follow," Tutts retorted.

Black's vision went from the buck-eyed expression on her friend's face to the mental escape she was offering her. *One hit! That's all!* Her thoughts defeated her as she took the pipe and lighter. Black lit its tip and as soon as the familiar taste of the smoke snaked down her throat, life didn't seem so bad. One hit turned into two, two turned into three, and three turned into…

"Goddamn, bitch, you wasn't the one taken a pussy poundin' from ya son's homie!" Tutts verbalized as she took the pipe by its scalding tip and snatched it from between Black's lips.

Buck-eyed, high as Venus, and holding the dark smoke inside her lungs as long as she could, Black crossed one leg over the other and sat as if she was the most dignified smoker in the universe. As she released, her words were laced with hints of regret. "Tutts, you remember way back in '93 when we first met?"

Tutts gave her a small smile as she absently patted her nappy hair. She seemed to be staring off into the cloud of smoke Black had exhaled. "Mm-hmm, girl, we was the shit back then, huh?" she sadly responded.

"We was. We was, baby girl." Tears came to Black's eyes as she stared into the pillow of smoke that only seemed to grow denser.

Both women stared deep into the foul smoke as their minds hurled them back to a time when shit wasn't so crazy, but before they slipped too far away, Black's words cast a demon into the room.

"Blow came home last week, Tutts. He murdered my husband in cold blood! Shot him down like a rabid dog in the streets."

***

1993

Messiah walked into the plush penthouse he shared with Pimpin Maxwell and their ladies, and as soon as his Gators sank into the plush carpet, he could sense an awkwardness that didn't fit into the usual bustle of the playa's den. His hand instinctively went for the banga on his waist, but he paused at the scene before him. His three girls along with Holly, Foxy, Sassy, and Cotton, Pimpin Maxwell's ladies, sat in various places of the living room. The atmosphere was sullen as all eyes rose to meet his, but it was Black's stare that told the tale that if they were doing more sitting on their twats than using them for compensation, the pimp lord of lords must've issued a hoe's off day directly from pimp heaven.

"Fuck you hoes got goin on? Y'all must think pimpin' on hold for the day or somethin'? Y'all hoes betta——"

"Let the girls be, young blood, and come let me put some pimpin' in ya ear real quick." Pimpin Maxwell's deep voice interrupted his stomp down.

The aroma of the Cuban-cut tobacco spoke to his senses before his vision found the relaxed demeanor of his mentor as he leaned against the wall leading to the back room. Pimpin was debonair as usual in a tailored pair of mint green slacks, tan dress shirt, and a pair of desert sand-colored loafers. Their eyes connected before the older man turned on his heels and disappeared down the hall.

Messiah departed with a glare that promised his wrath when he returned, but as soon as he made it to the threshold of his bedroom, he stopped in his tracks. Four suitcases were neatly lined up by his bed, and as his eyes surveyed the space he knew as home, his common sense spoke louder than any pair of lips could. *I'm being evicted!* His gut spoke to his mental. His eyes rose to find Pimpin Maxwell standing, staring out at the Dallas skyline as if he was trying to memorize it.

After taking a pull from the cigar, he pulled it from his lips. "Come over here and share this view wit' an ole playa, young'n, tell me what'cha see," he requested.

Messiah's feet felt like bricks as he made his way over to the man he'd grown to love and respect like a father, but he forced himself to wade through troubled waters and find his way beside the OG. He studied Pimpin for a few seconds, seeing that he wasn't gonna break the eye fuck he was having with the treacherous city that had robbed him of so much.

"You know something, baby boy?" Pimpin broke the awkward silence before pausing once more to savor the woody flavor of his addiction. "The game of baseball is a strange sport, cat daddy. In fact, it's one of the highest paid *contradictions* in the land of no liberty." Pimpin Maxwell chuckled.

"See, Major League Baseball has always been a pale man's sport, but back in 1947, they made a grand mistake in terms of Klan USA. They not only allowed Jackie Robinson to be the first Negro to ever enter Major League Baseball, but that one blunder broke the color barrier and created one of the biggest contradictions in sports today," he spoke as Messiah turned to look at him.

The young'n played with the ring on his pinkie finger as he studied his mentor. "I don't get it, OG. What any of that shit gotta do wit' you havin my shit packed and my hoes off duty?" he inquired with a controlled irritation.

Pimpin Maxwell blew a long stream of smoke before replying. "The lesson is found in the contradiction, Pimp. Dig me, baby, why would *any* bonafide playa inject poison into the veins of the game? See, niggas always screamin 'bout how fucked up their life was growin' up 'cause they mamas was dope fiends and they pappies wasn't 'round to teach 'em shit, but them same lames allow their actions to contradict the shit they complainin' 'bout."

Pimpin spat the words as if they were vulgarity within the mouth of a devout Christian. He turned to face his protégé and allowed his eyes to roll over him. Pimpin shook his head in disappointment. "Contradiction, son, just like Major League Baseball, it's a sport that's loved by white folks, but dominated by foreigners. The same people they don't want in their country." He paused and took a deep pull from his cigar before quickly exhaling the sweet smoke. Pimpin pointed the tobacco stick at Messiah. "Our people complain 'bout how fucked up shit is, but fail to understand that change should be more of a self-acceptance than a complaint! The same brothas that know what it's like not to have a father choose the streets over his own seed," Pimpin Maxwell spat before turning to face his protégé. He allowed his eyes to study the skyline once again. "You sinned against the game, daddy, and more disappointingly, you contradicted everything a certified playa stands for," he jeweled.

Messiah's expression was stained with confusion as he lifted his arms in a *what the fuck you talking 'bout* gesture. "Pimpin, I'm lost in the sauce, OG. Just give it to me absolute. A boss like myself deserves that much." Messiah was ready for the blade to fall.

Pimpin strode over to the side of the bed and retrieved an empty Nike gym bag and tossed it onto the bare mattress before his eyes drowned Messiah. The young'n's heart pounded against his chest as he began to perspire.

Empty! Empty! Empty! his mind kept repeating, but the rationality of the truth seemed elusive to what his heart wanted to believe.

"Where's my work, Pimpin? We're not gonna play with my pockets, OG." His voice was shaky, yet deadly. His mind went to the banga on his waist, but respect quieted that demon within him.

"Why you disrespect my home by bringin' that shit here?" Pimpin responded with a question. *"Never mix your hustles, cat daddy, we're not drug dealers. We're playas that prosper by the fruits of what's between a hoe's legs. Never bring poison 'round me or where we rest out heads."*

They both reflected on the jewel Pimpin once bestowed upon the young pup. Their eyes danced as their egos tilted on the edge of pride's mountain and with the wrong words, love and respect could evolve into what should never be amongst real niggas.

"That was a half a book, Pimpin. I fucked off all my loot on that shit!" Messiah hissed. His temperature seemed to be rising with each second and before he could tame the urge, he had the tool out and gripped tight in his hand. "Fuck my shit at, my dude?" Murder swirled in the air. *Fuck it,* he thought before aiming at the OG's chest.

"It's gone, Pimp. I crushed that poison and flushed it! It was that or give it to ya mama!"

I'm 'bout to whack fam. He in major violation! Messiah's mental was homicidal. But he knew that to kill the old man would kill himself internally.

Pimpin Maxwell stretched his arms out wide. "Go 'head and shoot, pimp buddy, go on and shorten my days for the sins of ya own game. I asked you to keep my place and your street activities separate, but you not only spat on a playa's request, you also endangered me and the girls' livelihood." Pimpin smashed the stub of the cigar against the window pane. "I flushed that shit to show you the last piece of the game, P. You may not respect it now, but you will when ya Gators reach their full shoe size," he reasoned.

Messiah's eyes were murderous, but as the seconds passed and melted into the silence, so did his intent. He lowered the pistol and shook his head sadly. "I've been a dope boy my entire life, my nigga. It's part of me, Pimpin."

"Pimp friend, the only things that's a part of a real nigga that he can't live without is his heart, brain, and his game," Pimpin Maxwell replied as their eyes fell to the four suitcases. Messiah tucked the tool back on his waist before walking over to the cases that held his life's possessions. "So this is it, huh, me and my girls are on our own?" He chuckled at the irony of his predicament.

Pimpin's gaze seemed to cloud over as he made his way back to the window. "This is the last and most critical lesson of the game I can give you, cat daddy. The rest has to be learned by experience," he spoke over his shoulder. But it was the tone of his voice that caused Messiah to fix his eyes on him. Smoked swirled around his bald head as he spoke. "This last piece of game will be essential to your future endeavors. See, the worst thing a playa can do is allow his woman to despise the weakness of his game and thinking capabilities while at the same time beholding the playerisms of the next playa. A bitch wants a king that can take her to the next level, daddy-o. It's not all 'bout pussy and dick. Playa's jewels, cat daddy," Pimpin Maxwell blessed him before turning and allowing his eyes to connect with the man-child he'd grown to love. He raised his hand and snapped his fingers three times before turning his admiration back to the crooked city of Dallas, Texas that sat twenty floors down.

Messiah found the action strange, but digested it as his dismissal. He bent to retrieve two of the suitcases, but the entrance of his three women gave him a better idea. *Let these hoes do the labor while I think of my next move!* he thought.

"Candy, y'all each grab a suitcase so we can blow this spot," he demanded as if he was sho'nuff and hadn't just been evicted.

Candy and Creamy stepped forward, but the only assistance he received was a cool breeze upon his warm face as they strode past him. Creamy approached Pimpin as Candy's frightful eyes ping-ponged back and forth between them and Messiah's heated gaze. Little did he know, while he was out playing the field, Pimpin Maxwell's ladies had been working the insecurities of his girls.

"Messiah, baby, one day you're gonna be a sho'nuff playa classically, but right now you're just too young to understand this game." Creamy didn't even have the decency to look him in his eyes as she did what only a hoe was born to do. "Pimpin, Foxy n'em have spoken of the glories of your management and me and Candy would truly feel honored to bless ya game with our services," she confessed while handing him a nice bankroll. "I know that this measly thirty-nine hundred ain't shit in comparison to what your girls bring in, but we're some thoroughbred whores that know how to fuck for a buck," she said enticingly.

Pimpin Maxwell didn't give the hoe the respect of his eye contact as he studied Black. "And you?" he inquired.

"Nigga, I would neva give you or these treacherous hoes the satisfaction of humiliating my baby," Black seethed.

Pimpin figured as much and nodded his respect. Without taking his eyes off of Messiah, he spoke. "You hoes serve him proper, like the boss he is."

Both women seemed timid as they made their way before Messiah, but it was again Creamy that was the voice of the duo.

"Messiah, you are a——"

"Silence, hoe, I don't need ya verbal!" he spat as he snatched up two of the suitcases. His eyes were twin seas that submerged the vision before him so deeply into his mental that it branded his thoughts.

Pimpin Maxwell bit down on his stump of a cigar as he studied the young'n. "This will only make your pimp hand strong, Messiah.

Now we'll see where ya game takes you. You're either goin' to take the city of Dallas by storm or wind up a victim of the storm. It's nothin' personal, son, only a day's work!" he stated.

But Messiah had already walked out.

***

Dream's lips were tight around his dick head as she swallowed him and played with his nuts.

"Damn, shawty, you got that soft touch!" Fatso gritted as he grabbed a handful of her weave and forced her mouth down further on his length. His eyes rolled to the back of his head as his toes curled inside the Retro's on his feet. His pants were at his ankles as he fucked her mouth. He was on the edge of no return when she pulled away from him with a popping sound. "Fuck! Why you stop, ma? I was just about to get that shit off," he whined like a big sucka unaccustomed to a bad bitch's mouth technique.

Dream giggled as she climbed to her feet. She was as jazzy as ever in a G-string and baby tee that barely covered her perky breasts. They'd barely made it into the apartment before Fatso was all over her and though she felt some kinda way about crossing Sunjay, she knew she had to be a big girl until the deed was done. She'd been babysitting the successful hustler for the past six weeks before he'd finally brought her to where he rested his head.

"Wait, papi, let me use the little girl's room and when I come back, I'ma fuck you till them J's pop off your feet," she purred.

Only a special kind of nigga can resist the seductions of a bad bitch, and outside of securing a bag, there was nothin too special bout Fatso.

"Hurry up, lil mama, you got the boy's nuts smokin'! I'm trying to slide up in that and see if you're worth a Birkin or two," he shot as he watched her ass cheeks jiggle as she made her way to the bathroom.

Dream paused at the threshold of the door and glanced back at him with seduction exuding from her gaze.

"A Birkin? That's cute, but this pussy at least worth a Peugeot," she challenged while running her tongue over her upper lip.

Fatso kicked off his shoes and slid his pants and boxers the rest of the way off before laying back and stroking himself to an erection. Dream laughed before leaving him to his business.

This pussy worth ya life to my man, she thought as she slipped into the living room and unlocked the door. She then grabbed her purse and slipped into the bathroom to let her nerves calm down.

***

"Messiah! Messiah, wait!" Black shouted from behind him.

Messiah's pain fueled his feet to carry him as far away from that place as they could carry him.

Black caught up to him. "Boy, you ain't hear me callin' you? I'm too old to be runnin' afta yo' young ass!" she rasped, out of breath.

Messiah kept his eyes straight and held his silence, but the woman that gave birth to him was not to be deterred. She jumped in front of him and placed her hands on his chest.

"Boy, you're about to piss me off. Now I know how you're feelin', but *I* ain't the one that done it to you. No matter how I live my life, I'm still your mama!" she admonished with that *don't make me whoop ya ass* look.

Messiah had stopped in his tracks and the heat in his eyes were lakes of fire as he glared at her. "My mama?" The question came out more of a statement. "You ain't been my mama since my daddy di——"

She slapped the remaining words out of his mouth. Messiah tensed as if he were battling the urge of his gangsterisms.

"I brought you into this world, Negro, and I'll kill you as sure as my husband is dead if you ever - *ever* - raise ya hand at me, Messiah!"

Black's voice had taken on a deadly timbre and within her stare, Messiah could see a love so deep that it gave birth to how far she'd go to ensure his respect. At that moment, as cars sped by, Messiah deflated. He dropped the suitcases and allowed a river to stream from his left eye until the right followed suit as if they were in a race.

"Why us though, ma? Why *everybody* we love end up fuckin' ova us? Huh?" he cried without blinking.

Black studied him until his pain melted all the protections she'd placed on her heart, and there on the corner of Poke Street, she pulled her son into her embrace.

"I couldn't tell you, baby. I couldn't tell you if I wanted to," she whispered. Releasing him, Black cupped his face in her hands, forcing him to look up at her. "I know this hurts, baby, but you gotta shake it off!" She used her thumbs to wipe his tears. "Understand this, Messiah: you should never, never sell your soul for love or the cheap thrills of a pussy hole! One thing about pussy, son, is it can become as wet as you make its possessor, it can push out a baby, and it can even make you rich if your game is tight enough, but the one thing pussy can't do is give you love or loyalty! Only the bitch that it's attached to can give you that, and even that should be under great scrutiny," Black jeweled him before flipping the script.

She released his face and sat down on one of the suitcases. She pulled out a pack of Newport 100's and pulled one free. Lighting it, she glanced out at the passing cars as they flew by.

"Tame that bitch in you, lil daddy. Every man has her somewhere inside him. That bitch is called your emotions! Envy, jealousy, and hate are bitch traits, Messiah! When Pimpin knocked you for ya hoes back there, you shoulda shared one of them ole cigars wit' him and congratulated him for takin' them snake bitches off ya hands. But instead, when the hoes defected on you, you allowed that bitch in you to cause you to think irrational." Her words were as sharp as the edge of a scalpel.

Messiah's guard went up and his pride spoke through him. "Fuck you talm'bout, Ma, what else was I s'posed to do?" He paused and took his beeper off his waist. He glanced down at the same number that had been paging him for the past few weeks. *This hoe Liberty just won't ease up!* He shook his head at the thought.

Black knew who it was without having to ask.

"Nigga, ya silly ass was so hurt that you got us walkin' up and down these street, and you got the keys to Pimpin's Benz in ya pockets." She chuckled at the surprised expression on his face. "And if you plan on recovering from the hand Pimpin Maxwell just dealt you, I suggest you quiet that bitch in you and keep her tamed. Master her!" She spoke with passion before climbing to her feet and tossing the unlit cigarette. "That ole girl that keeps pagin' you is dyin' to be managed, but your simp ass so worried about ya heart that you're not seein' the profit in ya pocket! Get it, Messiah? Profit in my pocket?" She laughed as she began to walk away.

"Where you goin', Mama?" he asked, confused by her sudden departure.

"I'm goin' back for my senses! Didn't ya black ass just hear me say you got the keys to Pimpin's Benz in ya pocket?" She stopped and glanced back at him. Shaking her head in amusement, Black stared at her baby. "Just like ya daddy, all the heart in the world but not a lick of sense!"

***

Sunjay eased the door open to the apartment and slid in as silently as the moon trading places with the sun. The F and N clutched tight in his gloved hand, he followed the familiar sounds of Dream's love song until he was at the doorway of the bedroom.

"Yes! Yes! Right there!" she cried as he peeked through the crack in the door.

He watched as her back arched and heaven was called down into the space she shared with another man. Yet, he continued to pump, his own sense of ecstasy beckoning him forward. Dream wrapped her arms around him and pulled his head down into the crook of her neck.

Damn, this nigga has some good di—— Oh shit! she thought when she looked up to find the penetrating gaze of Sunjay. She began to panic and slapped Fatso's shoulder, but he only pumped faster. "Oh my God! Gun!" she shouted, finally getting his attention.

Confused, Fatso glanced down at her before following her frightened stare.

"'Sup, blood, she got some heat huh, brah?" Sunjay laughed at Fatso's clumsy attempt to roll away from her. With the speed of a mongoose, Sanjay was around the bed with the banga aimed at play-boy's noggin. "Uh-uh! The coroner will find it funny if she gotta piece ya dome back together, startin' from here to that wet spot you just made in the middle of that bed, my G, Let's not be stupid," he gritted as he reached down and snatched the black .380 off the floor that dude was obviously going for.

"Say, you know who I am, dawg?" Fatso stuttered.

"Please don't hurt us. Please!" Dream's theatrics were grade-A and before anyone could wrap their mind around what he was doing, Sunjay's aim diverted slightly and he fired.

The sound of her body hitting the floor was the testament of the devil's presence. Without looking behind him, Fatso knew that Dream was either dead or well on her way to talking to God or the devil. His eyes grew big as he threw his hands up.

"Say, playboy, it ain't no need for all that. The bread and work is right there." He nodded to the floor nervously.

Sunjay took a step back and glanced in the direction he was in-dicating, but he saw nothing. He chuckled before the gun jumped in his hand. The F and N spit and knocked a chunk of Fatso's side off. He fell to the floor in a heap.

"Fuck!" he shouted as he clutched his body and whimpered. "Fuck you do that for? I told you where the shit was at!" he rasped.

"Nigga, you think it's a game!" Sunjay spat while standing over him with evil intent in his stare.

"What you talm'bout, mane, the shit is in the stash under the carpet! Just go over there and pull the corner of the carpet up and it's a false board in the floor! Come on, fam, I'm 'bout to bleed to death!" Fatso's cry was pleading.

Sunjay's eyes flickered from him to the corner before he shrugged his shoulders. "Thought you was playin wit my G, blood." He chuckled. "But that's not what I'm here for."

"Man, what you talm'bout? What else you want?" Fatso moaned.

Sunjay kicked him in the wounded side. "Bitch nigga, quit cryin' like a bitch and listen! I know you got that work, but I want more than that! See, you niggas talk too much when ya dick wet and you never know when the devil is listenin'. I know you got a meetin' wit' ya plug this week. I need details."

"Awww, man, I can't! They'll kill me! Look, it's three bricks and——"

Bocka!

Fatso's knee exploded into a mess of bone and white meat.

"Fuuuuck!" he cried as he grabbed his knee.

"Look, playboy, my next shot gonna close ya curtains. I'm tryin' to let you live ya life. You may have a permanent shit bag, but at least you can still see a bag or two. What's up, homie? I ain't got much time. I'm sure *someone* done heard all these fireworks and called the law." Sunjay was getting antsy. There was a moment of contemplation, but when Sunjay decided to count his losses and rock him to sleep, Fatso saw the resolution in his stare. As soon as he raised the tool for a head shot...

"A'ight, a'ight. Look, Friday the thirteenth it's gonna be a delivery at the storage place off Poke. The truck will be a decoy, but the next car in at eight o'clock will be the real deal. But man, you don't know who you're fuckin' with, these people will murder your entire family!" Fatso declared.

Bocka! Bocka! Bocka! Bocka!

The F and N spit long flames with each caress of the trigger. Four slugs sang the fat man to sleep as Sunjay tucked both bangas on his waist and rushed to the corner of the room. He knelt down and pulled the carpet back and just as the dead man confirmed, the false board was as noticeable as a white man in a Black Panther's convention.

"Dream, come over here and help me with this shit," he called over his shoulder.

Dream popped up from the floor with a serious attitude. She crossed her arms over her chest and stood her ground.

"Nigga, fuck you! You shot too close to me, Sunjay. What if ya stupid ass woulda killed me on a fluke, huh?" she snapped.

Sunjay paid her no mind as he tried to figure out how to get the spot open. Impatient and out of time, he used the bottom of the gun and smashed it into the plywood. It crashed in easily. He gazed down into the hole and his dick began to stand up at the sight of the three books of boy and neat bundles of hundreds.

"Well, at least come clean your cum off playboy's dick before them people gets here. DNA a mu'fucka these days, bae," he chuckled.

Chapter 10

"Hello?" Her feminine tone was skeptical, but still caused memories of their past to flood his mental.

Yet Messiah's heart was as black as a locked basement with no windows, cracks or lights. "Why you keep blowin' my shit up, bitch? Didn't I tell you to get lost?" he spat vehemently.

There was a long pause before her soft reply. "Why you handlin' me like this, bae? I just miss you," she sniveled. "I've apologized sooo many times, but you're so hurt, you can't see that you're killing me, baby. Just give me a chance to make this right, please, baby!" she cried.

Messiah held the cordless phone to his ear as he gazed out at the zoo of the projects. He and Sunjay were posted in East Dallas projects, thuggin' with Sunjay's cousin, Taco.

"Apologize? Give you a chance to make it right, huh?" Messiah chuckled as he watched Sunjay serve a smoker. "Bitch, the only chance you deserve is the chance of findin a different hobby! Stop ca——"

"I'll do *anything*, Messiah, just tell me what I gotta do!" she whined.

Messiah smiled mischievously as the words replayed within the confines of his mind. "Anything, huh?" he inquired as Taco stuck his head out the door and beckoned for them to come in.

"Anything, bae, anything! I just want us back," Liberty reiterated. The maliciousness within his laughter should've warned her of his crooked intent, but love will always be the kidnapped of common sense.

"That's a bet, mama. If that's fa sho', meet me at the La Quinta Inn tomorrow. We'll talk and see where we can go from here," he relented as Sunjay walked past, counting the bread he'd just made. Their eyes locked and Sunjay nodded his head in question at the crooked grin on his potna's face.

"'Sup, nigga, why you lookin' like the Joker out that movie Batman?" he chuckled with inquisition.

Messiah playfully big faced him at the same time that Liberty's heart slipped from her lips.

"I love you, pa."

"Yeah, we'll see." Messiah's callousness repelled her confession. Without waiting for a response, he ended the call and followed Sunjay into the apartment.

The living room was filled with weed smoke as the gang rotated blunts of exotic and did what only a room filled with gangstas would be doing. The sounds of clips being locked into place and various types of automatic artillery being cocked resounded within the small space. Taco laid the stick across his lap before glancing at Sunjay.

"Lil bro, you sho' this shit official, or you got us piped up on some humbug shit?" he inquired, causing all eyes to fixate on the young killa. Sunjay took the street sweeper off the floor and admired it before ignoring the question and the questioning stares completely. Instead, he turned his gaze to his ace.

"Dawg, you know you been outta touch wit' the streets. Don't be dry on no prove something shit just 'cause that pimp nigga got you on yo' dick." He studied his day one.

Messiah accepted a blunt from Murda before lifting his shirt to reveal the twin burnas on his waist. "Nigga, worry 'bout ya bitch. You and all these niggas know I'm wit' the shits. Just 'cause I sell pussy don't mean I won't dirt somethin'," he pledged.

Sunjay smiled before breaking his stare with a confirming nod. "Two niggas, one heart, brah." He gave it up for his nigga. Looking up at the clock on the wall, he stood. "The question is, are you otha niggas wit' it?"

***

"Wait, wait, hold up!" Justice spoke breathlessly as she broke the kiss.

"What? What's good, shawty?" Lamont's nature was as hard as stainless steel. He had her down to her bra and panties and the only thing on his mind was how tight that young pussy would be.

Justice wiped her mouth and glanced around the room in wonder. *What am I doin'? Am I ready for this? What will Messiah think?* Her mental was aflame with questions.

There was a knock at the door.

"Y'all a'ight in there?" Porsha asked with her ear to the door's surface.

"Yeah, we good, Porsha." Justice confirmed. Her eyes went to Lamont. *"Bitch, I dare you to fuck him!"* Porsha's voice played in her head, but it was the pinkie promise she'd made so long ago that had put the brakes on the moment of pleasure's exchange for her innocence.

"Promise me you'll wait on me." She could hear Messiah's voice in her mind as if he'd made a room there and was speaking within it.

Lamont ran his fingers through her hair as he kissed her neck. "'Sup, boo? I ain't gonna hurt you. Trust me," he spoke between kisses as his hands massaged the peach just beyond the material of her panties.

She was as wet as the Pacific, moaning from the combination of his lips and dancing hand that had somehow slipped underneath the thin barrier that protected her femininity from nature. His fingers played a tune on her clit that was foreign, but delicious to that side of her that she wasn't in touch with. Before she knew it, she was pantiless. Things became a blur as dude stole her thoughts with each kiss. She wanted to stop him, but that monster was untamable when fear was defeated by the feeling of that first nut. Justice bit her bottom lip and wasn't prepared for heaven intermingling with hell when…

"Ahhhhh! Lamont, it…it…" She got lost within the pain as the head of his nature passed her ocean.

"Damn, you tight, baby," he growled.

Her nails dug into his back and unbeknownst to either of them, Porsha's ear was still glued to the door and heard each word.

"Damn, lil one, let dem do they thang. We got our own room to be in," Dunte, Lamont's brother, whispered as he snuck up behind her.

Porsha smiled as she turned around and took his hand in hers, placing it between her bare legs. She wrapped her arms around his neck and allowed the freak in her to bleed into her eyes. "Awww. Him miss Mama!" she cooed in a baby's voice. "Come on, let Mama put the baby to sleep. I hope you know how to eat pussy, 'cause I have a buffet you can eat from all night." She giggled as she pulled him toward the back room.

***

The moon was up and full. The gates rolled open and the Lexus coupe eased through. Junebug navigated the whip toward the back of the storage unit before pulling to a stop and killing the ignition. He glanced nervously toward smoke in the passenger's seat.

"Mane, you say that nigga Fatso ain't answer when you got at 'im?"

The dark-skinned cat sucked his gold teeth and shook his head in confirmation. "Naw, naw, that fat-ass nigga been M.I.A. all day. Nigga hit us last night 'bout this bidness and now he on some funny activity, fam. I'm tellin' you, yo' people ain't right. This shit just don't feel right."

"Chill, cuz, let's just see what the bizz is and if shit crazy, we'll dip." Junebug soothed the tension.

Just as his words left his mouth, the headlights of a black Ford Bronco illuminated them as it pulled in front of the Lex.

"Why these dumb mu'fuckas got they beams on a nigga like we're in a police lineup, cuzzo!" Smoke fumed before patting the p.89 in his lap.

Junebug shrugged as he lit a Newport and watched as the driver of the truck jumped out. The man was thin with multicolored dreadlocks that were tied into a bundle on top of his head. The passenger door opened and another Jamaican with long dreads swinging about his face stepped out. Both men strolled to the front of the truck and stared out at the Lex as if they could see its occupants. After a moment's observation, the passenger slapped the hood of the Bronco. In formation, three other dreads filed out of the back seat. Each man brandished an assault rifle that was equipped with a hundred round drum. The man with the multicolored dreads whistled and waved Junebug and Smoke out.

The two goons exchanged suspicious glances before Junebug shrugged and pushed his door open. He slid out into the night and waited for Smoke to follow suit. Once both men were out, Junebug took the first step into the unknown.

Smoke wasn't so trusting. He studied the strangers for a moment longer before relenting and reaching in the backseat to get the duffle bag. He followed his potna and once they stepped beyond enemy's lines, the three Jamaican shooters spread out around them.

"Wagwon, Star, where's de fat man?" Multicolored inquired as his eyes swept their surroundings as if expecting some gangsta shit to pop off.

"Fam tied up wit' some other shit right now, so he sent us to get the bidness done. You've seen me wit' brah at a couple of the movements so it ain't like I'm a stranger, huh?" Junebug rolled the dice with fate.

The tension was thick as they studied each other. The dread strolled closer before his brethren joined him. They began to speak in their patois dialect as the foreigner with the long dreads used his hands to stress his point. They seemed to be in a heated debate and the extras seemed to make Smoke nervous.

"Cuz, fuck these boys talm'bout?" he whispered as his hand inched forward with a forced smile on his face.

Junebug was more in tune with the malicious glare the other Jamaican fixated on them. Smoke glanced to him for guidance, but it was the dread with the multicolored dreads that spoke up.

"Ah Star we gon' do business or jah gon' stare at meh brethren like him crazy, hmm?" he stole their attention.

Junebug nodded at them before nodding to Smoke. The man tossed the duffle at the dread's feet, sending the tension up another degree. The offense shone brightly in the Jamaican's stare as his partner spoke rapidly in a harsh tone. The lead dread raised his palm to tame his lions before shouting, "Benjie!"

At his command, one of the shooters ran over and with one hand still aiming the baby choppa, he used the other to snatch the bag open. Stacks of big faces stared back at them. The shooter reached down and pulled one of the stacks out before tossing it to the dread with the multicolored dreads, who caught it with one hand. The man flipped through the bills until he was satisfied.

"Jah good, mon. De fat mon should inform us next time so dis discomfort don confuse tings," he spoke with a smile before turning and heading for the back of the truck. "Come!"

He summoned them to follow. Junebug and Smoke found him opening the back of the truck at the same time that his crime partner ran around and jumped in the driver's seat. From the opened hatch, they watched as he started the truck, pushed the lighter in, and pumped the brakes simultaneously. Junebug and Smoke's confused expressions were identical as a pressurized sound released and the floor of the Bronco popped open. Both men were mesmerized as the dreads lifted the floor to reveal a hidden compartment. He pulled out a similar duffle bag as theirs and set it on the ground. After nodding his consent, Smoke squatted and opened the bag to reveal ten compressed books of pure coca. Smoke smiled, but in vain. Confusion eased into his expression as the red dot centered itself in the middle of the dread's neck.

"What the——"

Btttttaw! A spray of buck shots interrupted the proclamation. *Bocka! Bocka! Bocka!*

Tu! Tu! Tu!

An orchestra of different guns lit up the night. The dread's body shook as he danced his last dance, and seeing the chunks of flesh being knocked from dude's body caused Junebug to vomit. He dove to the pavement and scurried underneath the truck, but the smoke was up.

"Jah wan death, huh? Huh, fun boi!" one of the Jamaicans shouted as the different sounds of gunfire intermingled in a deadly synchrony.

In the darkness, Sunjay smiled in bliss as long flames spat from the pipe like the fire kiss of a dragon. The street sweepa's recoil was so powerful that he jerked with each finger fuck. Beside him the gang gang stood with red or black bandannas covering the bottom halves of their faces as they showed no mercy. Blood splattered the side of his face as the man to his left took one to the dome. Sunjay's heart cracked as he witnessed one of his childhood friends crumble to the asphalt. *Damn, D-Dawg, I got ya kids, blood!* he thought as he cried internally. Out of his peripheral, he caught the shadow as it blurred past. *Fuck?* he thought as he recognized Messiah dive to his stomach. He watched his brother from another mother take aim at something that was out of sight. The move confused him. *Fuck brah got goin; on! These dread heads tryin' to make sho' none of us have an open casket, and this nigga shootin' at their feet?*

His thoughts couldn't have been further from the truth. Messiah began firing underneath the truck and the cries of agony that intertwined with the gunfire brought a smile to the crazed killa. Junebug attempted to crawl from underneath the truck, but as soon as his head appeared, the side of it burst into a spray of blood and gray matter. In the midst of the madness, another sound joined the deadly sound of the reapers singing. For a moment, that stick talk was eclipsed by the silence as the squad tried to place the growl that had joined the fray. Sunjay was first to recognize the danger.

"Watch out, nigga!" He reacted just in time to snatch Messiah up and out of the way before the Bronco turned him into a pancake.

In their thirst for blood, Sunjay and the gang hadn't noticed their adversary retreating and going for escape. The motor sounded like a lion's roar as the driver mashed the gas in reverse. Sunjay released his bro and didn't waste time getting to the business. He waited until the reckless driver sped by before running toward his target. Aiming, he began to squeeze. The windshield exploded, but the powerful pipe had too much power for the young killer. With each explosion, the steel jumped.

Scurrrr! The driver ducked down and simultaneously threw the gear into drive. He stomped down on the gas as he attempted to navigate without watching the road.

Poooofishh!

The truck swerved and slammed into the side of a storage unit. Without warning, Messiah flew past Sunjay and over to the driver's side, where the bloodied Rasta was attempting to escape from the hands of fate.

Bocka! Bocka! Bocka! Bocka!

Messiah's finger molested the trigger.

"You niggas hurry up. We got the work and the loot. We need to ghost this spot before we end up holdin' court in the streets!" Taco shouted.

Sunjay and Messiah shared a silent moment as their eyes met.

It ain't no turnin' back now that blood on ya hands, blood. Sunjay's thoughts spoke through his pupils.

I'm on my dick, fam. I need to make somethin' happen! Messiah's thoughts exuded from his.

Chapter 11

Next Day

Fifty bands and two books of raw! his mind kept repeating. Messiah laid flat on his back in the hotel room, staring at his cut of the lick they'd hit.

"Never mix your hustles, cat daddy, we're not drug dealers. We're playas that prosper by the fruits of what's between a hoe's legs!" He reflected on the jewels Maxwell had gifted him.

"Mane, fuck what brah talm'bout, this ain't the seventies. I'ma do it all for this bag," he whispered as he grabbed a handful of dead presidents and tossed them in the air. He stared up and watched each bill tumble and twist in their descent, and as they fell around him, he wondered if he'd somehow developed parasomnia. He feared sleep because every time he closed his eyes, all he saw were the faces of the dead and visions of himself drowning in blood. *Fuck sleep. I'll sleep after I run this check up!* His thoughts brought a smile to his face. He thought of every man or woman that had ever fucked over him and vowed to put his dick in their faces once he got off his knuckles. Messiah glanced at the burna lying beside him and knew he'd made a deal with the opposite side of God.

Btttting! Btttting!

The phone disturbed his thoughts. He allowed it to ring a few more times before snatching it out of its cradle.

"Yeah? Yeah?" he answered.

"I'm on my way, baby, give me 'bout twenty minutes." Liberty's words were hurried.

"Bitch, what's the point in callin' to let me know ya whereabouts if you ain't already where you need to be? Get here!" he demanded before placing the phone into its place. *Let's see where ya game takes you, playboy!* he thought before snatching two more handfuls of loose bills and once again making it rain down on himself.

***

The club vibrated with music and a lively energy as the clubgoers danced and had a good time.

"Awww shit, East Dallas up in this mu'fucka!" DJ BoBo fed the atmosphere.

Mu'fuckas went crazy as Mystical's "Man Right Chea" blasted from the speakers.

"The gritty grove up in dis biiiiatch! I see you, Big J, do ya thang, my mans!" The DJ shouted out a group of wild young cats who began twisting their fingers in their gang signs as a short, muscular man in a fire red Kani unit saluted the man that worked the turn tables.

"The man right chea, man right chea! What ya gon' do?" Mystical's hype ignited the crowd.

"I see the Gator boys puttin' on for the wicked west, sho'nuff, playas! I see you, Black Rat!" DJ BoBo poured gas on the already lit fuse. He began to blend Lil Kim's hit into the mix and the women joined the fray.

"Beta, Gangsta Boo, I see you niggas ova there puttin' on for the KROOKED! Shout out to the nutty noff!" The DJ showed love before Eight Ball and MJG's "Showin' Love" turnt up the beat.

"Hoes in the club showin' love / shakin' that ass..."

"Heyyyy, bitch, that's my jam!" Cola, Dream's bestie, shouted as she threw her hands in the air and snapped her fingers to the beat.

Sunjay sat back in his seat, a Chicago Bulls snapback resting so low on his head so that one couldn't see his eyes. A thick, golden pitbull's head pendant complemented the thick herringbone necklace that glimmered under the dancing lights of the club as he sipped straight from the bottle of Moet and enjoyed the sight of his team turning up.

"Y'all mu'fuckas rep that shit. I see you lil niggas ova there in the VIP! Sunjay, Murda, Trap Boy Freddy - one time for the stiff cliff!"

The acknowledgement set flame to the scene. Murda popped a bottle and laughed as champagne sprayed the two women standing closest to him. Sunjay could feel the envious stares of the street, but his cockiness was what blindfolded him to the fact that even the most savage niggas out of the slums could become prey.

As they put on, no one noticed how one of the niggas in their clique positioned himself to face specific people. Inside his necklace was a small cam called "a bird's eye view". It was a gadget the Bureau of Investigations used for their informants on the streets. The small camera caught it all.

Someone tossed a pile of loose bills into the air. Sunjay nodded his head to the beat as he glanced up at the fluttering bills. The camera snapped away. Dream sat beside her man, dancing in her seat while taking sips from her glass.

"South Oak Cliff!" Murda shouted over the crowd. Their entourage became rowdy.

"That's my hood!" they shouted in union.

Sunjay cracked a crooked grin as he tilted the bottle to his lips. His eyes were closed as he savored the taste of the bitter drink. When he opened them, his vision captured heaven in the form of a 5'7" goddess. Her skin was so dark it shone under the glow of the club's lights. It wasn't the predatory glare she was giving him that spoke to his dick, but more the private message her body was sending him as she danced and rubbed her hands over her most intimate portions. The dance floor was filled, but in that moment, the world ceased to exist as their eyes fucked each other.

Sunjay's eyes took a brief intermission as he glanced to see if Dream was on to him. She was tipsy and paying him no mind as she and Cola high-fived. Her preoccupancy allowed him to recapture heaven. When their eyes met, Chocolate gave him a seductive grin before ending her seduction and strutting away from the dance floor. He watched her head toward the public restrooms, her ass cheeks seeming to jiggle without much effort. She paused and glanced back at him from over her shoulder before disappearing around the corner.

Sunjay waited a few seconds before leaning over to reveal his intentions to Murda. His boy laughed and dapped him up. He'd spied the energy between bro and the chocolate seductress. Sunjay slid from the booth before kissing Dream on the cheek and slipping into the crowd.

As he slid through the sea of people, his mental should have been filled with erratic thoughts, but his gut castrated the moment. *Somethin' ain't right!* he thought before pausing and instinctively reaching for the fo'-five on his waist. He allowed his eyes to sweep his circumference. Couples danced around him. Some were so into the spirit of the moment that it looked as if they were fucking on the dance floor. *I'm trippin', mane, that drank fooly!* Sunjay's mental silenced his paranoia. He made his way to the restroom, but couldn't shake the feeling of being watched. He paused once more to give the crowd another glance before pursuing the heaven he prayed would rain down so powerfully onto him that he'd testify to a God he'd never believed in.

As soon as he entered the restroom, he was greeted by "Hit dice!" Someone shouted as the cubes landed on the number of the gods. "Seven till eleven, I'm gettin' to that bag!" a light-skinned, freckle-faced cat exclaimed before snatchin' his bread off the ground.

Sunjay nodded at him and dapped the few hustlas he knew from around the city.

The heaven he was pursuing was standing by one of the open stalls, rolling her eyes as a stocky cat shot his shot.

"I'm sayin', lil mama, I'm tryin' to change ya life and you actin' like a nigga ain't out here runnin' this check up," he capped as he flashed a bankroll at her.

Shawty crossed her arms over her ample breasts and twisted her lips in that *I'm tired of hearin' that line* way. Her eyes found Sunjay and ate him up. His nugget rings and earrings glistened under the dim lights. The red Guess pants and white and red Guess shirt complemented his dark skin. The lady ran her tongue over her top lip and stepped into the stall. Playboy that had tried his hand had watched the display with hate in his heart.

"Well, fuck you too, bitch, you ain't *that* fine anyway!" he spat with emphasis on the proclamation.

The room exploded in laughter as Sunjay joined her in the stall. He paid dude no mind as he closed the door in his face with a slam. He and the goddess faced off with anticipation feeding their energy.

"What's ya name, lil baby?" he asked as his eyes fell in love with her sex appeal. The tight leather mini rode high up her thighs and the skintight, black half-shirt she wore looked as if her nipples swelled any more, they'd burst through the material. Her thick thighs glistened and as his vision fell to the knee high boots, one word drifted through the alleyways of his mind: *freak!*

"Does it matter? Names only steal the fun from the mystery, so why not just allow pussy and dick to say the things our lips shouldn't? I mean…" She paused while stepping over to him.

Queen pushed him against the door and slipped her hand down his pants. As she played with his nuts, she bit her bottom lip.

"Wasn't that yo' bitch you was all hugged up wit' in the VIP?" She smiled wickedly as she felt his dick throbbing in her hand.

As she seduced him, Sunjay noticed two things: one, the silence was thick whereas just moments ago, there was a whole dice game in progress. Secondly... *This hoe tryin' to dominate the kid!* he thought as he turned the tides in his favor.

Unexpectedly, Sunjay reached out and snatched her by her long braids. "Come here, bitch!" he growled as he yanked her head back.

"Auuuh!" A soft cry of surprise escaped her lips as he began to suck her neck.

Queens's hands had their own navigational system as she hurriedly undid his pants. As Sunjay yanked her skirt up around her waist, their energy created a tornado of mixed emotions within their disregard for the envious.

"That nigga Sunjay be wildin', fam!" Freckle-faced exclaimed as the sounds of rough sex serenaded the room.

"Fuck Sunjay, I got somethin' for his cappin' ass," the stocky cat spat his venom before pushing past the onlookers and out the door.

"'Sup wit' Brock?" one of the dice shootas asked with an expression of disgust for the homie's statement.

Freckle-faced shrugged while counting his earnings. "Sucka shit ain't eva deserved a nigga's attentions, my dude," he responded.

"Yeah, do that shit, boy, you…you…ohhh!"

The passionate cries of the goddess caused all that heard them to feel some type of way.

Freckle-faced shook the dice. "Money on the wood makes the gamblin' good!"

***

The knock was soft against the door as Messiah glanced around to ensure he'd stashed his treasure and everything was acceptable for the vision of a bitch he aspired to seduce. Content, he opened the door and backed away just in case there was a surprise on the other side.

Liberty stood wrapped within a trench coat that she'd had tailored to fit like a dress. It stopped mid-thigh, but the sash that held it closed hung low at the ends. Her wet and wavy hair was pulled back into a bun so tight that her already chinky eyes seemed half-mast. Two chopsticks were stabbed into an X inside the bun and as she stepped passed the point of no return, Messiah mentally saluted the hoe for the effort.

God may have created bad bitches, but the devil the one that knows how to use 'em! he thought as she closed the door behind her.

"Lock it!" He smiled with the demand.

"What, you think I'm gonna set you up or summin'?" she asked with a mutual grin.

Messiah's eyes fell to the white peep toes that allowed an observer's view of her pedicured feet. She'd applied some sort of glitter to them and as his vision found hers, he tossed the banga on the bed.

"If you would've, you would've been the first one to realize the stupidity of it," he spoke matter-of-factly.

He watched her observe her surroundings. She walked over and ran a hand over the corner of the bed before glancing back at him. "May I?"

Messiah made his way over to the chair beside the bed and took a seat. He crossed his leg at the ankle and gazed up at her. "Your choice."

She took a seat and crossed one leg over the other before her eyes left him and fell to the carpet as if she'd lost her nerve. Messiah allowed her to feel the pressure of his gaze before bossing up.

"Look, bitch, surely you ain't went through all the trouble of cleanin' that pussy and fixin' ya hair just to find ya'self in my presence and stare at the carpet?"

"I…I just wanted to apologize for…for…" She tried to rationalize the irrational, but her words were lost somewhere between a lie and the truth.

"For what, hoe? For fuckin' ova me? For allowin' anotha nigga to run dick in you when you vowed to keep ya funky pussy hole exclusively for me? What you apologizin' for, bitch?"

His words burned her and caused her eyes to become baptized with tears.

"I neva meant to hurt you. Baby, I fucked up and I know I hurt you, but damn, Messiah, you ain't perfect!"

His eyes found her with a peculiar gaze before he burst into deep laughter. He laughed so hard that his stomach hurt. Liberty's confusion was written all over her face, but his laughter melted it into a boiling anger.

"What the fuck is so funny!" she demanded with a bounce of her foot.

Messiah rose from his seat while attempting to compose himself. *Bitches always on some victim shit!* His thoughts were official.

"You gotta get up outta here, Ms. Lady, before I do somethin' I'll regret," he spoke between chuckles. He walked to the door and unlocked it before throwing it open. The silence caused him to glance back. *This hoe thinks it's a game.*

Liberty's eyes were wet as she stared at him. Within his play for the door, she'd done exactly what he'd expected her to do. She'd snatched up the pistol he'd earlier discarded. *"It's never the sculpture that should be praised, baby, because without the sculptor, what would it be other than a useless piece of clay? You must remold every woman you allow into your orbit. Her mind is your putty. Create what you choose!"* He thought of the boss game his mother had blessed him with. He'd known how Liberty would react to his heartache. He'd learned early on in his life that a woman's emotions were a true playa's navigational system. As he stood there, face to face with the woman that yearned more than anything for him to forgive her, Messiah dug deep down within the waters of his internal chaos and found the thoughts of his slain father drowning in his own blood. He thought of how his Queen had fallen from glory and landed on planet rock. He called on his pain and within that hurricane of pain, rain fell from his eyes while Liberty cried for a chance at redemption. He slowly made his way back to the chair

"Why you do a nigga like that, ma? You was my heart! Was a moment of dick worth the sacrifice of my heart? My love? You're a thief, ma. You stole a nigga's heart only to run off wit' it, set it down on the ground to collect dust, and it was all in the name of satisfyin' the cry of ya pussy! What kinda robber are you to steal what's mine before bringin' it back to me as if I'm the type of nigga that'll accept damaged goods!" he cried without breaking the stare.

His pain crushed her and in that moment, Messiah realized that betrayal wasn't always intentional. For a mu'fucka that lacks self-control, pussy and dick outweigh what should never be tainted. He watched the empty gun fall from her hand as she made her way to him, and though his tears were merely manufactured, hers were born from something primal and real.

"I'm so sorry, Messiah, I didn't mean to do that shit! I was stupid, baby, so, so stupid for crossin' you. I need you, boo!" she submitted before leaning down and hugging him as tight as she could.

Messiah laughed internally, but allowed his body to tremble with his artificial tears.

138

"Don't cry, pa, I got you. Let me make it up to you...please?" Liberty's plea was his cue.

"Naw, hell naw, you're just tryin' to play me again. You love that nigga!" His Dr. Jekyll and Mr. Hyde theatrics kicked in as he pushed her away.

"What! No! I don't love anyone but you, Messiah, I promise!"

"Bitch, you're a serpent, and I fear anything that slithers. You might got the nigga outside, waitin' to come stick me for my chips!" he declared.

She was caught off guard by his sudden emotional change. She watched as he snatched up the tool and stormed to the window. Messiah stared out of it suspiciously as if he was expecting an ambush at any second. "Hoe, you tryin' to set me up? Huh!" he roared before spinning to face her. In three long strides, he was in front of her with a feral look in his eyes. "Huh, bitch, you think I'm stupid or somethin'?"

"No!" she shouted in fear. "I'd never do you like that, baby, you gotta believe me!"

"You know what?" He paused and tossed the pistol back on the bed. Messiah aggressively snatched her by the arm and pulled her toward the door. Liberty tried to dig her heels into the carpet to counter his intent, but he was relentless.

"What? Wait! Just give me a chance!" She stumbled over her words. "I'll do *anything*, Messiah!"

She dangled the temptation before him. Messiah stopped abruptly before releasing her from his grip.

"Auuuh!" Liberty cried as she fell to the floor.

Messiah stood staring down at her through hazy vision. Her proclamation had snatched him from the present and down into the treasure chest of his past.

"This a jewel you'll be able to cash in on for the rest of ya life, playboy," Pimpin Maxwell spoke over a lungful of cigar smoke.

It was a sunny Sunday evening and they reclined in the confines of the older man's new Aston Martin. They were valeted on the hoe stroll, observing whorism as it's finest.

"Always study yo' bitch, baby boy. She's the closest thing to a nigga outside of his mama and big mama. These clowns out her today only see the ass and titties of the hoe, but neglect the vitality of her mind. See, when the hoe is happy and respects ya game, she'll never defect on you because she becomes possessive of the feelings you give her and don't want the next bitch to share that same feeling. Yet, when you begin to rob the hoe of who and what she is naturally, when you become so lost within your feelings that you trick ya'self into believing that you can sexually domesticate that wild pussy, and most importantly, when you force the hoe to lie to you because she fears the reactions of her being solid with you, she'll become the most dangerous thing known to playaism. If you're a jealous, insecure-ass nigga, yo' gal will be a jealous, insecure bitch, and there's no way you'll be able to build a solid stable with that kinda energy. Never allow ya emotions to transcend ya game, playboy."

"Anything, papi," Liberty tempted him. She'd noticed the faraway look in his eye and mistaken his reflections for him considering her offer.

Anything? Her words snatched him back to the present. He added a fallacious uncertainty to his glare. *It's either now or never!* he thought as he studied her. After a brief pause, he extended his hand to her and Liberty accepted the gesture with apprehension. Once to her feet, Messiah led the lady to the edge of the bed and nodded for her to have a seat before he followed suit, cutting his eyes at her.

"You gotta make this right, ma. We'll always be crooked if you don't take the first step in straightenin' the path that you changed the direction of," he whispered as he massaged her hand.

"But what you want me to do, Messiah? Just keep it real, pa!" she sniveled, defeated.

Messiah released her hand and reached behind them, and when he turned back to her, he had the phone in his hand. His eyes searched hers in a moment of contemplation. He could see the confusion mastering her mental as she glanced down at the receiver he held out to her. "What, you want me to call someone or somethin'?" she asked.

"I'm sure you ain't forgot cat daddy's math, so add 'em up. I want you to get a cool grand out his parts, hoe," he offered the bait.

Liberty lived within a moment of perplexion as her eyes found his. "How the fuck will I do that?" she asked, astonished. "I mean, we cool, but we——"

"Dig this," Messiah silenced her. "Look, you can either place a three course meal of deception, fuckery, and an cold slab of lie pie before me and rely on your expectations of me getting full off it, or…" He paused and took her hand in his before placing the phone in it. The young playa fixed her with a curious expression as he rose and headed for the door. "Or you can cater to the broken portions of my heart that you victimized during the moments of my irrational love for you. That nigga will pay you whatever you demand if you suck, fuck, and freak his mind, body, and spirit into submission. Manipulate each one of those portions of that sucker before you kiss him to sleep and the john will pay you for the shit you woulda done for free!" he spoke over his shoulder.

"But we ain't like that! We're cool, but baby, he——"

"Bitch, I ain't concerned with yo' domesticated relations wit' cat daddy!" he spat while flinging the door open. "You gon' either get it right or get out my sight. Either direction you choose, you'll have to pay yo' dues," he jazzed before turning to face her. Though his face was as void of expression as a poem with no substance, he smiled internally as his eyes captured Liberty's shaking fingers dancing over the buttons on the phone. After a brief moment…

"Baby!" she cooed into the receiver, but looked to Messiah for acceptance. He nodded his encouragement while thinking, *A bitch with no morals is a true playa's paradise. As long as the hoe lacks principium, a boss like myself can extort that quality!*

"Bae, you know I been missin' you, I just been dealin' wit' a lot. My granny sick and they askin' for all this money to get her some kind of procedure done. I'm so through——"

Her words caused him to smile as she paused and crossed her legs with a false dignity. Messiah was mesmerized by the sight of converted emotions. It was his first time seeing a hoe be a hoe in raw display.

"I'm at the La Quinta Inn and I'm naked, playin' wit' this pussy. I'm as wet as a lake, daddy, what you gon' do?"

Her sexual prelude caused Messiah to shake his head. *Hoes!*

***

"Hit dice!" were the first words that greeted him when he entered the restroom, but it was the cries of passion emitting from the shaking stall that caused him to frown in confusion. The sound of the door closing alerted the crowd of hustlas of company.

"Oh, shit!" Freckle-faced hissed.

All eyes shot to the newcomer and in that moment, chaos was born. Hustlas stumbled over each other as they snatched burnas off the floor along with the bread they'd placed on the gamble. In seconds, the room was empty, save for one unlucky straggler.

"Damn!" he spat.

"Ole Lil Walter, when you touch down, baby?" Detective Spinx chuckled. He knew exactly when the young gangsta had been released from TYC. He'd been the one to send him there. "I see ain't much done changed, baby." He smiled as both their eyes fell to the burna that was stuffed down the front of the young'n's pants.

"Mannn, Spinx, stall me out, brah, I ain't doin——"

"Ohhh shittt!" Chocolate's cries of euphoria inturrupted his plea.

Both men's eyes shot to the stall, in the thralls of ecstasy, Sunjay was as clueless as ever to the threat, but his naïveté was Lil Walter's salvation. Spinx nodded for him to ghost the spot. Surprise splashed across his face for merely a second before the young'n remembered that blessings were rare for niggas from the ghetto. He ran for the exit, but Spinx caught him by the back of his shirt.

I knew this shit was too good to be true! he thought as the detective reached around and relieved him of the .357 he had on his waist.

"I'm still the law 'round this mu'fucka. Let me get this off ya, lil daddy." He laughed before slapping Lil Walter in the back of the head.

Young'n knew the reprieve was better than a cold jail cell and with that acceptance, he made his escape.

Back in the stall, Sunjay gave one last stroke before pulling out and shooting his spirit onto the seductress's ass cheeks.

"Damn, bitch!" he growled while jacking himself empty. *Fuck is it so quiet around this bitch?* His instincts were primal.

He didn't have to wait for an answer as the door crashed in. With his dick still hanging free, Sunjay went for the tool he'd rested by the toilet, but it was a frivolous quest.

"Do it, nigga, I'm burnin' to leave yo' lil ass leakin' in this bitch!" Spinx spat as he aimed the .357 at him.

"Oh my God, I have nothin' to do wit' this nigga, please don't kill me, I'll do *anything*!" Chocolate cried with a fearful but suggestive expression on her face.

"Shut up, bitch, and get yo' nothin' ass up outta here!" Sunjay growled.

Chocolate's confused vision found Spinx and to her relief, he nodded his consent.

"Maybe anotha time, lil lady. Right now me and ya boy got some bidness to tend to. Ain't that right, Sunny boy?" His words were mocking as his eyes locked into the young killa's.

Chocolate wasted no time taking her leave. She was so in a rush to be gone that she forgot that her dress was pulled up over her ass cheeks.

Spinx laughed as the door clicked shut. "'Sup, lil daddy?"

"What, you here to take me down or what?" Sunjay gritted while extending his arms, crossing his wrists one on top of the other.

Spinx tucked the pistol and stepped into the stall. He leaned against the broken door and crossed his arms over his chest. *Lil nigga a gangsta, but he ain't stupid enough to kill an officer of the law!* he thought as he watched Sunjay lean down and recover his banga.

"What you gon' do wit' that, knuckle head, huh? You gonna kill a Dallas detective in a club full of cameras and people?" He smirked with the question. Sunjay reflected the smile, but maintained his fifth amendment. "Oh, you wanna be a gangsta, huh? Huh?" he spat in mid-stride. He'd lost his control and before he could tame his crooked intentions, he snatched Sunjay up by the collar and slammed his back against the wall.

The young wolf's eyes became slits that reflected a murder scene, but it was more of the kiss of the cold steel under his chin that warned Spinx of the possibilities. Yet he pressed on.

"Pull the trigga, punk! Do it!" he spat. "That's what I thought. You ain't no gangsta." He chuckled menacingly, yet he released Sunjay with a shove.

The young goon watched as the detective dug into the inside of his suit coat and came out with a manila envelope. "My number is in here along wit' a lil surprise from me and a few of my associates. It's in you and ya boy Messiah's best interest to get at me, better sooner than later, playboy," he concluded before turning and making his exit.

***

"Saaayy, ain't yo' name Dream?" Brock asked with a disarming smile.

Dream and Cola were on the dance floor putting on a show that had spectators anticipating them going over the edge with their freakiness, but they left a lot to the imagination as they continued to grind against one another.

Dream jumped in surprise. "Nigga, you betta ease up before my nigga see you being disrespectful!" She snaked her neck. "How you know my name?" Her eyes searched the crowd for Sunjay, but he was nowhere to be found.

Brock gave her a surrendering smile as he tossed his hands in the air. "Whoa, lil mama, I ain't lookin' for no smoke. I just came ova here to let you know that yo' dawg-ass nigga in the bathroom gettin' his dick sucked by some thick, sexy-ass bitch! I know you a good girl to that nigga. That's why it fucks wit' me to see how he out here fuckin ova you. I'd neva——"

Dream stormed passed him in hot pursuit of Sunjay's dawg ass.

Brock laughed at his own fag-ass actions. "That's what the hoe-ass nigga gets for thinkin' he the shit," he whispered to himself before stepping behind a yellow bone sista that danced alone.

Renta

Chapter 12

Liberty woke to the light snores of Messiah as he slept in the chair beside the bed.

He used me! Now he sees me as a hoe. Nigga don't even wanna get in the bed with me now, she thought as her eyes watered. She felt like a slut, and as she threw the cover off her naked body, all she could think of was how she'd fucked, sucked, and fucked some more the night before. She'd allowed Lil Woo to do things that were beyond taboo, but just as Messiah had predicted, the man had coughed over a cool thousand without much of a protest. It amazed her because she'd been giving him the pussy for months and outside of the few hundred he'd blessed her with on occasion, most times she was left with nothing but a wet pussy. Messiah had opened her eyes to the value of what lay between her legs and would soon introduce her to the woman inside her that she feared accepting due to the tainted judgements of others.

Feeling himself being watched, Messiah's eyes popped open alertly. He allowed his vision to adjust to the sun slipping through the thin curtains before turning his eyes to her.

"What's the bidness, ma, where you goin'?" he asked as he watched Liberty rush into her trench coat.

She tied the sash before looking at him, searching his eyes for the disgust she knew he now harbored for her. "Why, Messiah, why'd you have me do that shit, huh? Now you hate me and think I'm a hoe." She rolled her eyes as she went for her purse.

Messiah stood and made his way to her. Taking her hand into his, he began to kiss each fingertip while gazing into her eyes.

"Can I ask you a solid question that deserves a solid answer?"

Though she was confused, ashamed, and skeptical, Liberty nodded her consent.

"I don't know sign language, Queen. A woman knows how to verbalize her truths because she understands that being indirect leaves too much room for being misunderstood. So, what's up? You gonna keep it G wit' me or not?" he reiterated while pulling the sash loose on the coat.

"Yeah, bae, I just don't want you to hate me for what I did."

"Fuck all that. Look, did you enjoy yourself?" he asked.

Liberty's face balled up in confusion until his clarification transformed into an expression of surprise.

"Getting fucked. Sex. Do you enjoy it?" The look he gave her warned of the consequences of deceit.

"Huh? I mean, yes, I like sex, but——"

Messiah silenced her by placing two fingers against her lips.

"Chill. I don't judge you for who you are, Ms. Lady, but it's a sin to proclaim to be the breed of bitch you not. Don't ever be ashamed of what you do wit' your pussy, mama, as long as you're getting more than merely a nut for it," he gave it to her before pushing the trench down and off her shoulders, It fell into a pool at their feet.

Messiah took her hand and led her toward the bathroom. She wanted to protest, but curiosity was an addictor of persons and when Messiah was added to the equation, Liberty was an addict to that addiction. He pulled her into the small bathroom and released her before turning the shower on, and only when it was at the perfect temperature did he turn to face her. Without breaking eye contact, the young playa undressed slowly. Naked as Adam was in the Garden of Eden, Messiah extended his hand to her.

"Most bitches attempt to hide the hoe in them because they fear being rejected. They've been taught that if they are anything less than who society wants you to be, then you're unworthy of love, but that's because you're tryin' to be loved by the kinda people that can't appreciated you as a woman first, a Queen in title, and a bonafide hoe in nature," he jeweled as she took his hand. He admired her for only a brief moment before pulling her into the hot shower with him.

"Messiah, don't play with me. *Please* don't. I know you think I'm a hoe and don't want me, and that's——"

"Shhh!" He placed a finger to her lips, cutting her short. Messiah took a towel and bar of soap off the rack and began to create a lather. He propped Liberty's foot on the edge of the tub as he allowed his eyes to molest her stature. He placed the soapy material between her legs. "Ma, the type of nigga I've become has opened my eyes to what true love is. Love is accepting the truest nature of a person. See…"

He paused while massaging her essence with the towel. He cleaned from her clit to just before her asshole.

"Most mu'fuckas would see a flaw in what you did because they don't love *you*. They love their *perspective* of who they think you should be. I won't lie to you, ma, and tell you that I can love you as my gal or wife because every bitch wasn't created for that title, but I do vow to give a fuck 'bout you and reserve a portion of my heart solely for you."

His game was the gospel. Liberty moaned in ecstasy as he took a stroll through her mental.

"Liberty, you just made a band for somethin' you woulda done for free! You wanna know why the act of you givin' this pussy to anotha nigga touches my heart? Huh?" He worked the towel over her clit with pressure. Messiah sucked her neck. "Hmm?" he growled while slipping a finger inside her garden.

"Tell me! Damn, I missed yooouu!" she moaned.

"It's because in the act of you doin' it, you didn't lie, cheat, or keep it secret. It's because in doin' what you already enjoy, you sacrificed self for what *I* needed. Only a boss bitch can fully submit and help her nigga get it out the dirt!" he spoke in the crook of her neck.

Liberty's leg shook as she wrapped her arms around his neck and grinded against his plunging finger.

"Only in becomin' a real nigga am I able to truly appreciate the type of bitch you are, ma, and I need you as my bottom in order for me to get us to the top, but the only way for me to love you in any fashion is by you provin' that you'll protect my heart with all of yours." He nibbled her neck as his dick saluted her.

"I will! How? What I gotta do?" she cried as her body called for him to enter it as deeply as he could journey.

Messiah reached behind her with the soap and towel and began to clean between her cheeks.

"Tell me, shawty, will you sacrifice self for the success of what you can envision us becomin'?" he wanted to know.

Liberty was lost within him as she nodded her head yes. "I'll do any—— Ohhh!" She lost her train of thought as Messiah slipped that dick inside her with a curving deep stroke. She bit his neck, but just when her lower lips squeezed him...

"What's wrong!" she cried in surprised confusion.

Messiah slipped from within her waters and turned his back to her. He handed her the towel while reflecting on a rare gem Black had blessed him with. *"Listen, baby, a bitch won't respect you if you keep ya dick in her all day. Feeding the freak in her will only give her an addiction that will eventually lead her to cross you for whoever else that can best satisfy what you created in her. That's why so many men and women cheat or get crossed. It's because their other half placed so much into the freak in them that the call of pussy and dick becomes stronger than their pledge of love and loyalty. Tame ya dick, Messiah. You let a hoe be a hoe without yo' dick and she'll respect the boss in you versus the trick in the next man. It should be a privilege to fuck you, baby! You'll meet thousands of women, son, and no matter how much more beautiful some are than others, pussy is pussy no matter which bitch it's attached to!"*

The touch of the towel against his back brought him back from the words his mother had buried into his memory. Liberty's legs shook from craving him, but she was too confused to ask why he'd deprived not only her, but also himself.

"When you get this dick again, you're gonna appreciate it like a boss bitch should, but until then..." He paused and turned to face her. Messiah took the towel out her hands and began to wash his ass. "Go count my trap and make sho' the number right before properly choosin' up, hoe." He nodded toward the room.

Liberty was taken fast, but as the past fourteen hours replayed in her mind, she laughed and stepped out of the shower.

Messiah slapped her on the ass with only one thought on his mind. *What they gonna do wit' me now?*

***

The day was sunny as Black and Creamy stood between two semi-trucks at the truck stop.

"I'm through with the life, Creamy. I made a promise to my son that I'd never step foot on another stroll again, and that's a promise I'm gonna keep."

Black's words were tainted as she held the crack smoke down. She exhaled and passed the stem to the white woman that had stolen her dignity with the introduction to an escape that she'd never be able to escape. Creamy used a pusher to clean out the residue in the burnt glass pipe before placing it to her lips, and just as she lit its tip, a car pulled into the truck stop.

A tall, thick Queen slid out the passenger's side and began fixing her clothes. She caught their eye and waved before heading to find her next trick. Tutts was a bad bitch and was rumored to have been the hardest hustling bitch on the stroll. Her techniques in sexual taboos were top notch and the bankroll she handed over to Sweet Eddie, her pimp, were as fresh as new money coming straight out of that U.S. Treasury.

"You remember when we were that young and tight? Girl, you couldn't tell us shit!" Black exclaimed with an insecure glance down at herself. The dope man had stolen more than merely her self-worth with his blessings and those same blessings had become her sadistic savior.

Creamy's bug-eyed expression was alert. She felt no insecurity. Her consistent high fed her self-inflicted delusion of beauty.

"Girl, I don't know what you talkin' 'bout. A motherfucker will *still* pay his rent money for this hot twat!" she exclaimed as she pointed down at her essence.

Black laughed, but her mind had just given birth to a new idea. *That hoe Tutts will be a nice trophy for my baby's stable.*

***

"I'm tellin' you, Gator, I'll find the sons a bitches that did this shit and make sure the bidness is tended to!" Blow vowed as he reclined in the leather office chair behind his desk. He held the phone away from his ear as the old man raged his frustrations.

Sunjay sat on the other side of the mahogany furniture, taking deep pulls from a blunt of heat as he listened. *This nigga a snake that needs his head cut off!* he was thinking when Blow ended the call and glared at him.

"What I tell you 'bout smokin' that shit in my office, lil nigga?"

Sunjay merely reached down, picked up the duffle bag off the floor and sat it on the desk. "It's all there, my G." He ignored the question and got straight to the business.

Blow's eyes fell to the bag as if it was a virus. "Get that shit off my desk, Sunjay. You're gettin more disrespectful wit' age!" he spat before swatting the heavy bag off his place of business. "Thought I told you not to kill nobody, Sunjay. Now we got these dread head mu'fuckas on the rampage. Damn, mane, you *always* fuckin' shit up. Maybe I shoulda gave Messiah the job."

Blow's words were the words that fed Sun's demons. He shot to his feet with it on his mind. He hated the comparison.

"Naw, *maybe* yo' snake ass needs to stop bitin' the hands that's feedin' you, fuck boy! Fuck you talm'bout? I don't believe in takin' a nigga down without whackin' somethin'. I don't believe in the witness pandemic!" he spat with his hand down by the butt of his banga.

"What it is, fam? Hope you boys——" Messiah's words trailed off when he witnessed the battle of prides. He hurriedly closed and locked the door before rushing over to defuse the bomb that had potential to take down half the ghetto.

"Whoa! Say, fuck you boys got goin' on, fam?" He pushed his way between the two men.

Sunjay took a drag from the exotic before leaning down and using Blow's desk as an astray. He snubbed the blunt and turned to leave, but had one more thought for the older gangsta. Turning to the man, Sunjay exhaled the cloud of smoke from his lungs. "Nigga, after this shit we got poppin', I ain't fuckin' wit' ya no mo'. It's somethin' 'bout you that ain't right, and before I have to lay you down, I'ma slide back."

He severed ties that should have been bound by the links of loyalty, respect, and realism, but within the life of a crook, one second of a misunderstanding could be the crack that lets the devil in. Sunjay's eyes went to Messiah. The confusion in brah-brah's face told him he had some explaining to do, yet, in spite of his secrets, Sunjay knew that Messiah was riding with him till the axle broke. "Let's mash out, dawg." He cast the choice into the atmosphere before turning and making his exit.

Messiah's confused expression diverted to Blow, the old man had evil playing within his pupils and that spoke to the young'n's spirit. For some reason, Messiah had always had a strange suspicion of Blow, but he was their ticket out of the hood, so bro quieted his gut and got to the bag with dude.

"You niggas can't just walk away. I made you lil niggas and before I see y'all workin' or gettin' money wit' the op, I'll put that work in myself!" Blow spoke without making eye contact.

"Made us?" The words slipped from Messiah's lips in a river of disbelief. "Bro, you ain't did shit for me and bro but put a pack in our hands! You ain't out in these trenches wit' us while we gettin' to it, and you may wanna tame that gangsta shit you spittin' before you invite the boogeyman to ya front door, OG, blood on that," Messiah seethed as he backed out the door.

The last thing he heard before his exit was Blow's vow of bloodshed.

***

"'Sup, lil mama? I know yo' nigga ain't let yo' lil sexy ass out the house by yourself. He either a lame or too confident for his own good." A tall light-skinned cat with long braids shot his shot.

Liberty kept it pushing as she strolled through the Parks Mall. Messiah had given her five bands to get work clothes and a few items for him, but as she swayed her hips in seduction, the only thing on her mind was how she could make a play for her admirer's bankroll. She glanced over her shoulder to ensure he was watching as she gave him a prelude to a sexual intermission.

"Bro, she out ya league. Look at that bitch. She Mona Lisa bad!" one of the dudes with playboy chided him.

"Mona Lisa was a painting, fool!"

"Yeah, but she was still a bad bitch, brah. Fuck you think all them white folk fuckin' off all that cake on just a picture of that hoe?" they argued.

"Bet I get shawty!" Light Skin challenged as they followed Liberty.

She'd noticed all the shine the three cats flaunted and had spotted the Benz they'd showed up in. Since the light-skinned brotha was the driver, she set her sights on him.

"Damn, ma, you got a nigga followin' you through this bitch like you a human navigational system or somethin'. All I'm askin' for is five minutes of your time," he called to her.

Liberty cut her chinky eyes at him and blessed him with a suggestive smile, but kept it moving. *Just around the corner, keep followin' me, lil daddy,* she encouraged him in her mind. To her delight, he did! All the way to the ladies' room. Liberty stepped in and waited, a black widow awaiting her prey, and just as she'd anticipated, the man's audacity overrode his mannerisms.

"Damn, a nigga gotta come in here and kiss yo' ass just for a minute of ya time?" His sarcasm was complemented with an innocent smile.

"That's cute, but before you can get to the ass, you gotta pay for my time, lil daddy," she proposed.

The look of shock on dude's face was priceless and fed Liberty's promiscuity. She dropped her bags on the floor before turning to face the restroom's mirror. The slut in her stared back at her as she gripped the edge of the porcelain sink. Playboy's nature surged in his pants as he watched her pull her dress up over her naked ass cheeks and look back at it, Liberty began to make her ass clap. "But talkin' is boring, boo, when a punk few hundred can get you up in this wet pussy." She raised up on her tip toes and ran a hand down her ass crack.

"Few hunnid?" Light Skin smiled, his weakness for a bad bitch evident. He pulled out a knot of money and held it up. "Baby, I can change ya life!" he exclaimed as Liberty righted herself and stalked over to him - dress still up over her ass and waxed kitten on display.

She reached up and relieved him of the knot before pulling him into one of the stalls. A nigga with an untamed ego would always fall victim to a pretty face and some good pussy.

***

"What? Why the fuck you didn't tell me that shit *before* we put the work in, Sunjay!" Messiah spat as he slammed a fist into the dashboard of Sunjay's Fleetwood. Sunjay had just opened his eyes to the treachery of Blow's greed.

Sunjay gripped the grain as he coasted down Poke Street., he understood his potna's frustrations, but wasn't feeling the abuse of his new whip.

"Say, blood, hold that down. I know you heated, but watch how you handle my shit, fam," he shot with a quick glance at his bro. "I didn't tell you 'cause the nigga Blow was on some sneaky shit. The boy feel like Gator chumpin' him so he wanted me to hit one of his plays. He wasn't expecting me to lay them boys down. I was gonna tell you, but shit been crazy for both of us." Sunjay pulled the Lac up to the side of the spot he and Dream had copped in Woodtown and killed the ignition.

Messiah glanced around before his eyes found his day one. Sunjay busted down a Swisher and seemed to have a lot on his mind. As Messiah watched him twist the blunt, he noticed the long scratch running down the side of his face. *The nigga always into some shit!* He shook his head in amusement.

"You know them dread heads gonna want some smoke ova this shit, brah, and——"

"Nigga, I don't give a fuck 'bout no smoke! I'ma——"

"See! That's what the fuck I'm talm'bout!" Messiah lost his composure so quickly that his words began to run together. "My nigga, just 'cause you're a killa don't mean you quit givin' a damn 'bout the mu'fuckas that love you! These people will whack our folks for our sins. Don't you get it, my dude?"

Sunjay lit the stick and sucked the soul out of it before allowing Messiah to see the shit within his eyes that he wished he didn't have to reveal. Their eyes danced and that's when it all made sense to the man child in the passenger's seat. *My nigga soul gone!* His mental was troubled waters. Sunjay dropped his head as he exhaled the spirit of smoke.

"Look, Sunjay, you're my day one nigga and I'll neva turn sour on you, but you can't fault the world for the decisions of every mu'fucka that fucked ova you. You down bad out here, family, and lettin' these streets eat you up!" Messiah gave it to him like a man, but Sunjay's next words froze him.

"I'm glad you're a positive nigga and all, fam, but you may have to save the sermon for after we meet again in the afterlife, 'cause them white folks gonna bring the chair back for out asses!" He shook his head as he reached underneath the seat and pulled out the manila envelope Spinx had given him the night at the club. "That fuck boy detective Spinx gave me this and told me we need to get at 'em," he spoke over a deep pull of the good. Sunjay tossed him the package as if it was a bomb he wanted away from him.

Messiah snatched it out the air with a humorous smirk on his face that told his potna that he wasn't digesting the depth of his claim. He watched Messiah open and pour the contents out of the envelope. "Mane, what the fuck is this!" he spat in disbelief.

A stack of pictures tumbled into his lap and as he flipped through each of them, his heart sank a little deeper into the ocean of his chest. He and Sunjay walking into Blow's club, then leaving with duffle bags. Play by play scenes of the night of the lick they'd just hit. Messiah lying on the ground firing at the op. Drug deals...there were up close pictures of it all!

"Brah, tell me I ain't seein' what my eyes are seein'." Messiah's words were bathed in disbelief.

Sunjay chuckled while pushing his door open and stepping out into the day's humid sunshine. He stared out at the life of the ghetto and allowed his thoughts to escape from his lips.

"If they wanted to crush us, we woulda been sittin' in West Tower already, blood. These pigs playin' dirty. They on some mo' shit."

Messiah had figured that much and as he shut his door, the only thought that went to war with his mental was *what they want?* He glanced over at Sunjay and studied the scratch before swallowing the initial shock of the flicks.

"Brah, it's too many variables to this shit: Blow, Spinx's hoe ass, the Jamaicans…" He paused as they made their way to the front of the house. "We got too many niggas at our heads and we ain't even seen no real fetti yet, bro. Look…"

His words trailed as he grabbed Sunjay by the arm to prevent him from opening the door to his kingdom. His eyes found his potna's in question. Messiah glanced around before allowing the boss in him to flow from his tongue.

"I got a plan, fam. We gonna shake this fag Spinx and make shit right with the dreads," he revealed.

"What 'bout the boy Blow?" Sunjay was skeptical.

"I got a cake we can bake for daddy-o, but first we gotta get our bag up!" Messiah's words were his prophecy.

Sunjay nodded his agreement as he put his key into the lock, but Messiah had one more inquiry. He tapped Sunjay's arm until their eyes connected once more.

"Dawg, what happened to the side of ya face?"

Sunjay's hand instinctively went to the scratch as he chuckled. "Aw, this ain't shit. Dream's bitch ass just got on some extra shit at the club the other night."

Renta

Chapter 13
The Next Day

"Dis, my beautiful child, is called de tear of Saint Marie. It's a rare stone from the mud of Sierra Leone. It was only two of these beauties ever found and dis is one of those two. Yuh know what makes these exquisite stones so powerful, so priceless, Keisha?" Gator asked his studious daughter. He held up the eight carat sparkling diamond and stared at it in admiration. A disco ball of color danced over his face as he praised the beauty that only pressure could create. "In 1998, a village of beautiful Africans, young, old, and the forced worked the mines down there on the west coast of Africa. This was around the time that the Revolutionary united front, a rebel guerrilla group, mounted a savage attack and killed thousands of civilians and mutilated even more. At that time, daughter, The Sierra Leone Special court was created to try war crimes and—

"Mother"— Keisha's voice silenced through his history lesson. Gator's dark eyes trailed from the sparkling jewel and found the curios gaze of his sixteen year old daughter. Her eyes were trained on the big diamond as if it was one of the seven wonders of the world.

"I remember de stories she told me of her homeland, de diamond in de mud." Her words were soft as she took timid steps in her father's direction. Keisha reached out and took the stone from his rough hands, instantly falling in love with its brilliance.

"Yes, little one, before me and yuh mother fell in love in the isles of Jamaica, she mined the soil of her home country. Yuh mother is de reason I'm now the possessor of this precious stone and it came at a great price of her and her poor family's existence there in that corrupted land."

Gator's words were distant as if the reflection had transported him across the seven seas and deep into the dark tunnels of Africa, where the blood of many had been spilt over the pressurized minerals. He observed the awe within Keisha's glare as the diamonds symmetry awakened somethin in her that he knew all too well: *obsession*!

"How much is it worth, Papa?" Her words came out in a breathless timbre.

"Somethin of this mag——"

Gator's words tapered off as one of his workers entered the study with two young boys on his heels. The old man's vision swallowed them within the inky blackness of his pupils as the silence spoke its peace. His attention fell upon Sunjay's transfixed gaze. The boy was locked in on the diamond in Keisha's hand and even she had noticed the boldness of the stranger's stare.

"Dis must be de messengers of de man dat robbed and spilt de blood of my brodas."

Gator's words were deadly as he tapped Keisha's arm and without being told, the young girl placed the diamond back into a velvet pouch with many smaller stones. She excused herself with curious study of Messiah, but a swift elbow to Sunjay's arm as she passed. Gator laughed as he waved for them to have a seat.

"De streets say yuh been looking fa meh - or yuh superiors, should I say?"

Sunjay moved to find a seat, but Messiah grabbed his arm.

"Naw, we're our own boss and we'd rather stand, if that's cool with you, homie?" he spoke for both of them.

Gator studied him before nodding his indifference. His eyes fell to the two duffle bags in each boy's hands. He nodded.

"Yuh own boss, hmm?" he inquired before sitting back in his seat and crossing his arms over his chest. "From what I hear, yuh work for a mon dat is employed by *me!*" he emphasized the word.

"Yeah, we *used* to get money wit' brah, but that's neither here nor there," Messiah cleared the air before lying his bag on the floor and nodded for Sunjay to do the same.

"Wha's dis?" Gator smiled menacingly.

His worker rushed over and opened one of the duffels and pulled out a kilo of dope. He glanced up at Gator, who never broke his stare with Messiah. There was something about the man child that he was drawn to.

"How did yuh know dis was mine? Most importantly, how do you know of me period!" he spat, ready to give the order to have the two boys slain.

Messiah stretched his arms out wide as if he was an eagle soaring under the sun. He knew his plan had the potential to be deadly, but for the slight chance of cutting out the middle man, he was taking the gamble with the guillotine.

"Look, OG, we're street niggas and the streets talk. Yo' rep proceeds you and we respect this shit you puttin' down in the trap, but we out here gettin' it how we live. When we got it in the mud for this shit, we didn't know you was involved, but dem boys we laid down was clearly Jamaican."

"So, even after you noticed they were of my heritage, you killed them anyway?" Gator tested his gangsterisms as the sounds of rushed footfalls spoke of danger.

Four armed Jamaicans rushed the room with menacing intent glowing in their eyes. Without warning, one took aim at the two boys.

"JonJa!" Gator's booming voice demanded all their attention.

"Him boy die for de blood of our brethren!" the wild boy spat.

"Yuh question my demands, JonJa?" The threat was evident.

The young Jamaican at eased and glared at Messiah. Though fear surged through him, externally he was as placid as still waters. Gator's sharp eyes took not only notice of that fact, but Sunjay's smirking face. *De boy is de devil!* His mental echoed the realization as he took in the boy's eagerness to meet the reaper. The older man looked to Messiah for the answer to his question.

"Dig, G, death don't give a fuck 'bout a nigga's ethnic group. Me and my brotha——" He paused to nod at Sunjay. "We come from the dirt of this city, and was taught that when the bullets flyin', it's not 'bout who's shootin. It's 'bout gettin' to that bag, whether it's our blood stainin' that money or the op's."

Gator's eyes danced between the two boys as he tried to figure their angle. "So why not just keep what yuh boys take and keep yuh mouths shut rather than gambling with yuh lives?" he inquired. *Say de wrong thing and you're gonna die!* he thought as he stood to his feet and made his way over to them. He toed the two bags. "This isn't all of the possessions."

Messiah nodded his agreement. "All we can speak for is our cut. We steppin' to you 'cause even though we could ball for a minute wit' this shit, at the end of the day, we need a bonafide plug." He revealed his chess move.

Gator chuckled with a nod. "And Blow…didn't he put yuh on? Wasn't he good to yuh?" he questioned their loyalties.

Sunjay's face contorted in response, but he'd promised not to mention Blow's sins to the man he'd fouled.

"Blow put us on and this is fa sho'. We salute playboy, but this ain't 'bout loyalty. Even a diligent worker has to one day become an even better boss," he broke his silence.

Gator strode passed them, but paused in the threshold of the sitting room's door, his back to them and anticipation in the air. He spoke over his shoulder.

"Evil his many faces, but even Satan respects balls."

Part II
The Bag of Diamonds

A poor man walked down the street mumbling about how broke and down bad he was. "If I had a few dollars, God, if you help me climb out this low down dirty shame I've become, I'd be appreciative." He said a silent prayer, but the only answer he received was a cold gust of wind that caused him to pull his tattered coat tight.

"Well, fuck you too!" he grumbled in frustration. He strode the cold streets in search of a meal. It mattered not if it came from a sympathizing heart, a discarded, nearly empty bag of chips, or merely a cold bone with a bite of meat found in a dumpster. He walked and grumbled and walked and grumbled until his feet felt the soft fabric of a black pouch. "The hell?" he whispered, bending over to retrieve the small bag. The soft velvet felt good to his rough hands, but when he opened it, he cursed God in disgust.

"Goddammit! Who the hell would put glass inside such a beautiful bag!" he gruffed before tossing the bag back to the street and cursing his way on down the street.

Minutes later, another man down on his luck walked down that exact street mumbling, "God, I know I've sinned, but all a nigga ask is for just a lucky day and a blessing! I'll truly appreciate it, ole man," he prayed as he walked in the exact direction of the first bum. Suddenly, he came upon the black pouch. "This bag sho' is pretty, maybe I can sell it for a mint or two," he whispered while picking it up. The bum opened it and his eyes grew as big as an owls. "Lawd have mercy! Diamonds!" he shouted and did a funky little dance.

Days later, that first bum was still prowling the streets in search of a blessing when a cocaine-white Bentley pulled beside him. The window eased down and to his surprise it was the second bum. "This can't be right! Jimmy?" he asked his longtime enemy.

Jimmy, the second bum, smiled a veneered smile as he stuck his head out the window. "Ole Black Pat, fancy seein' ya out her in the cold, ole buddy." He laughed more at his own good fortune than at the cold reality of the streets.

"How'd you... I mean, what's goin' on?" the first bum stammered.

The second street walker allowed his eyes to soften as the truth came forth. "Man, you wouldn't believe this shit! I was strollin' down the street and stumbled over a black pouch that was filled with diamonds!" he exclaimed.

The memory of the pouch he'd assumed was filled with glass flashed through his mind. "Now you slick, low down, snake! Them was my diamonds you stole and I want 'em back!" he tried his hand.

Jimmy, the second bum's, confusion was evident until he figured that the other man must've stumbled upon the bag, but didn't know what he'd found. He smiled bright. "Well, brotha man, take this as a life's lesson, baby. Sometimes the blessin' is right there in front of ya, but it's up to you on how you look at it!" the man shouted before speeding off into the night.

The grumbling bum fell to his knees in tears. "I ain't gonna shit, shave, or bathe till I see some betta days! My dog done bit me, the cat won't lick me, and God, yo' funky ass done tricked me!"

Chapter 14

It was October sixteenth, the year of 1995. It had been a year plus since Byron De La Beckwith had gotten convicted of the 1963 murder of civil rights leader Medgor Evers, but it was a day that even the slain man would be proud of. On that beautiful day in October, history was being repeated. The great Louis Farrakhan had organized the Million Man March in Washington, DC. Hundreds of thousands of black men showed up for the rally, but in the crooked streets of Dallas Texas, another victory was being manifested.

"Bitch, I said bend ya funky ass ova and assume the position before I wring ya funky ass neck!" Sweet Eddie demanded to the amusement of the other pimps that found their leisure out on the stroll of North Dallas.

Tutts was one of the most desired hoes on the stroll, but only a true jeweler can recognize the authenticity of a diamond versus the brilliance but artificialness of a cubic zirconia. As Messiah sat silently within his teal green Jag, he appreciated the sculptors that had chiseled away the barbarism from his two step. He watched through the tinted windshield as the bowlegged beauty bent over and allowed the man she worked for to defame her. Sweet Eddie reared back and placed a swift kick to her ass. The woman crashed to the stoned pavement in agony, and to add salt to the open wound, Sweet Eddie reached down and twisted Tutts's finger back so hard that it was no doubt broken.

"Bitch! A broken finger is better than a late regret on any given Sunday!"

The pimp's words drifted through the cracked window. Messiah's eyes fell to the ember at the tip of the twisted blunt as he gave it mouth to mouth. The AC threw snowballs at them as he and Liberty sat, observing the depreciation of a rare gem. Kush smoke snaked from his nose and lips as he watched Sweet Eddie rear back and slap spit from Tutts. The surrounding pimps laughed at the spectacle of their fellow pimp layin' the law down on his top earner.

"Why'd you slap the hoe, Sweet Eddie?" pimp Suave G inquired.

Sweet Eddie glared down at the whimpering woman.
"I slapped the hoe for all the shit she done when I wasn't lookin'!" he capped before tossing the five hundred dollars she'd handed him. "Bitch, it's principal in ya potential. Don't disrespect me wit' no short change when I know that funky pussy hole got long range. Get ya funky ass up, and you bet' not return to civilization until you got a pimp's trap right!" he laid it down.

Tutts climbed to her feet and hobbled away from the circus he'd created out of her dedication to his occupation. She made it about twenty steps around the corner before an angel fell from an earthly heaven. Liberty's appearance spoke of class and her mannerisms was that of a boss bitch. Her slanted eyes fell onto Tutts in wonder.

"Excuse me, baby girl, but you deserve better," was the first thing that came to Tutts's ears. The soft words flowed from Liberty's soft lips like red wine spilling from an expensive bottle of the good shit.

"Yeah, well, I don't know you and you surely don't know enough about me to know of what I deserve," Tutts spat without breaking her stride.

Liberty found it hard to keep up with the lady. The four thousand dollar Brian Atwood nude heels were made for class rather than dash.

"I just might not know you as a woman, but I surely know enough about life to know that you deserve more than that display of disrespect that I just witnessed," Liberty spoke matter-of-factly.

They turned the corner before Tutts stopped and fixed her with a heated stare. *This bitch judgin' me?* she wondered as their eyes danced.

"Bitch, *paleeeease!* You don't know nothin' 'bout the life I live! Yo' prissy ass must not be from 'round these parts, so let me enlighten yo' naive ass 'bout somethin' before one of these nothin'-ass pimps introduce you to a life of white slavery!" Tutt's placed her hand over her aching finger. She'd laid her vision on the blood red silk dress that Liberty wore. The short collar spoke of chinoiserie, the style of a Chinese influence.

Stereotyping had always been ninety percent away from the truth of a person and as Liberty burst into laughter, she recalled Messiah's words.

"You must always be presentable, ma. You're the reflection of who I am as a man, boss, and mack, and a lot can be said of how a nigga's bitch carries herself! The memory was fresh as she composed herself.

"Fuck is so funny? Who are you anyway?" Tutts demanded.

"She's my Earth. Now I need to find the wind and fire to complete the galaxy that orbits me."

Messiah's voice caused the unsuspecting woman to jump in surprise. Her eyes bounced from him to Liberty.

"Nigga, and who the fuck is *you*?" Her eyes digested his aura.

Messiah stood leaning against the side of the Jag. He was clad in a pair of white slacks complemented by a silk long-sleeved Versace shirt that was completely unbuttoned to display his cut up stature. The thick Cuban link was weighed down by a nine ounce gold and diamond pendant in the shape of a key. Her eyes briefly fell to the teal green crocodiles that covered his feet before his words molested her mind, heart, and pussy.

"I'm the Sun, Queen, but beyond entity, I'm here to introduce you to a heaven that will always appreciate what most niggas depreciate"

Tutts's eyes bounced back and forth between God and Goddess in awe. The vernacular, the dress code, and play was the separation between the people that she'd grown accustomed to within the life of whorism.

"I don't give a damn 'bout heaven, because if the devil catches me talkin' to you, he'll make me beg for a blazin' pit," she spoke before attempting to escape the inevitable.

Messiah was next to her in a few strides and without an invitation, he took hold of her broken finger. The pain shot up Tutts's arm and caused her to pause in her stride. Messiah squeezed the throbbing digit as hard as he could until he felt it pop back into place.

"Oh my Goddddd!" Tutt's cry was primal as she attempted to pull her finger free, but Messiah held tight.

"The devil has no dominance over a God, mama, and you've made my point exactly. Why would you wanna make sacrificial decisions for a devil?" he asked while gently massaging the ache from her hand.

Tutts cried softly, not from the agony of the physical, but from the spiritual mirror Messiah was placing before her.

"Ma, you slave day and night to get this cat's trap right. You've allowed your actions to prove that the love of your heart surpasses the value of ya pussy by sacrificin' your essence for the livelihood of a nigga that can never appreciate your clarity. Why though?" he asked as he released her hand.

The pain had ebbed into a distant reminder. Tutts crossed her arms over her breasts as she studied him beyond his profession.

"Aren't you a pimp? What makes you any different from the first, last, and every other slick-talkin' nigga that's promised heaven on earth?" She rolled her eyes with the question.

Messiah gave her an innocent smile before reaching up to fix her unkempt hair.

"No, I'm not a pimp, lady. I'm a mack, and the differences can't be found within the convo, but more in the quality of the nigga. See, a pimp sells pussy, but a mack sells the dream that only *you* can bring into reality. I don't wanna own you or your pussy, baby. I just want the keys to your heart and mind so I can change your perspective."

Tutts didn't react when he stepped into her space and kissed her forehead. His next words were the waters that baptized her apprehensions and opened her mental.

"Alfred Nobel was a Swedish chemist that invented dynamite in 1886, and after he became rich off of his weapon of mass destruction, the man gave his fortune to an idea of what we now know as the Nobel Peace Prize," he spoke before suddenly stepping away from her and walking toward the foreign car.

The further away he moved, the emptier Tutts felt. Messiah swung the door open for Liberty to get in the driver's seat before he made his way to the rear door. He nodded for Tutts to make her way to him. Without question and filled with curiosity, she found herself back before him. Messiah slid into the comfort of the car before closing the door on her. Confusion was a dominating storm within the woman's mind as the car's motor came to life in a soft purr. Seconds passed before Messiah's window eased down, and to her surprise, he extended a green apple to her.

"The same mu'fucka that created the explosive that destroys shit is the same mu'fucka that promotes world peace!" He chuckled as she accepted the fresh fruit. "My point is, that analogy is what I see in you. A woman of confliction and contradictions. You love and dedicate yourself to a nigga that can't love you because when he looks at you, all he sees is how many niggas you've fucked versus the reason behind your sacrifice." Messiah blew her a kiss before tapping the driver's seat head rest. The Jag backed out at a slow crawl as the twenty-two inch blades reflected off of the pavement. "You don't have to create something that has the potential to destroy your world just to advocate for your own peace, mama. Loyalty should never become the definition of stupidity, but always the gift of a righteous bitch. Serve daddy-o his dismissal papers and I'll meet you here tomorrow."

The window eased up and the teal green car blended into traffic.

***

"Hurry up, brah, I ain't got all day!" Lil Zetti spat with a quick glance around.

He stood on the curb serving a fiend and knew he was out of line for the act. Ever since Sunjay and Messiah had secured the plug, Blow and his squad had been coming through shooting shit up. Sunjay had warned him about making himself a target, but... *Shid, I need this quick hundo!* he thought.

"A'ight, youngsta, let me see what'cha got. Ya know these lil niggas been out here sellin' Planters peanuts and candle wax. I ain't 'bout to be a victim of my own addiction, ya hear?" the smoker spoke from the driver's seat of an old Toyota Corolla.

Lil Zetti frowned in irritation. "Say, Bug, you doin' too much, my boy. Hurry up and pick 'em so we can get out the street. You know Spinx's bitch ass on a war path!" he fumed before pouring eight stones of crack in his palm and putting it in the window.

The fiend was studious as his eyes scanned the euphoria that had stolen the meaning of life from the ghetto and made itself the god that not only the smokers, but even its distributors praise.

"Well, they look good, but——"

"Man, what you gon' do? You want 'em, or this some kinda game you runnin'?" Lil Zetti interrupted him.

"Well see, Zetti, the thang is, my Social Security check ain't——"

Smack!

Before Lil Zetti could react, the fiend had slapped the bottom of his palm, causing the eight stones to fly up into the air.

Scurrrrr! The tires burnt the asphalt as he mashed the gas. The car swerved dangerously in the smoker's haste to get away.

Bocka! Bocka! Bocka! Bocka! Bocka! The banga jumped in his hand as Lil Zetti chased the speeding car, but it was a frivolous quest. The old Toyota had bent the corner and made its escape.

"Bitch-ass nigga, mane!" Lil Zetti spat in embarassment. *How'd I fall for the oldest trick in the book?* he thought.

He tucked the Glock and made his way to the bench in the small park of the Jets and sat down to twist one. Lil Zetti was an eleven-year-old shoota that had the best of both worlds, Sunjay had instilled the gangsterism and Messiah made him promise to not only stay in school, but also obtain knowledge. He'd even gone as far as enlightening the boy that the education his teachers would give him was based off of Euro American and Caucasoid history. *"You'll get the real history from the oppression that you were born into,"* he'd told him.

"Zetti Tyrone Jackson, boy, come over here and give ya mama some love!" a dingy, snaggled woman called from behind him.

Lil Zetti didn't bother to look her way. He continued to roll the blunt as Felicia made her way around the table. His mother seemed more broken every time he saw her. The pain and shame of the reality had numbed his heart long ago and as his eyes found hers, Lil Zetti wondered what drove his queen to exchange her dignity for a high that she'd have to travel too far away from family, morale, and love to reach.

"'Sup, Felicia?" he acknowledged before running a flame over the moist blunt of good.

His mother attempted to give him a stern expression as she watched him put the stick to his lips and spark it.

"Zetti, don't *eva* forget I pushed you out this pussy. You ain't had me!" she spat as he exhaled a stream of smoke.

Lil Zetti chuckled sarcastically. "What's up, Ma? I know you ain't come all this way to give me the history of my birth."

Felicia smiled. "Well, I need a wake, nothin' major, baby, just a lil somethin' to get my blood pumpin' until I can make somethin' shake."

Lil Zetti shook his head but knew there was nothin' he could do. "What you got, Ma? I blessed you the last six times!" He hoped the request for compensation would deter her from pressing him for the work, but her response was a reality of the ghetto that no man was safe from.

"Come on, baby, you know Mama down bad right now, but I'll make it up to you!" she cried, her addiction overpowering morale.

"Felicia, you've paid me so much *I'll make it up to you's* that I'm rich off the shit. Come fuck wit' me later after I re-up. I got you, Ma."

"Mannn, come on, Zetti, I'm achin' baby, look." She paused and allowed her eyes to sweep the park before her eyes met his again. Felicia placed a hand on her son's knee. "I'll suck ya dick. Them lil girls ain't——"

Before she could complete the sentence, the blunt flew from Zetti's hand as he jumped off the bench and rushed his queen. Before he could tame that darkness within him, he had one hand around her throat and the other gripping her chin so tightly that her lips puckered.

"Bitch, you bet' not ever…" He tried to shake the tears from his eyes. From somewhere deep, the child he never had the chance to be cried so powerfully that his tears wrapped themselves around his heart, and pushed themselves inside.

"Ole bad-ass Lil Zetti, I know that ain't ya mama ya got hemmed up like some common dopefiend," a relaxed voice called from behind them.

Zetti's blood froze at the sound of Detective Spinx's voice.

"Lil brah, don't be out in the hood this week, and if you are gonna be out there, don't be dirty. DPD been gettin pressure from up top and now them hoes takin' down everything wit' a lil color to their pigment." Messiah's words echoed within his mind like a loud scream in an empty hallway.

His mental did inventory of everything he had that could get him placed in them cold bracelets. *The banga, an ounce of hard, half a zip of corn!* Lil Zetti did the only rational thing he could.

"Fuck you, Lil Zetti! I hope he locks yo' mu'fuckin' ass up!" Felicia shouted as he flung her to the side and took off in a dead sprint.

Spinx didn't hesitate to give chase. "Uh-uh you lil mu'fucka, yo' lil ass goin' to jail today!" he spat.

Lil Zetti cut through the breezeways and trails of the apartments that only its natives were privy of. He glanced behind him and saw that Spinx was on his heels. Without warning, he cut left and tossed the burna without slowing down. Without the tool digging into his side, the boy was able to better maneuver, but the harder he ran, the more Spinx pushed himself. They came out a narrow wedge of the building and that's where the gods smiled upon the bad guy. Sweat poured down Zetti's face, but he'd spent his life in those bricks. He knew the places that would accept him with open arms.

"Hey look, Lil Zetti runnin' from the laws!"

Both men heard the squeals and laughter of the kids surrounding the ice cream truck. Lil Zetti jerked to the left, causing Spinx to follow suit, but at the last second, the young boy went right. Spinx ran into the back of the ice cream truck with a bang.

"Hey, buddy, watch it!" the truck driver screamed.

Spinx paid him no mind as he drew his service pistol. He was out of breath as he spun around the truck and aimed. The crooked detective made it halfway around the truck before he heard the tell-tale sounds of fleeing footsteps. He rushed around the truck just in time to see an apartment door slamming shut. He wasted no time running toward it and preparing to kick it in until realization robbed him of the urge.

Ms. Betty, Sunjay's grandma!

He reupholstered the gun and knocked. He knocked once more before the door opened to reveal the old woman, Ms. Betty was dressed in her Sunday's best as she smiled up at him

"Heeeeyyy, baby, how ya been, Gerald? Haven't seen ya round these parts in a time. In fact, I ain't seen ya at church in a good while. How's ya mama Tracy?" she asked while standing firmly in the threshold.

"How you doin', Ms. Betty? I know I ain't been ta church in a while and I been meanin' to get up there, but work been kinda hectic. Mama been doin God only knows," he replied while trying to look around her and into the apartment. "Ms. Betty, I don't mean to be rude and cut this chat short, but Im kinda in the middle of something. Have you seen Zetti Jackson?" he asked the rhetorical question.

Ms. Betty's expression was a confused one. "You talkin' 'bout Lil Zetti? Felicia's son?" she asked.

Spinx nodded with a defeated look on his face. He knew the hood protected their own and he would never win.

"Naww, baby, can't say that I have, but if I do, I'll let him know you lookin' for him, ya hear? I wanna see yo' handsome butt in church on Sunday too. Ain't nobody too busy to get em some lawd in they life, but I'm gonna close this door, baby, I'm lettin' my air out."

Detective Spinx nodded in defeat before waving and going on about his way. "A'ight, Ms. Betty, you take care."

"And get ya some water. It's hot out here, baby, you don't want to catch the stroke," she said before closing the door and locking it. She made her way back to the old worn couch and reclaimed her seat in front of the television.

"Zetti, come on from back there, and if ya think yo' lil narrow ass gone be leavin' this house, you got anotha thang comin'!" she scolded before turning her attention back to her stories.

***

Entry: 8

By now, winter is melting away, but life has become a nasty bitch with no remorse for who she fucks over. Yet every bitch has a weakness, Messiah. It's just that when men become so enchanted with the portions of a bitch that they can't deny, the weakness becomes their own while their strength becomes that weapon the bitch uses to slay 'em. A man's money used to be the tool he used to capture a woman's attention, but now women has their own bankroll and do more for a no good-ass nigga than he's ever done for ten bitches in his entire life. A nigga used to use some good dick to keep a bitch fiendin', but now women are so dizzy from the lack of men that they don't know which one they crave more: the hard dick of a solid man, or the plastic cock and flickering tongue of a butch bitch that wishes she was born with a male organ. Everything that used to be abnormal is now normal and what use to be normal is now alien.

So it's never about how much of a bitch life is, baby. It's more about you findin' that weakness in that bitch that you can use to your advantage. The key to this bitch called life, son, is not found between her legs or under her bosom. It's in the mere fact that life is a hoe you'll never be able to control. You have to treat life as you would every other woman. You allow her to be her! If you see that the bitch is dick craved and wild, never attempt to domesticate her! Allow the bitch to embrace her whorism and you get more than merely a nut out her pussy hole. You have to allow a woman to be who she naturally is or she will portray to be who she's naturally not and that's a lie you could've done without. Life is no different, baby. By now you know that it was Blow that killed your father, and I can't apologize for my part enough. He must pay for his sins, baby. His release is near and I won't be able to co-exist within a world with a man that stole somethin' so precious from us. I wish I could paint you a perfect picture, son, but I can't! Life is just a bitch that don't give a damn about me just as much as she don't give a damn 'bout you!

Mama

Chapter 15

Friday

Vroom! The six hundred growled.

"Awww shit, look at this damn fool Sunjay!" Murda shouted when the fire red stunt bike flew by and down the street in wheelie position.

Sunjay had always loved motorcycles and as soon as his bread was right, that's the first thing he copped. The hood was out in full effect and as they watched him turn the bike around, Murda and his twin brother, Bam, shared a chuckle. The only thing that separated the two boys in appearance was the black bandanna Bam never left home without. He kept it in his right pocket with a claim of it bringing him good luck.

"Say, you see this boy, brah!" Murda was lit, but Bam's lips was twisted up in that *"yeah, whateva, nigga"* kinda way as he trained envious eyes on the oncoming machine.

Scurrrt! The bike flew up onto the curb and bounced down onto both wheels.

Scurrrrr! A dragon's breath of smoke rose from the rough sex the rear tire was having with the asphalt.

"Yeah, I see the nigga, fam, but why that nigga always cappin' on a nigga like we lames and shit?" Bam's envy was louder than the hiss of a deadly snake as he watched the felines from the block fawn over the glossy machine.

Murda glanced over at his brother curiously. He knew his twin and main man didn't rock like that, but the hate was new and he made a mental note to check that shit when he and Bam were alone.

"'Sup, Blood, what that B like!" Sunjay's jewelry game was sick under the rays of the sun. He locked the set up with Murda and turned to do the same with Bam, but the gangsta ignored the gesture with a suck of his teeth.

"Fuck I look like, homie, one of these hoes or somethin'?" he spat before walking away.

They watched him walk over to Porsha and slap her on the ass. She smiled back at him as he leaned forward and whispered something in her ear.

"Say, dawg, why yo' blood always actin' like a bitch!" Sunjay spat the words as if they were a bad taste in his mouth.

Murda cut his eyes at him. He wasn't feeling the heat coming from Sunjay, but understood the pride of men.

"You know how bro be, but it ain't shit though. What's good wit' you though, stuntman? I see you doin' big thangs." He nodded toward the bike.

But Sunjay's eyes were on Bam as he and Porsha made their way over to the green electricity box that every housing projects had, and as his eyes fell to the black bandanna that hung from the goon's back pocket, he spat on the ground.

"Yeah, whateva, my dude, but dig." Sunjay paused to adjust the .40 on his waist. He tapped Murda's shoulder and nodded for him to follow him away from the crowd. "Look, fam, I got a lick that can set us straight for the rest of our lives!" He seemed nervous as his eyes swept the hood.

"Whats bracken', Flame, spit the shit out!" Murda was always on go mode for a bag.

"What you know 'bout diamonds, fam?" The words slipped from Sunjay's mouth and earned him a look of bewilderment.

***

The sun burned bright in the heavens as the Jag crawled to a stop a few feet away from the group of playas that stood on the stroll choppin' game. The block of Harry Hines was alive with the hustle and pussy was the highest commodity. The Isley Brothers beat low in the car, but enough to vibrate the teal green monster that squatted on the twenty-two inch big heads. Four sets of eyes drifted toward the whip as it idled for a few seconds before Liberty slid from the driver's seat in raw beauty. Her hair was stylishly wild and blew out like the mane of a male lion, but the panda bear black and white quarter mink that encased her femininity paused all activity. The coat was held in place by a fashionable belt with a huge medusa head for the buckle, but it was the dangerous cleavage on display, coupled with the trail up her bare legs that told a seductive tale of a pantiless pussy and a heavenly destination for the right compensation. She allowed the six inch stiletto heels to guide her to the rear door of the whip, and being careful not to chip a nail, she cracked the door. A thick swirl of smoke escaped from the crack before the door opened to his heaven, and the baby powder white Gators were the first sign that a god had arrived.

Suave G tapped Sweet Eddie's shoulder as Messiah slid out of his throne.

"Say, pimp, ain't that the lil nigga you tried to knock for that hoe Candy?" he inquired.

A look of confusion tainted Sweet Eddie's facial as he squinted under the heat of the sun. Messiah's after midnight-hued pants and shirt were offset by a cloud-white jacket, but it was his smile that spanked the baby. He'd fucked off ten bands on a gold and emerald encrusted top and bottom grill that played a strange trick on the eyes when he blessed one with a peek.

"Yeah, that's the chump, but I've never seen the dame on his arm. She must be as green as a string bean to have fallen victim to the game of a toy pimp." Sweet Eddie got a few chuckles from his fellow pimps.

Red Bone Tyrone, Suave G, and Earl the Pearl were all bona fide playas that had slayed hoe strolls from Dallas, Texas to Melrose, and each man respected the dynamics of whorism. Sweet Eddie chuckled as the young playa made his way over to where they stood.

"Big bidness, gentleman, I'm Messiah the Jeweler and I'm out her pushin' my campaign that's as sweet as French champagne." His intro was the interlude between respect and cockiness. Messiah extended his hand to Redbone, who was highly respected in the lifestyle.

The OG had diamond-kissed rings on all five fingers and the clarity of each stone spoke of his taste as he embraced the younger man. He pulled Messiah's hand closer for inspection, his eyes studying the heart-shaped VVS diamond on the young'n's pinkie before he released him with a chuckle. He gave Messiah a brief nod of approval.

"Pimpin Maxwell's boy. I've heard a lot 'bout cha, Tyke, and now I see ya keepin' ya game tight." His light voice contradicted his 6'4" height. The velvety lightness of it carried as he nodded at the Jag.

Sweet Eddie popped his collar. "I'ont know 'bout all that Jazz you kickin' out ya ass, Red Bone, but if Junior don't check his hoe, my game gonna imprison the hoe for reckless eyeballin'!"

Sweet Eddie's words caused all eyes to shift to Liberty. She never broke eye contact as she boldly gave the pimp a seductive smile. Messiah chuckled before fixing the man with a gaze.

"See, playboy, that's where you got the game fucked up, I'm a special kinda nigga. Dig." His words played in the air as he reached into his pocket and pulled out a small green apple. "See, the reason niggas try to regulate their hoes' attention is because insecurities lead them to feel inferior in the presence of a true playa's playaism. Niggas feel like if their bitch sets eyes on the glam of the next nigga, she'll magically disappear. But it's not the appearance of the playa that will hold the hoe captive. It's his nature that's the abductor," he jeweled the older pimp before handing the apple to Liberty.

Her promiscuity pervaded the air like a strong spray of perfume as she stepped in between the men and undid the belt. The fluffy material fell open, causing all eyes to rove from her perky titties down to her waxed oasis. She allowed the coat to slip from her shoulders before spreading its expensive fur on the ground. Liberty sat spread eagle on top of it, pussy lips pouting and on full display.

"Sayyyy, cat daddy, what kinda kicks you gettin' outta playin' slick tricks!" Suave G inquired while adjusting his hardened nature.

Confusion intermingled with raw lust within his and Sweet Eddie's vision, but Earl the Pearl and Redbone Tyrone kept their eyes trained on Messiah. The younger playa smiled at the vet pimps. In that moment, he understood what had allowed the playas to survive so long within a game that held no promise.

180

"Yesss! Mmm!" Liberty's moans were a silken melody that had the power to reveal the sucka in any man that held the quality.

Messiah didn't have to glance down at her to know that her essence was kissing, saturating the fruit, and in moments she would submerge it within her warm folds. His eyes drifted across the street to the game room and that's where he found an angel gravitating toward his godhood. His eyes flickered to Redbone before touching Earl the Pearl. Both men shared a knowing chuckle that caught Sweet Eddie's attention.

Tutts perspired lightly but even the light sheen didn't taint the natural beauty she was gifted with.

"Whore, you betta get back to my bidness before——"

"It's ova, Sweet Eddie. I'm divorcin' ya ass!" Her words were firm when she cut him short.

"Hoe, you say what! You 'bout to make me——"

"See, playboy, that's the cause of ya loss." Messiah paused the man's barbarity while stepping in between him and Tutts. "It's niggas like you that makes boss hoes go rogue, or confuse the bitch so much that she runs off in search of chicks with plastic dicks," he gritted.

"Fuck! Yassss!" Liberty cried as she worked her clit at a frenzied pace. Her lower lips bulged from the imprint of the apple that gently peeked from between them.

"Nigga, I don't know what jazz you tryin' to blow out ya trumpet, but you betta mind ya bidness before shit gets ugly!" Sweet Eddie growled.

Messiah took a step closer without breaking their stare.

"Listen, my dude, let me give you a spiel to help you heal, 'cause no matter how fucked up you are 'bout blowin' this hoe, you've been cut from her future duties," he jeweled before pointing a thumb back at Tutts.

"Nigga, fuck you talm'bout? My stomp down is wit' this hoe. You ain't——"

"Let the boy speak his peace, Sweet E, you know how this shit go!"

Earl the Pearl smiled a wicked smile, but the hand he'd slid in-side his suit coat was the only motivation Sweet Eddie needed to regain his playerism.

He wiped invisible lint off his shoulders before lookin' up at Messiah with fallacious security in his gaze. Messiah chuckled at the attempt before serving him up a cold piece of boss shit.

"A hoe gon' be a hoe at the end of each day, playboy, whether it's a hoe wit' a dick, the feminine type wit' a clit, or a freak that was born wit' both sexes. A hoe is a hoe. You can keep ya foot in a bitch's ass, treat her with class, or run dick in the bitch deep enough to touch her heart, but after she's free from ya rovin' eyeballs, the hoe gon' do only what that pussy leads her to do, and that's be a bonafide hoe!"

"Preach, son, that right! That's right!" Redbone Tyrone smiled like a proud father while snapping his fingers.

Messiah stepped around the man he was about to strip of his pride, and made his way over to where Liberty lay splayed over the eight thousand dollar mink. Her eyes were half-mast as she arched her back, in harmony with ecstasy. He gazed down at the bitch he once cared for, for the opposite reasons of why he now loved her. Her head raised and when their eyes met, her juices oozed from her peach. Without breaking the connection, Messiah spoke more to Tutts than to anyone else.

"When a nigga depreciates a woman, she loses surety in self and comes to a fork in the road that can either lead her down a path of becomin' a boss bitch that's worth more than just her pussy, or in the opposite direction and down a crooked path of uncountable sex partners and so many heartbreaks that she forgets that she's a woman altogether." He paused to nod down at Liberty. "A broken bitch will adopt the ways and perspectives of a nothin'-ass nigga and begin to poetize the fact that since a man has no respect for his dick, and it's deemed normal, she doesn't have to have any respect for her own pussy." He chuckled at the same time the apple burst from Liberty's fountain in a splash of wetness.

"Ohhh myyyy!" she cried as jaws dropped at the force of her explosion.

I gotta have this hoe! was the thought of many of the men that had gathered around to observe the spectacle. No one ever expected that to have been Messiah's intent from the alpha of his approach, but when he spun on his heels, his intent became clear to all that had the brain to comprehend game personified. He strolled over to Tutts and ran a hand down the side of her face.

"By the time the bitch realizes she's worth more than a nigga's dick and a good nut, the man she wants to respect her and see the clarity of her heart will only see the hoe in her, and that makes him fear the possibilities of what could happen if he entrusts her with his weakest portion."

His words stirred a tropical storm within her that escaped from her eyelids. Messiah leaned forward and kissed each wet stream of salty water.

"You know why I gave you the apple? Why I use them as my signature?" he probed.

Tutts nodded her head to confirm her naïveté and received an emerald smile from the man she knew she'd never betray.

"Though they never spoke it into existence, the apple is used as a symbol of the forbidden fruit that the serpent used to open Eve's eyes to the value of her pussy and in return, she used it to open Adam's eyes to his very own nature," he spoke before leaning his head back so she could see his neck. "See that?" He pointed at his throat and swallowed. Tutts witnessed the small ball go up and down. "That's called Adam's apple! It's the piece of the fruit that got stuck in the lame's throat as a reminder that if a playa fails to open the eyes of his bitch, with the right game and appearance, a serpent has the glam to lead her to betray her God."

His words were the gospel. Messiah trained his gaze on the captivated woman. He extended his hand to her.

"You got something for a real nigga?"

Tutts reached under her dress and slipped a bankroll out of her pussy before attempting to hand it to him, but the look of disapproval Messiah gave her confused the moment. He pushed her hand away.

"Don't be disrespectful, hoe, that ain't how you get me my trap!" His reaction baffled everyone that witnessed the resection, but his next request was a tribute to the days of old. He nodded toward Liberty.

"Let them pretty lil shoes carry you over there next to ya wife-in-law," he demanded.

Tutts made her way over and stood over Liberty. Messiah waved a dismissive hand.

"Now, put my cash flow deep in her pussy, hoe."

All eyes bounced from Tutts down to Liberty's bold paradise, yet Tutts didn't hesitate. She squatted down and spread Liberty's damp folds. Her wife-in-law smiled a mischievous smile as the knot of money disappeared inside her thieves' paradise. Messiah made his way over to the two foundations of his mackin' and stood above his enterprise.

"Now retrieve my bankroll, hoe, and from now on, that's how I want my pennies." He paused to wag a finger down at Liberty's cunt. "Fresh out the womb like a newborn, 'cause a hoe gonna either break bread or play dead, and if she choose to play dead, all she'll get from a real playa is a jagged stone for a tombstone without an engravement to tell who she is!" He laid down the law before accepting the moist loot from Tutts. Messiah sniffed the bankroll and smiled. "Smells like this shit could never be the root of all evil. It's the people that *don't* got it that manifests the evil." He laughed.

"Preach, P, talk that shit!" Redbone Tyrone shouted.

***

"I hate that nigga!" Bam spat as they watched Sunjay crank the bike as a high yellow girl with a juicy ass straddled it behind him.

Porsha leaned against him with his arms around her small waist. She could feel his rigidness poking her and though she had a mind to tend to that for him, his words unnerved her. Porsha pulled his arms free and turned to face him. Bam's hands instinctively went to her plump ass once his arms were back in place.

"What's the deal with this otha shit you on? What's ya beef wit' Sun?" she asked, more curious than actually giving a damn.

But Bam knew of her history with the killa and mistook curiosity for concern. "What, you on one 'cause I ain't fuckin' wit' ya nigga or somethin'? Fuck that nigga!" he spat while pushing her away from him.

Porsha frowned in confusion. *Fuck wrong wit' this nigga!* she wondered before spazzin' on him.

"Nigga, Sunjay ain't my nigga, and neither are you!" She put her hands on her hips while snaking her neck. "Just 'cause you gettin the pussy don't mean you owed no loyalty from a bitch. You niggas always on the lame shit! Like, yo' dumb ass be stashin' yo' work in the park like these niggas you out here fuckin' wit' ain't starvin' enough to steal!" She giggled while watching Sunjay zoom down the street on the motorcycle.

"Just like Sunjay's rotten ass be stashin' shit at Ms. Betty's crib like niggas got too much heart to rob an old lady!" Porsha was on her shit as she rolled her eyes and stormed off. "Lame-lame, be quiet!" she spat over her shoulder. The lady never considered that she'd just revealed a secret to the devil.

Renta

Chapter 16

Saturday Night

"Fuuuckkk meeee!" Porsha's cries of pleasure were hungry, enflamed by the erotic strokes of some good dick. *"Oh my God, Messiah, you in my stomach wit' this dick!"* she moaned while digging her nails into his chest.

Neither one expected Justice to have come home early from her trip to Houston. She wasn't supposed to be back for another three days, but she'd missed her hubby. Now, as she crept through the house with overflowing eyes, her heart cried for what she knew she'd find. As silently as a panther on the hunt, the betrayed woman made her way to the Italian imported couch and tossed the cushions. Betrayal robbed her of rationality as her small fingers wrapped around the cold metal of the Glock 16 that Messiah kept there for quick access. With her heart cracking with each step, Justice found her way through the house that no longer felt like a home.

"Yeah, yeah, yeaaaah!" Her best friend's love moans greeted her as the door eased open to hers and Messiah's bedroom.

"Yes!" Porsha's head was thrust back in ecstasy as she rode him. The silky sheets were a mess around her waist as she bucked on Messiah's nature. Love and betrayal had a head on collision as she stood frozen in place with so much pain and too much hurt. That level of treason could taint the heart of even the strongest of men, but for a woman, the need for revenge ran as deep as the island of Atlantis that was submerged beneath the Atlantic Ocean.

Boom!

The first shot threw Porsha forward in a wet spray of blood and open flesh.

Boom!

The second shot flipped her off the bed. Messiah popped up off the mattress, the sweat and dark stains of Porsha's blood causing him to look almost translucent underneath the glow of the moonlight that came through the window. Justice stood as still as a scarecrow on a windless night as their eyes spoke in ways their lips couldn't.

187

"You crossed me first," were the only words that Messiah could think of.

Justice cocked her head to the side in a strange curiosity, but she was beyond words.

Boom! Boom!

"Why!" Justice screamed as she popped up out of a dead sleep, squeezing her hands together as if she could still feel the gun there. The knock at her bedroom door caused her to snap back and glance around. Sweat shone like a soft glow on her skin as she reminded herself that it was only a dream.

"Justice, are you okay?" JoJo's question entered the room before his physical.

"Yeah, Dad, just ah bad dream." She fell back against the mattress with a huff.

JoJo stepped in and allowed his eyes to explore the room before landing on his baby girl. He smiled at the checkered quilt his wife's mother had gifted her.

"I heard yuh scream and..." His words trailed off at the sight of the light film of perspiration. JoJo strolled over to the bed and took a seat at the edge of the place Justice had spent many sleepless nights.

"Yuh don' have to go, yuh know." His words were gentle as he used his fingers to move a strand of damp hair out of her face.

Justice giggled. She loved her father wholeheartedly and knew he'd always see her as his little girl. She also was privy to him worrying about her. She'd moved out of their house the year before and started college at the U of H, and the old man had gone to visit her at least three times a week. Last week was her last semester at the school and she'd decided it would be her last week in the city of Houston as well. As much as she'd tried to grow without it, Messiah was a piece of her heart that she had to see the conclusion of. Justice had gotten accepted to the University of North Texas and she knew that JoJo didn't like her decision, but wouldn't stop her from spreading her wings.

"Dad, stop worrying so much. Aunty Jonice and Jazzy are——"

Her words died off at the thought of her favorite cousin. After Jazzy's trial, it was as if their family had turned their backs on her, and Justice vowed to herself that she'd make it up to her and find the child Jazzy had had while locked behind those walls. "I'm okay, OG JoJo. It's not like I'm moving across the world."

They shared a laugh at her use of the handle the streets had given him.

"That doesn't make me worry less, Daughter. Yuh mine and will always be my baby girl, mama." He chuckled at the face she made. "The dreams get worse, mama, I can tell."

His eyes spoke the words neither of them wanted to verbalize. Though her dreams and visions weren't always spot on, they had always held a figment of the future within them.

Justice nodded her confirmation. "Yes, and at times I have these visions of home." Her words were low.

"Trinidad?" JoJo's question was skeptical.

Justice nodded again before her eyes drifted closed. After a brief moment of silence, her father smiled.

"Well, Basdeo Panday's in office and is our first Prime Minister of Indian ancestry in Trinidad. Maybe that's not such a bad idea." He snickered at the indirect suggestion.

Justice laughed at the slick suggestion before turning onto her side and pulling the quilt up to her chin. JoJo nodded as his eyes took in the room he'd watched his baby girl come into her own in.

"Yuh still think about him, huh - the boy?" He knew her better then she knew herself.

Justice gave him a bashful smile, but wouldn't lie to him.

"I made him ah promise and my heart holds close to it, yuh know? I still love him and don't even know if he remembers me, Dad." Her facial expression was unsure.

JoJo studied her face before rising and doing the unexpected. He walked out the room.

***

12:30 a.m.

The dark figure moved through the room like a shadow.

Fuck this boy keep the fetti at? he wondered as he stopped at a vase filled with waxed flowers. As silent as a ghost, he pulled the flowers out and glanced down into the dark void of the glossy clay. *Empty!*

He laid it down and rested the flowers on the carpet before moving on to the couch. Tossing the cushions and lookin' underneath the couch entirely, his mind ran wild.

It gotta be 'round here somewhere. Where would I put my bread if I didn't want it to be found?

His mental was a spider's web as he searched. Suddenly, it hit him. *The kitchen!*

The man made his way to the kitchen and started with the drawers before working his way to the cabinets. The figure climbed onto the counter and went to work, pushing containers and condiments aside in a desperate search of forsaken treasures.

Bingo! he thought at the sight of the thick Wal-Mart bag that was stuffed deep in the back of the cubbyhole. He pulled the bag free of its hiding spot and opened it. "That's what the fuck I'm talm'bout!" He kissed the rubber banded hundred dollar bills.

"Sunjay, baby, what you doin' in there?" Ms. Betty's soulful voice turned a burglary into a possible capital murder.

The dark figure jumped off the counter while simultaneously upping the strap.

Damn, Ms. Betty! I gotta kill yo' nosy ass now! Panic convinced him that even with the ski mask concealing his identity, the old woman that had watched him come up in those trenches could still recognize him. He aimed the banga toward the darkness and waited. *I'm leavin' wit' this bread, fam!* His thoughts were homicidal.

"Baby, is that you?" Ms. Betty reiterated as she rounded the corner in a floral house coat. "Lord have mercy!"

Boom!

The flame shot from the barrel. The kitchen lit up briefly and the last thing the figure witnessed before making his escape was Ms. Betty's falling body.

***

When JoJo returned, he had a small bundle in his hands. He seemed almost embarrassed as he reclaimed his seat at the edge of the bed. He handed her the package and as Justice sat up, she smiled. *Aww, Daddy bought me a departing gift!* She giggled at the thought. "Aww, thank you Dad!" she squealed as she pulled the string on the gift box and opened it. There was a stack of letters and one white waxed rose. She picked up the first letter and frowned.

"Daddy?" Her smile had disappeared at the sight of the sloppy handwriting. She would recognize it anywhere. She glanced up at the man she loved more than life and the confirming nod he gave her sliced a gorge through her heart.

"Why though?" she asked, confused and frustrated.

"Read it," was JoJo's only response. He watched as Justice ripped the missive open and began to read.

You remember the times we'd just thug under the street lights, the long cold nights? I miss that shit. Sometimes I lay awake all night thinking of how you'd put ya J's on and sneak out to come tell me how much you love me. JoJo woulda beat both of our asses if he knew how we'd sneak up to that attic and get lost within that sixty seconds, but it would be an ass whoopin' I'd take a million times if for only a few more stolen moments with you, Justice Catrina. Life has taken me on a crazy path, but I'm on all ten, mama, still out here bad and me and Pimpin Maxwell ain't as close as we used to be. Sunjay is living his dreams of being a kingpin and me? Well, let's just say you wouldn't be so proud of me. This my sixtieth letter with no response, but it's real, baby. Porsha told me how you gave ya promise to ole buddy down there in the big city. Guess pinkie promise don't mean so much when there's so much distance and time between two people. Well, ma, I'm up! I miss you, ma, that's all. The son of a dopefiend.

P.S. The wax rose will serve as a reminder, real love will never die.

Justice's eyes brimmed with a waterfall that she held at bay. She held JoJo captive inside her stare until he spoke his piece. "A father will never feel another man is worthy of his baby girl...*never!*" he vowed without regret. He reached over and wiped a fallen tear from the corner of her eye. "You're grown now, baby, and I still see you as my little princess. See, for a man, the love of a woman, no matter if it's his wife, lady friend, or daughter, is a possession he wants to hold captive for as long as he can. His ego loves the energy, that feeling of being Superman if only in the eyes of those few women. I'm no different, baby girl."

His truths ran deep. Justice nodded with a smile. Not only did she understand, but she could never stay angry with the old man. She wiped the river from her eyes before smelling the wax rose as if it held a fragrance.

"You'll always be my Superman, Dad, and thank you." She sounded relieved.

JoJo's eyebrow rose high on his face. "For?"

"For savin' the man from being socked in the jaw for forgettin' me!"

They laughed.

***

"You sure you didn't recognize him, Ms. Betty?" Spinx asked for the third time.

The old woman swatted him away.

"I told you ova and ova again, I ain't seen no face. Now don't ask me again, ya hear!" she admonished. "Who called the law anyway?" she inquired.

But before he could answer the question, Sunjay and Messiah rushed into the apartment with murder on their minds.

"Fuck happened to my big mama, blood?" Sunjay was on his shit.

"Sunjay Carter, ya betta watch ya mouth in my damn house! Yo' ass ain't too big fa no ass whoopin', ya hear?"

Ms. Betty's stern stare did little for the untamed gangsterisms of her grandson. He rushed over and hugged her tight as he could.

"B-boy, ya gonna squeeze the soul of Jesus up outta me!" she wheezed.

Sunjay released her and glanced over at Spinx and a pudgy white cop that stood by observing the display of affection. At the sight of Spinx, their last encounter replayed in the walls of his mind and the look the dirty pig gave him told him that he, too, remembered.

"Get out!" Sunjay spat.

Detective Spinx chuckled before nodding to his partner. "Ms. Betty, if you remember something that can help us, give me a call," he spoke before making his way to the door. Spinx paused as he was passing Messiah. "'Sup, baby, long time no see!" He acted as if they were old friends. Messiah fixed him with a blank stare as the man leaned in and whispered, "I know you got my lil message. It's in you and ya boy's best interest to get at me. Let's say…" He paused to look at his watch. "Tomorrow at the William's Chicken down the street. And don't forget, *pimp*…my time is money."

"Gerald Spinx, it's time ya went on home, don't you think?"

Ms. Betty's words received a wave over his shoulder as Spinx made his exit. As soon as the door closed, Ms. Betty reached back and slapped fire from Sunjay's mouth. Both he and Messiah stared at her bewilderedly.

"What I do, Mama? I ain't——"

"Come on!" The sixty-six-year-old woman cut him off and made her way to the kitchen. They followed as Sunjay glanced at Messiah, who gave him a perplexed shrug. Ms. Betty paused in the middle of the small kitchen and waved her frail hand in a wide arch.

"Now, I may not be the smartest woman that Plymouth Rock landed on, but I know as sho' as Jesus is black that nobody's breakin' into an old lady's house fa condiments in the seasoning family!" she spat.

Sunjay glanced up at the ceiling that the intruder had shot to scare his grandmother. *Whoeva did this shit knows my G-lady. That's why they ain't leave her dead and stankin'!* he thought as he tuned back into her rant.

"All I's heard was the shot and my blood pressure must've shot through the roof! I blacked out and when I came to, Gerald Spinx was standin' ova me like I was the dead resurrection." She waved her hand dramatically.

She was still on a war path when Sunjay's eyes found Messiah. The man was staring so intently at whatever had caught his attention that Sunjay's curiosity over powered his attention. His vision followed his bro's and when he found the object of Messiah's captivation, his mind snatched him back to the last time he'd seen the piece of cloth.

"'Sup, Blood, what that B be like!" he'd acknowledged them as he locked the set up with Murda and turned to do the same with Bam. He remembered the hate radiating from the young goon.

"Fuck I look like, nigga, one of these hoes or somethin'?" Bam spat before walking away.

As clear as day he reflected on the black bandanna that Bam kept in his back pocket for good luck - the same black bandanna that was snagged on the drawer of the counter. His eyes drifted to Messiah and in that moment, both men knew that the display of vengeance had to be done in a way that surpassed the ordinary. Sanjay's only thought was, *Damn, hope I ain't gotta whack Murda too!*

"Sunjay! Sunjay Carter, don't ya hear me, boy?" Ms. Betty's voice was tinged with anger.

Sunjay was as lost as a car with no navigational system. "Huh? Naw, I didn't hear you, Granny."

Ms. Betty placed her hands on her wide hips before flaring up at him. "Boy, I've been knowin' ya since ya had shit in ya Pampers and were pissin' in ya bath water, so don't play me like I was born the day afta last Sunday! What ya ass done had in my cupboards that one of these no good heathens wants? And either you done told 'em you had it here or ya dumb ass done told one of them fast-tailed gals, and they told it."

She paused to catch her breath. Ms. Betty made her way over to the black bandanna. From the look on her face, she'd just recognized it.

"And it makes no sense for ya to be runnin' ya mouth 'bout ya business like ya lips a faucet with a leak. I taught ya better than…" Her words trailed off as her heart cracked in half. *This Irene's son's rag that he likes to carry!* The recognition was like a heavy punch to the chest. "Lord have mercy, Sunjay, this——"

Her words died in her throat when she turned to address her grandson. Sunjay and Messiah had left with the silence of a cathedral at prayer time.

Renta

Chapter 17

2010

The black book fell from Messiah's hand and crashed against the floor in a flutter of pages. He was in shock.

Blow killed your father! Blow killed your father! The words were a never-ending mantra within the hallways of his mind.

Pimpin Maxwell shook his head in awe. "Say, young blood, that mother of yours is something else! The lady done recorded the world of pimpin' and whorin' in its purest state." The words spilled from his lips in wonder.

Messiah's eyes went to the fallen book. After they'd left the cemetery, they'd found themselves camping at Messiah's five bedroom estate, plotting on a quick solution to the beef that was aflame in the streets. Sunjay stood and began to pace the marbled floor as if the act could help him think.

"What I don't understand is if Justice was snatched up out this hoe and the nigga that did it invited you to some kinda weirdo party, why the fuck we ain't piped up and standin' ova that boy yet?" he asked while tossing his hands in the air in that *nigga, what up!* kind of way.

Messiah shook his head as he fell back against the couch and exhaled a long whoosh of breath. "Fam, that was the first thing I had the squad do, but the spot empty, wasn't shit there but a face mask the cocksucka left behind to taunt me."

Sunjay laughed as he spun on his heels to make another lap around the room, but when he looked up, something caught his eye that caused him to spin back toward his main man.

"My dude, they got down on you, cool, but I know damn well if a mu'fucka came up in ya safe heaven and snatched sis up out this bitch, that camera up there caught it!" He pointed up at the corner of the room.

At that moment, it was as if someone had thrown a cold glass of water in Messiah's face as he shot to his feet with a wild look in his eyes. Sunjay's bewildered expression followed him out of the room as he took off in a dead sprint.

His eyes landed on Pimpin. "Fuck's up wit' brah?"

Pimpin shrugged. "So much been happenin' I think the man forgot he had the camera system." He chuckled in amusement before climbing to his feet and following in his 'protégés wake.

Sunjay glanced up at the eye in the sky and shook his head. *How a nigga forget he got cameras?*

***

Gator took each step with care as he made his way down to the dark basement. It had been years since he'd been down there. When his wife died of cancer, he'd taken all her belongings down to the dark hideaway to help him cope better with the reality that he didn't want to accept. He hummed an old Jamaican folksong as the darkness enveloped him. The only source of light he had came from the flickering flame that danced off a thick candle he carried.

The old mansion had one of those deep basements that was usually used in castles, and one had to trek through a long brick corridor in order to reach their destination. Gator finally reached the oak door and paused to sweep his dreadlocks from his face, the slight must that wafted from underneath the old wood caused him to scrunch his nose. *I have ta get someone to come clean de place*, he thought while sticking an ancient iron key into the keyhole and twisting it until he heard the bolt turn with a click. He used his shoulder to push the door open before stepping in and holding the candle out in front of him, the old man paused in the doorway and allowed his eyes to take in the cluster of memories he'd stuffed into boxes. Some were stacked as high as the ceiling and in other places, cluttered in corners.

"Yuh've lived a long time, old dawg. It's 'bout time yuh hang yuh guns up." He made his way over to a stack of boxes and pulled the lids back on the first one he came to.

The first thing his eyes captured were his wedding picture. *So beautiful...precious!* His eyes watered at the thought. Gator lifted the picture from its dusty captivity and thought of how much he missed his Queen. As he stared down at his and his wife's smiling faces, he relived their last moments together. *I'll always love you, baby!* his heart cried.

"Mmmph! Ammmah!"

The sudden splash of noise frightened him. He dropped the glass picture frame. It shattered into a thousand pieces. The Jamaican man's instincts became acute as he eased the baby Glock from the small of his back. His thoughts became dark. "Who dere? hmm?" he shouted.

"Mmmph! Mmmmph!" The jumbled mumble became more persistent the closer he got.

Clutching the Glock tight, Gator rounded a tall pile of boxes and it was there that his vision beheld a sight that stole his breath. "In de name of Haile selassie!" he called on the name of the Rastafarian divinity. His eyes swallowed her. She was dirty and had lost so much weight that he almost didn't recognize her, but it was the light he'd always admired in her eyes that convinced him that she was really there, tied and gagged in his basement.

"How'd yuh get here? I...I...Messiah has——"

"Yuh shouldn't go snooping around, Papa. Yuh find tings yuh wan looking for." Keisha's tone held a tinge of sadness.

Confusion played over his features as the pieces of the puzzle began to snap into place within his sharp mind.

"Keisha, why yuh invitin' de devil into my home?" Gator shook his head in disappointment.

Though he couldn't see her, Keisha smiled wickedly with a slight shake of her head. "Papa, yuh old and age has made yuh weak!" she spat as she took a step closer. "And dere's no room for weakness!" she whispered.

Darkness clouded Gator's eyes as he gritted his teeth. "Weak!" he spat.

In the midst of turning to confront the seed of his loins, Keisha moved with the speed of a striking cobra as she wrapped her arms around his neck in a brief embrace. There was merely a brief flash of silver when she broke away. The bound woman gazed up into the eyes of the only man that had the power to rescue her, but time took on a slow motion effect as the gun fell from his hand. Gator stumbled forward a few steps before turning to the woman he loved more than life. Keisha had a second's glance at the bloody smiley face the box cutter created before his hands shot to his slit throat in an attempt at staunching the blood flow. His eyes were wide in surprise as blood shot through his fingers, and a river of pain ran a race down both of their faces.

"I'm sorry, dada, I will always love you. Please understand!" she cried as rain stormed down from the dark skies of her eyes.

With a flash of silver, the corrupted seed swung the deadly blade with a killing blow, causing Gator's face to burst open. With a perfect spinning slice, she finished him. The night dimmed in his eyes as he tumbled forward and crashed into her. Together father and daughter crumbled to the floor in a bloody mess. Gator's lifeless body landed on top of her, knocking the air from her lungs, but the pain of her heart made deeper love to her mind. As she sucked in precious gulps of air, the deranged woman cried a heartfelt melody while wrapping her arms around her father's slit neck.

"I'm sorry, Papa, so sorry. Now yuh won' miss Mother anymore."

***

Marcella had a smile on her face as she listened to the success of her older brother, but it pained her to hear how far her mother had fallen from grace. Though she'd grown to hate the woman for leaving her trapped in foster care, she'd never forsaken the fantasies of their reunion. She'd always wondered about Messiah's outcome and as she stood outside the HiHo corner store, she was almost stunned to hear of her estranged family and how life had spun so far out of control. *I guess there's a blessin' in some of the worst storms?* She accepted the fact that growing up in the system may have been more of a blessing than the curse she'd always deemed it to be. "You say Messiah is doin; good for himself, huh?"

She continued to smile to keep him off guard, but it wasn't necessary. Fast Freddy was as high as the reunion tower and the fifty dollars she'd offered him was heaven inside a crack pipe for him.

"I'm tellin' ya, sweet thang, that ole boy is as groovy as a ten cent movie. Just the other day I seen the man in a Rolls Royce as fresh as grass in the mornin' time when the honey dew makes it moist. The nigga is pimpin' hoes out that there club he got out in the country!" The old fiend's lips were as loose as a prostitute's pussy after turning ten tricks. His eyes were glued to the Grant she held in her clutches. *If this hoe tryin' to play fast for this cash, I'ma have to get real physical!* he was thinking as he smiled at her.

"You wouldn't happen to know where he stays, or where I can find Black at, would you?" she inquired.

Fast Freddy smiled that rotten-toothed smile and allowed his eyes to speak the words that they both knew would keep his tongue loose. Marcella shook her head at the hustle, but pulled a twenty from her purse nonetheless.

"Damn, nigga, you can't be trying to break a bitch!" Marcella threatened while slipping her hand into her purse as if she had a hidden weapon. Fast Freddy's eyes followed the move before gazing back up at her. He began to shuffle from foot to foot, his addiction eating away at his patience.

"Look, I'on know where cat daddy rest his head, but I know his club is that big ole buildin' in Arlington they call Peepin Toms, and Black done lost her marbles! Last I heard, she was laid up in some nut-house?" He gave up what he knew.

Marcella studied him as if she could separate the truth from a lie from his body language. Reluctantly, she handed the money to him and as soon as it touched his hand, Fast Freddy did his tap dance.

"Well, cutie," he began before pausing to stare at her. "Has anybody ever told ya you looks just like Black?" he asked with a peculiar look on his face.

Marcella smiled before turning on her heels and heading for her rental car. "So they say. Let's see if she says the same!" she spoke over her shoulder.

***

The three men stood around the plasma screen. Messiah had wound the tape back to the day his world was turned upside down. Taking a deep breath, he pressed play, praying that he'd find the answers to the many questions that had damn near stolen his sanity. The screen came to life in crystal clear footage as they watched Ms. Rosa exit the kitchen while wiping her hands on the dish towel. She made her way to the front door and opened it with a bright smile on her face. Messiah leaned closer to the screen as if the act would help him get a better glimpse of the robber of his peace. They could see the smile slip from Ms. Rosa's pretty face and seconds later, her head snapped back as if she'd been punched.

"Cold game on an icy plate they fed the ole gal," Pimpin whispered almost as an afterthought.

That's when shit became a hurricane of confusion, surprise, and more dominantly, that gangsta shit that was born within the room of gangstas. As the person on the screen stepped into view, Sunjay's confusion blossomed like a pink rose in spring time as he went for the FN on his waist, but Pimpin Maxwell beat him to the draw.

"Now, I don't know what kinda freak games is bein' played, but let's not get no blood on this here pretty carpet." Pimpin's voice was strained as he waved the pistol between the two men.

"What the fuck?" The words escaped Messiah's lips as his eyes bounced from the screen to Pimpin Maxwell.

"Ain't this a bitch?" Sunjay spat with murder in his stare.

"Yeah, that's usually what they call it when shit gets ugly. Now you boys chill while I give my spiel," Pimpin spoke as if shit hadn't just gotten funky.

To Be Continued...
Son of a Dope Fiend 3
-- Coming to a hood near you --

Submission Guideline

Submit the first three chapters of your completed manuscript to ldpsubmissions@gmail.com, subject line: Your book's title. The manuscript must be in a .doc file and sent as an attachment. Document should be in Times New Roman, double spaced and in size 12 font. Also, provide your synopsis and full contact information. If sending multiple submissions, they must each be in a separate email.

Have a story but no way to send it electronically? You can still submit to LDP/Ca$h Presents. Send in the first three chapters, written or typed, of your completed manuscript to:

LDP: Submissions Dept
Po Box 944
Stockbridge, Ga 30281

DO NOT send original manuscript. Must be a duplicate.

Provide your synopsis and a cover letter containing your full contact information.

Thanks for considering LDP and Ca$h Presents.

Coming Soon from Lock Down Publications/Ca$h Presents

BOW DOWN TO MY GANGSTA

By **Ca$h**

TORN BETWEEN TWO

By **Coffee**

THE STREETS STAINED MY SOUL **II**

By **Marcellus Allen**

BLOOD OF A BOSS **VI**

SHADOWS OF THE GAME II

By **Askari**

LOYAL TO THE GAME **IV**

By **T.J. & Jelissa**

A DOPEBOY'S PRAYER **II**

By **Eddie "Wolf" Lee**

IF LOVING YOU IS WRONG… **III**

By **Jelissa**

TRUE SAVAGE **VII**

MIDNIGHT CARTEL III

DOPE BOY MAGIC IV

CITY OF KINGZ II

By **Chris Green**

BLAST FOR ME **III**

A SAVAGE DOPEBOY III

CUTTHROAT MAFIA II

By **Ghost**

A HUSTLER'S DECEIT III

KILL ZONE **II**

BAE BELONGS TO ME III

A DOPE BOY'S QUEEN II

By **Aryanna**

COKE KINGS V

KING OF THE TRAP II

By **T.J. Edwards**

GORILLAZ IN THE BAY V

De'Kari

THE STREETS ARE CALLING II

Duquie Wilson

KINGPIN KILLAZ IV

STREET KINGS III

PAID IN BLOOD III

CARTEL KILLAZ IV

DOPE GODS III

Hood Rich

SINS OF A HUSTLA II

ASAD

KINGZ OF THE GAME V

Playa Ray

SLAUGHTER GANG IV

RUTHLESS HEART IV

By **Willie Slaughter**

THE HEART OF A SAVAGE III

By **Jibril Williams**

FUK SHYT II

By **Blakk Diamond**

FEAR MY GANGSTA 5

THE REALEST KILLAZ II

By **Tranay Adams**

TRAP GOD II

By **Troublesome**

YAYO IV

A SHOOTER'S AMBITION III

By S. Allen

GHOST MOB

Stilloan Robinson

KINGPIN DREAMS III

By Paper Boi Rari

CREAM

By Yolanda Moore

SON OF A DOPE FIEND III

By Renta

FOREVER GANGSTA II

GLOCKS ON SATIN SHEETS III

By Adrian Dulan

LOYALTY AIN'T PROMISED II

By Keith Williams

THE PRICE YOU PAY FOR LOVE II

DOPE GIRL MAGIC III

By Destiny Skai

CONFESSIONS OF A GANGSTA II

By Nicholas Lock

I'M NOTHING WITHOUT HIS LOVE II

By Monet Dragun

CAUGHT UP IN THE LIFE III

By Robert Baptiste

LIFE OF A SAVAGE IV

A GANGSTA'S QUR'AN II

MURDA SEASON II

By **Romell Tukes**

QUIET MONEY III

THUG LIFE II

By **Trai'Quan**

THE STREETS MADE ME III

By **Larry D. Wright**

THE ULTIMATE SACRIFICE VI

IF YOU CROSS ME ONCE II

ANGEL III

By **Anthony Fields**

THE LIFE OF A HOOD STAR

By **Ca$h & Rashia Wilson**

FRIEND OR FOE II

By **Mimi**

SAVAGE STORMS II

By **Meesha**

BLOOD ON THE MONEY II

By **J-Blunt**

Available Now

RESTRAINING ORDER **I & II**

By **CA$H & Coffee**

LOVE KNOWS NO BOUNDARIES **I II & III**

By **Coffee**

RAISED AS A GOON I, II, III & IV

BRED BY THE SLUMS I, II, III

BLAST FOR ME I & II

ROTTEN TO THE CORE I II III

A BRONX TALE I, II, III

DUFFEL BAG CARTEL I II III IV

HEARTLESS GOON I II III IV

A SAVAGE DOPEBOY I II

HEARTLESS GOON I II III

DRUG LORDS I II III

CUTTHROAT MAFIA

By **Ghost**

LAY IT DOWN **I & II**

LAST OF A DYING BREED

BLOOD STAINS OF A SHOTTA I & II III

By **Jamaica**

LOYAL TO THE GAME I II III

LIFE OF SIN I, II III

By **TJ & Jelissa**

BLOODY COMMAS I & II

SKI MASK CARTEL I II & III

KING OF NEW YORK I II,III IV V

RISE TO POWER I II III

COKE KINGS I II III IV

BORN HEARTLESS I II III IV

KING OF THE TRAP

By **T.J. Edwards**

IF LOVING HIM IS WRONG…I & II

LOVE ME EVEN WHEN IT HURTS I II III

By **Jelissa**

WHEN THE STREETS CLAP BACK I & II III

THE HEART OF A SAVAGE I II

By **Jibril Williams**

A DISTINGUISHED THUG STOLE MY HEART I II & III

LOVE SHOULDN'T HURT I II III IV

RENEGADE BOYS I II III IV

PAID IN KARMA I II III

SAVAGE STORMS

By **Meesha**

A GANGSTER'S CODE I &, II III

A GANGSTER'S SYN I II III

THE SAVAGE LIFE I II III

CHAINED TO THE STREETS I II III

BLOOD ON THE MONEY

By J-Blunt

PUSH IT TO THE LIMIT

By **Bre' Hayes**

BLOOD OF A BOSS **I, II, III, IV, V**

SHADOWS OF THE GAME

By **Askari**

THE STREETS BLEED MURDER **I, II & III**

THE HEART OF A GANGSTA I II& III

By **Jerry Jackson**

CUM FOR ME I II III IV V

An **LDP Erotica Collaboration**

BRIDE OF A HUSTLA **I II & II**

THE FETTI GIRLS **I, II& III**

CORRUPTED BY A GANGSTA I, II III, IV

BLINDED BY HIS LOVE

THE PRICE YOU PAY FOR LOVE

DOPE GIRL MAGIC I II

By **Destiny Skai**

WHEN A GOOD GIRL GOES BAD

By **Adrienne**
THE COST OF LOYALTY I II III
By Kweli
A GANGSTER'S REVENGE **I II III & IV**
THE BOSS MAN'S DAUGHTERS I II III IV V
A SAVAGE LOVE **I & II**
BAE BELONGS TO ME I II
A HUSTLER'S DECEIT I, II, III
WHAT BAD BITCHES DO I, II, III
SOUL OF A MONSTER I II III
KILL ZONE
A DOPE BOY'S QUEEN
By **Aryanna**
A KINGPIN'S AMBITON
A KINGPIN'S AMBITION **II**
I MURDER FOR THE DOUGH
By **Ambitious**
TRUE SAVAGE I II III IV V VI
DOPE BOY MAGIC I, II, III
MIDNIGHT CARTEL I II
CITY OF KINGZ
By **Chris Green**
A DOPEBOY'S PRAYER
By **Eddie "Wolf" Lee**
THE KING CARTEL **I, II & III**
By **Frank Gresham**
THESE NIGGAS AIN'T LOYAL **I, II & III**
By **Nikki Tee**
GANGSTA SHYT **I II &III**
By **CATO**

THE ULTIMATE BETRAYAL
By **Phoenix**
BOSS'N UP **I , II & III**
By **Royal Nicole**
I LOVE YOU TO DEATH
By Destiny J
I RIDE FOR MY HITTA
I STILL RIDE FOR MY HITTA
By **Misty Holt**
LOVE & CHASIN' PAPER
By **Qay Crockett**
TO DIE IN VAIN
SINS OF A HUSTLA
By **ASAD**
BROOKLYN HUSTLAZ
By **Boogsy Morina**
BROOKLYN ON LOCK I & II
By **Sonovia**
GANGSTA CITY
By **Teddy Duke**
A DRUG KING AND HIS DIAMOND I & II III
A DOPEMAN'S RICHES
HER MAN, MINE'S TOO I, II
CASH MONEY HO'S
By Nicole Goosby
TRAPHOUSE KING **I II & III**
KINGPIN KILLAZ I II III
STREET KINGS I II
PAID IN BLOOD **I II**
CARTEL KILLAZ I II III

DOPE GODS I II

By **Hood Rich**

LIPSTICK KILLAH **I, II, III**

CRIME OF PASSION I II & III

FRIEND OR FOE

By **Mimi**

STEADY MOBBN' **I, II, III**

THE STREETS STAINED MY SOUL

By **Marcellus Allen**

WHO SHOT YA **I, II, III**

SON OF A DOPE FIEND I II

Renta

GORILLAZ IN THE BAY **I II III IV**

TEARS OF A GANGSTA I II

DE'KARI

TRIGGADALE I II III

Elijah R. Freeman

GOD BLESS THE TRAPPERS I, II, III

THESE SCANDALOUS STREETS I, II, III

FEAR MY GANGSTA I, II, III IV

THESE STREETS DON'T LOVE NOBODY I, II

BURY ME A G I, II, III, IV, V

A GANGSTA'S EMPIRE I, II, III, IV

THE DOPEMAN'S BODYGAURD I II

THE REALEST KILLAZ

Tranay Adams

THE STREETS ARE CALLING

Duquie Wilson

MARRIED TO A BOSS… I II III

By Destiny Skai & Chris Green

KINGZ OF THE GAME I II III IV
Playa Ray
SLAUGHTER GANG I II III
RUTHLESS HEART I II III
By Willie Slaughter
FUK SHYT
By Blakk Diamond
DON'T F#CK WITH MY HEART I II
By Linnea
ADDICTED TO THE DRAMA I II III
By Jamila
YAYO I II III
A SHOOTER'S AMBITION I II
By S. Allen
TRAP GOD
By Troublesome
FOREVER GANGSTA
GLOCKS ON SATIN SHEETS I II
By Adrian Dulan
TOE TAGZ I II III
By Ah'Million
KINGPIN DREAMS I II
By Paper Boi Rari
CONFESSIONS OF A GANGSTA
By Nicholas Lock
I'M NOTHING WITHOUT HIS LOVE
By Monet Dragun
CAUGHT UP IN THE LIFE I II
By Robert Baptiste
NEW TO THE GAME I II III

By **Malik D. Rice**

LIFE OF A SAVAGE I II III

A GANGSTA'S QUR'AN

MURDA SEASON

By **Romell Tukes**

LOYALTY AIN'T PROMISED

By Keith Williams

QUIET MONEY I II

THUG LIFE

By **Trai'Quan**

THE STREETS MADE ME I II

By **Larry D. Wright**

THE ULTIMATE SACRIFICE I, II, III, IV, V

KHADIFI

IF YOU CROSS ME ONCE

ANGEL I II

By **Anthony Fields**

THE LIFE OF A HOOD STAR

By Ca$h & Rashia Wilson

BOOKS BY LDP'S CEO, CA$H

TRUST IN NO MAN

TRUST IN NO MAN 2

TRUST IN NO MAN 3

BONDED BY BLOOD

SHORTY GOT A THUG

THUGS CRY

THUGS CRY 2

THUGS CRY 3

TRUST NO BITCH

TRUST NO BITCH 2

TRUST NO BITCH 3

TIL MY CASKET DROPS

RESTRAINING ORDER

RESTRAINING ORDER 2

IN LOVE WITH A CONVICT

LIFE OF A HOOD STAR

Coming Soon

BONDED BY BLOOD 2

BOW DOWN TO MY GANGSTA